Lane Robins

RENOVATION

BLIND
EYE
BOOKS

Renovation
by **Lane Robins**

Published by:
Blind Eye Books
1141 Grant Street
Bellingham, WA 98225
blindeyebooks.com

Edited by Nicole Kimberling
Cover art by Dawn Kimberling

First print edition May 19, 2015
Copyright© Lane Robins

ISBN: 978-1-935560-36-4

The very moment JK Lassiter rolled up the U-Haul door, he had an audience. It surprised him, though it shouldn't have. This neighborhood, from what his boss, Dustin Davis, had said, was a mixture of students, university professors, and retirees—exactly the kind of people who'd be able to come home midday.

A curtain in a fancy bay window directly across the street twitched, then a stiff-backed man moved out to sit on his porch, a book in hand. The book rested on his lap, unopened. A prop. An excuse to let him watch as JK unpacked. An older couple in a hatchback made a slow circuit around the cul-de-sac, then re-treated into the first driveway off the main road—a go 'round to get a better look. The woman, grey-haired and stocky in her yoga gear, waved as she got out of her car. JK raised his hand, waved back.

Nosy neighbors, but friendly ones.

A nice change. So many of Dallas's neighborhoods were in-dustrial, or apartment dense, or made up of houses with three-car garages that let people pull in, pull out, without ever seeing their neighbors. There weren't a lot of places left like this one: houses built in the twenties and thirties, full of personality, with lots that might be small—no room for swimming pools or tennis courts, but enough space for backyard decks, a swing set or two beneath the shade trees, and the inevitable barbecue grill.

JK smiled, soaking in the scene. Like something out of a movie setting.

His boss had to have had the luck of the devil to find a house for sale here and at a decent price. Of course—JK turned back to the house—you got what you paid for.

Against the pretty backdrop of the other houses, his place loomed like a nightmare—the blight in the neighborhood.

First impression: a house built out of scraps and remainders. Brickwork here, stone there, grey shingles cascading down one side of the house, peeling yellowed siding on the other. A decaying privacy fence gaped like a row of broken teeth, edging a front lawn where grass went to die in long, brittle brown strands.

It wasn't that bad, JK reminded himself. Had to remind himself against the sinking of his heart. The house had been victim to a series of renters, a disinterested landlord, and most lately, to a couple who apparently had other things on their mind than home repair.

At the core, the building stood strong and attractive. It was just overwhelmed by too many influences. He could take care of that. He hoped. JK needed to prove that he could help Davis flip houses. If he did well, an entirely new career path would open for him. He wanted that path. Desperately.

JK wiped a sudden burst of sweat from his hairline, sheltered his eyes from the midday sun, and focused back on the elderly couple.

The husband offloaded potted plants, with blooms in shades of red, purple, and yellow. They made a brilliant splash of color against the grey cement drive. The husband and wife team carried the plants one by one into their garden around the side of their house, until JK lost sight of them. From JK's angle, he could see only that the side garden bloomed with roses and larkspur. But just that made him cringe at the front lawn he called his now, all dirt patch and weeds.

He added landscaping to his to do list. Get down good grass seed. A few tidy shrubs. Enough to add curb appeal. JK rubbed at the sweat on the back of his neck, felt a tiny breeze do its best to cool his skin.

The house to his right—all brick facing and dark blue siding—was quiet. No one peeked through the mini-blinds, or made ever-so-casual decisions to read outside on a too-hot day.

A child's play pool, filled with sand, sat in the front yard beneath a leafed-out live oak. From the branches, unseen but easily heard wind chimes dangled.

The house on his immediate left, between him and the garden-rich house, had dark curtains drawn across the front windows, and a high privacy fence around the back. It might have been empty, the owner off at work, except music played, muffled by window glass. Laid-back blues, melancholy and slow.

Not JK's taste, but pleasant enough. The house was one of the nicest houses on the block; sandstone at ground level and siding painted dark green above, squared white pillars and painted eaves. Though the distance and the darkness of the curtains made it hard to tell, JK thought the windows were the original leaded glass.

Overall, though, the neighborhood seemed to doze peaceably. For a moment, JK missed the noise of the construction crew, the jangle and clamor of it, the camaraderie of working near others.

Young women's voices, arguing, drew his attention like new players entering the stage.

One said, "You need to stop giving that woman money. You can't afford it."

"It's worth it." The intensity in her voice made the other woman pause before resuming.

The two women, college-aged, came down the road from the blind end of the cul-de-sac. One was tall, lean, and loose in her bones, sauntering easily in her high heels and jeans. Glossy black hair slid over her shoulders.

The other girl, equally tall, but brunette and curvy, JK pegged as the intense one, the one who thought the money well-spent. Something about the way she held herself, a sort of desperation in her shoulders, the way her hands clutched her sleeves. JK recognized that kind of desperation; she felt unhappy, trapped, and hungry for something that eluded her.

"I know what I'm doing, Inez," she said.

Inez replied, "No, you really don't. Your parents wouldn't want—"

The girls broke off when they spotted JK in the shade of the U-Haul.

Inez raised a brow, smiled, and slid her gaze up and down his body, checking him out as thoroughly as he'd ever been checked out. He shook his head and grinned at her.

JK wasn't worth that much of a look; tall, dark, and handsome, he wasn't.

Tall? Okay, he was tall, six foot six, and his job kept him fit enough, but his muscles pressed lean and lanky over his bones. Dark? Nope, his hair ran blondish, by virtue of the long hours he spent under the sun. Handsome? More amiable than good-looking.

"Hi," she said. "I'm Inez."

"JK," he introduced himself.

The other girl tugged at Inez's arm, and said, "I'm going to be late, and you know how Harrison is about that."

"Yeah, all right," Inez said. She flipped another wave JK's way, and said, "Welcome to the neighborhood. See you around."

"Yup," JK agreed, and watched them go, picking up their pace so they wouldn't be late.

He didn't have time to dawdle either. He had a schedule, and a truck to return before the end of the day.

JK pulled out the U-Haul's ramp with a clatter and tried not to be annoyed. He wasn't supposed to be unloading this himself: his brother Jesse had promised to help, but had been called in to work a murder. No rest for the wicked in Texas: they kept themselves busy. No rest for the policemen who had to clean up after the criminals either.

He leaned into the U-Haul, and felt the same dull surprise he had when they had loaded it. When he'd left home, left the basement, to come live with Jesse, all his possessions had fit in a single duffel bag. Now, JK needed five bags for his clothes, two of which contained nothing but his gloves: tan suede work gloves, white silk sleeping gloves, blue nitrile gloves for around the house, and the frankengloves he'd cobbled together for specific tasks.

He even had a couple pairs of striped wool ones, just on the off chance that Dallas ever aspired to the Maine-style winters JK had been used to. Enough gloves that he'd never run the risk of being caught barehanded. His own reluctant fashion statement.

Besides his clothes, his gloves, his random assortment of personal effects, there were five bulky bags of construction tools—his own, and the ones he'd borrowed from his boss for this home renovation.

As if thinking about his boss had summoned him, his phone rang, and JK fumbled it out of his pocket, grimacing. He knew why Davis was calling.

The U-Haul should have been full to the brim; JK should have picked up new appliances early that morning, but... that hadn't happened.

Davis started talking the minute JK answered. "What the hell, JK? I sent you to get good appliances and you walk away from them? And piss off my supplier?"

Dustin Davis had a deceptive voice. High-pitched and nasal—like something that should come from a weedy teenager. In reality, he was a sixty-something retired linebacker.

"They weren't good machines," JK said. "Looked new, packaged as new, but they weren't. Poorly refurbished, at best. Practically guaranteed to fall apart in a few months."

He said, "I've been dealing with Martin for years."

"They were fakes, boss. You know I need this job. You know I wouldn't walk away for no reason."

Davis sighed. "Proof?"

JK's head ached, throbbed; he closed his eyes. Remembered gloating over the profit to be made. *Six thousand this month alone, and for just a little labor, a willingness to bend a few laws, and the customers just kept buying. They wanted to be scammed, or they'd question his prices more...*

Not JK's memory. Martin's.

But the memory belonged to JK now, never mind that he didn't want it. He had been switching his gloves out—thin driving gloves for suede work ones, and his right hand had been bare. Martin had bumped into him. That was all it had taken.

His psychic sense had dragged Martin's memories back to JK's mind like the incoming tide—unavoidable, unstoppable. Every single time he touched someone, he learned their secrets. Without the gloves he wore, without the pills he took, he'd be at the mercy of the world, a drowning man in a brutal sea of other people's memories.

JK said, "The serial numbers on the machines didn't match the boxes. Odd for new merch, don't you think? Martin gambled that no one would look that closely."

He'd gotten good at explaining away how he knew things he shouldn't know. Without telling the strict truth.

Telling people about his abilities seemed a no-win proposition: either they thought him crazy, or they believed, and wanted to see him do it. Neither made him happy.

"God damn it," Davis growled. "*God damn it*. I'm gonna nail his ass to the wall. Five years we've been working together—" He hung up, still bitching.

JK sighed, firmed up his gloves, pushing down at the web between each finger.

He decided to unload the truck first, then move everything into the garage.

Traditionally, these houses were built sans garage, in a time before cars cluttered the streets, but JK didn't mind this one late addition to his poor house.

His personal possessions weren't worth much, but his tools? A garage was more secure and more convenient than any stand-alone shed.

He worked his way through his duffel bags, tossing them out of the truck—nothing in them could break—and had finished hauling out his work table, inching it gingerly onto a dolly and rolling it carefully down the ramp. It left him sweating and heat prickled, flushed, and loathing his gloves. Sweat slopped around inside the suede and made his grip loose.

He peeled up his shirt to scrub at his face, and grimaced at the stains he left on the worn, white cotton. JK loved his job, but God, it kept him filthy.

Wind chimes—discordant, melodious—jangled in the inconstant breeze. The day marched on. He clattered back up the ramp into the truck. One item left. Not technically tools, not technically his. Definitely his problem.

That damned entertainment center. It was a massive thing, solid oak, stained dark, and hammered together by Big Mike on the construction crew as a housewarming gift. JK hadn't had the heart to decline it, especially since Big Mike had listened when JK had muttered darkly about Craftsman houses and what the hell did he know... Big Mike had made the entertainment center in something he called pseudo-Stickley.

Davis said it was going to look great in the house—if JK could get it out of the truck. The piece of furniture loomed large, easily twice the size of a refrigerator. JK gave it a thoughtful shove. It didn't budge.

He could leave it, wait for Jesse to get off work, and hope that he'd be in the mood to drive across the city. Homicide cops kept crap hours.

The entertainment center was the only thing preventing JK from returning the truck, and saving Davis another day's charge.

JK wasn't ready for another setback, not so soon. Not over something this stupid. Not when Davis was already cranky, when JK had assured him he didn't need help unloading: he had Jesse.

In the sky, a tumble of jays chased off an encroaching raven with shrill shrieks. JK stretched, cracking his back, and flexing his fingers in the sweaty heat of his gloves. He licked salt from his lips and drained the last sun-heated mouthfuls from his water bottle and tossed it aside.

JK had the tools he needed: loads of drop cloths, the industrial dolly, the van ramp. If he could get the entertainment center on the dolly, then it could be guided down to the driveway. He was big; he was strong; he could do this.

Twenty minutes later, JK knew he couldn't. Sure, he'd brute-forced the piece onto the dolly, pulling the whole burdensome mass onto the ramp to follow him down. The wheels creaked but bore the weight, turning freely enough. He'd braced it from below, his shoulders pushed tight against the solid wood, used his own body mass and resistance to control the rate of descent as he skidded slowly down the ramp before it, every line of his body straining...

JK hadn't counted on his gloves, sweat-soaked, slipping a fraction. Just enough for the left glove to shimmy up his hand and bare his palm. JK had shifted his grip and come into contact with the wood.

"Don't drink while you're using the saw! God damn it, are you trying to make a widow outta me? Fucking selfish bastard! You cut your fingers off and I'll be the one picking them up, and we're out of ice—"

"Aw, don't be like that, honey, you know I can hold my liquor—not even liquor, s'just beer!"

The crash of a bottle, glass shattering, spattering his feet, flecks of foam in his beard. Scrubbing his face with his hands, not even shaking. What's her problem? I know what I'm doing...

JK jerked out of Big Mike's memories to find himself in serious trouble. He might have frozen in his downward progress while the memories held him, but the heavy furniture sliding down the ramp hadn't. JK was nearly overrun, his back bent painfully, the entertainment center pressing hard all along his side, his thigh, his knee.

He swore a breathless blue streak, his arms, shoulders, back all straining as the entertainment center bore down on him. Too late to escape its weight; even if he threw himself off the side of the ramp, he'd be too slow to avoid the entertainment center crushing his ankle. His knee. Maybe even his hip.

The worst part was he knew better. This wasn't a one-man chore. He'd let his eagerness get the better of him.

The center slid another six inches, wood groaning over metal, trying to roll over him, and JK found his breath gone, had a perfectly human vision of himself squashed beneath 400 pounds of oak planking. He should have taken the broken leg. Better that than a crushed spine...

Then another shoulder wedged itself beside his, pressing the oak up and away. JK sucked in a tremendous breath.

"Can you slide out from under it?" Deep, husky voice, already going tight with strain. "If we shove it back toward the truck, can you get out from under?"

JK gave a quick thought to angles of force and said, "That'll work."

The shoulder beside him tensed; a scarred, solid forearm flexed and bulged, a sinewy wrist went taut. A warm hand pressed against JK's lower back, tapping at his spine. "On three, 'kay?"

"On three," JK echoed, dizzy from the effort of holding the furniture away from himself. His could sense his knee, wedged tight against the wood, blooming with pressure bruises.

"One, two..."

"Three." They heaved in unison; the entertainment center ground hard against the truck's bumper and ramp, the dolly skewed beneath it, set metal to shrieking, but the pressure on JK's body eased.

He slipped toward his savior, felt the other man tugging his belt loops, steadying him and yanking him away even as they let the entertainment center fall, skid-scraping its way down the ramp and landing in the grass with a thud that shook the ground, woke dry dirt to dancing, and bounced the edge of the ramp into the air. The dolly crashed down a bare foot from them.

"Holy fuck," JK swore. He bent over, breathed deep, his gloved hands shaking where he gripped his knees. "Thanks, man. Dying by ugly furniture's no way to go."

He turned to give his helper a grateful smile and got stuck staring. And smiling. Probably like an idiot.

Savior-guy was kind of crazy good-looking. Better than a movie star. JK had never really believed they were real. But this guy, sweat springing to his hairline after his effort, was real enough to smell—the sharpness of citrus and sweat. Real enough to touch.

He wore ancient plaid flannels that snugged over his thighs and hips—repurposed PJ pants?—in dark blue and sooty grey. They matched his threadbare t-shirt, almost all the orange lettering worn off of the chest. JK thought it had once advertised UT-Dallas. Battered running shoes, unlaced, stained green at the edges, suggested his rescuer ran on grass more than pavement.

JK hastily clapped dust from his gloves and held out his hand. "I'm JK Lassiter. And I'm really not an idiot. It only took two of us to get it into the truck and I thought it'd be easier going down."

"More lethal, maybe," the guy said, a tiny smile blooming on his face, showing even white teeth. That was it, the final blow. JK felt his brain pop and disappear. Heat spiraled down through his guts.

"I'm Nick Collier. Your next-door neighbor." He tilted his head toward the beautiful sandstone house, the cords of his neck stretching as he did.

JK felt his grin stretch to silly levels. Nick, smiling in the comedown of an adrenaline rush, was the kind of gorgeous—short dark hair and light eyes and perfectly chiseled features—that made JK imagine an entire history of people walking into streets and falling off curbs and crashing cars in his wake.

Belatedly, JK realized Nick had shaken his hand, let go, and was peering into the truck. "You got any other monsters in there you need help with?" The wind ruffled his hair, teased at the edges and suggested if it were any longer, it would start to curl. Nick's thin grey t-shirt pulled tight between the broad, flat juts of his shoulder blades, highlighted his spine. JK thought about running his hands down that sharp line, then reined in the desire. That behavior belonged in nightclubs, not in a nice suburban neighborhood, with a nice new neighbor. No matter how attractive.

"That was the last." JK hated to admit it.

"That's probably for the best," Nick said. He rubbed his arm, the red scar on it. Compound fracture, JK thought. The bone jutting through the skin. He'd seen breaks like that on the crew. When Nick saw JK watching, he stopped all at once, dropped his arm to his side. He shifted, losing some of the ease he'd had. "Anyway, you good?"

"Thanks to you," JK said. He cast about, trying to think of something else to say, to keep Nick around even a little longer.

From the corner of his eye, he noticed his book-reading elderly watcher standing on his lawn. Nick gave a quick wave—all good here—and the old man nodded, climbing stiffly back up his porch steps, shaking his head. JK winced, imagining the broken bones that would have resulted if the old man had been his only shot at help.

"You bought the Barton house?" Nick said. "Hope you didn't pay a lot for..." He grimaced at himself, and rephrased, "I mean, it needs a lot of work."

"That's my job," JK said. "I'm the renovator." He swept another furtive head-to-toe glance over Nick. "So, you work at home?"

"How—" Nick dropped his gaze, took in his clothing, and grinned without shame. "I guess I'm not exactly office-appropriate."

"Well, you were coming to my rescue. I promise not to hold it against you. And hey, you totally carry off the look. You've got the whole rock-star-glamour thing going on—" JK heard himself and winced. Fuck. A pretty face, a little near death, and he devolved to idiocy.

Nick was half-smiling at JK though, so at least he amused Nick.

Still. He could do better than that. JK stuck out his gloved hand again, said, "My boss, Dustin Davis, likes to flip houses. And I'm the one he tapped to remodel a long-neglected architectural gem."

Nick's half-smile morphed back into a full grin, showing teeth, crinkling his eyes. "Good news for the neighborhood. This house is an eyesore."

"So you're saying I can only improve it, no matter what I do?" JK said, smiling. He couldn't seem to stop. "Seriously, though. I'll be using some heavy machinery—compressors, mechanical saws, that sort of thing. I don't want to make your life miserable if you work from home—"

"Don't start before nine a.m. and we're good," Nick said.

"Nine a.m., check. I can do that," JK said. He looked at Nick's shirt, the slow rise and fall of his chest, the faded letters stretching side to side. "You go to the university?" Reassessed the other man's age. Closer to thirty than twenty. Probably over the edge of thirty. "Teach there?"

"I teach," Nick said. "History, School of Arts and Humanities. But I'm on sabbatical for the summer and fall semesters. Working on a book." He rubbed at the back of his neck, uncomfortable with the topic, JK thought. That scar showed on his forearm again. Looked recent. Still red. At least within the year.

JK said, "That had to hurt."

"It's getting better," Nick said. "Lots of physical therapy."

"Tell me saving my dumb ass didn't set you back."

Nick shook his head. "Really, it's all good. Good enough if you want help—"

"Won't say no." JK scrubbed his gloves against his pants, and Nick's gaze snagged on his wrist, the paler drift of skin, and the faded ribbons of color, oh—

When JK had first started wearing gloves, he had been worse than useless. Back then, it had taken three layers of gloves for him to feel safe. Fumble-fingered didn't begin to describe the result. He broke glasses, plates, couldn't pick up coins, couldn't even pick up a book reliably. His sister-in-law, Hannah, who'd prescribed the gloves to go along with his new meds, turned around and prescribed making friendship bracelets.

JK wore what Hannah called his master-class bracelet; a rainbow chevron that ended in bright pink ties. Nick couldn't stop looking at it.

Nick had gone stone-faced, and while that looked good on him too, JK couldn't read that blankness. Couldn't tell if Nick was going to be the kind to recoil or shrug. Too much to hope for that he'd flash a rainbow pin of his own? JK's hands twitched. A single glove off, a single brush of flesh and he'd know everything...

Instead he focused on Rule #1—never take the gloves off—and soldiered on, refusing to hide. Not this. He had too much else to keep secret. "Problem?" he asked, let his voice edge toward sharpness.

Disappointment tasted sour in his mouth. Not just because Nick was hot—it wasn't like he was seeing white fences in their future—but because he'd felt like the guy could be a friend.

Nick's eyes flared wide. "Oh. No. I mean, I'm neither self-loathing, nor a hypocrite, so no. No problem at all." He shook his head, flustered but sincere, and JK's disappointment faded.

Nick rubbed at the scar on his arm, stared past JK at the Barton house and said, "You ever have a day where it's like the universe has been crapping on you for ages, and suddenly it's like... it forgives you? For whatever it is you did?"

JK's throat felt tight and thick. He thought about the basement and his parents, back beyond that to the accident itself. The crash through the ice on the pond, that shock of impossible cold and his friends screaming and trying to grab the hockey sticks thrust at him, but his numb hands refusing to close. Sinking deeper into black water. The equal shock of waking when he'd expected to be dead, the discovery that his life had changed irretrievably. He had to swallow twice before he could find his voice. JK said, "Yeah. Yeah. I get that."

JK finessed the house key out of his pants pocket, always tricky with thick gloves, and glanced up to catch Nick watching him struggle, frowning slightly. Probably wondering why he hadn't taken the gloves off. The usual spurt of embarrassment didn't last; JK was thinking ahead, thinking about fitting the key to the lock, to opening the front door. *His* front door for the summer.

He felt a little like a kid given a key to a treasure chest. Grinning, he climbed the porch steps, bouncing a little on the scarred wood—sturdier than it looked, didn't need replacing, only stripping, sanding, and staining.

Nick followed in his wake, and when JK turned back to share his excitement, he found Nick's gaze lingering along the length of his body. Caught, Nick shrugged and said, "Construction keeps you fit."

JK caught Nick's gaze slipping over the seam of his jeans, and smiled. "Yep," JK agreed. "You want someone to lift heavy things, I'm your guy."

Nick glanced meaningfully at the fallen entertainment center, and JK shrugged. "Lifting, I said. That was lowering."

"Just open the door, caveman," Nick teased.

The lock stuck, of course it did. JK hadn't seen a single thing in this house that didn't need some work. Didn't dim his anticipation.

He swung the door open, stepped into the dimness and...

Recoiled.

Reeled.

It felt like a car accident might. *Impact*, a hundred separate sensations culminating in one giant shriek.

He froze in the doorway, gloved hand locking tight around the key.

"Whoof," Nick said, stepping back. "Hot in there, huh?"

Very hot, JK realized distantly. The AC had been turned off; the house radiated stale heat. And the heat had raised ghostly scents: the smell of cooked meals, hot plastic, dirty carpets, cigarette smoke, wet dog...

JK concentrated on the small sensations, trying to get out from under the big one, that horrible paralytic sensation that something terrible had happened here. Even with his gloves, even current on his pills, he felt the house screaming at him.

What had Davis told him about the house?

Nothing that had raised red flags. Nothing to cause this sort of impression. The Bartons had a bad marriage; he left her—good riddance—and she sold the house as fast as she could, didn't bother clearing it all out. Sour, Davis had said about her. Like she made drinking vinegar a habit.

"Get the AC on," Nick urged. "Open the windows, air it out some."

AC, JK thought. *Yes*. The house felt stifling; sweat crept down his spine and beaded at his hairline just standing in the doorway. The interior temperature must have been over a hundred degrees. He still felt cold in his bones.

It took more effort than he wanted to admit to take that next step, to walk across the three-foot tile "foyer" and the fourteen-foot space of old carpet to reach the thermostat.

For a moment, he saw a middle-aged woman, shoulders hunched, lighting a cigarette in the stairway, scowling at nothing. A roaring voice rose out of the center of the room, and a scrabble of dog claws and jingling collars responded.

JK shook the sensation off, kept thinking about Jesse telling him this job was a bad idea, and a core of stubbornness steadied him. If he wanted to be independent, he had to start taking risks. He was twenty-eight, not eighteen, and he had a job to do.

The AC churned to life, groaning, protesting the work ahead of it. JK set it for eighty-five. He'd lower it by increments throughout the day. He didn't want to blow out the ancient HVAC unit before he had a replacement lined up. Focusing on details. Closing out the sensation of the house itself.

He would rebuild it—scrape out the old memories. It could only get better from here.

JK joined Nick on the porch and said, forcing a lightness he didn't feel, "Want to see how bad the garage is?"

"Can't wait."

When JK opened the small garage, he made a show of it, aware of Nick watching him. He pulled off his t-shirt—the high temps, outside the house and in, provided enough of an excuse. Nick whistled at him, an appreciative light in his eyes that chased the chill from JK's bones. Then he stretched low and pulled the door high.

Nick's eyes skated past him, and his brows rose. "Don't people usually take their stuff when they move out?"

JK looked into the garage and said, "Oh crap."

Dealing with Mrs. Barton's leftovers in the garage had seemed like a petty annoyance the way Davis had made it sound, a matter of a handful of boxes, the things her husband hadn't bothered to take with him when he left her.

But this—

The clutter of Barton's life took up nearly the whole one-car garage. Two dozen boxes filled the space, along with seven bulging black plastic trash bags, and an enormous broken-down recliner that reeked of smoke.

"Damn," Nick said.

"It's a good thing I didn't bring new appliances." JK adjusted his gloves and waded in. The garage, he discovered gratefully, had little of the horror of the house. It was hot, crowded, and dusty, but it didn't ping his deeper senses.

"You have a plan?" Nick asked.

"Clear enough space that I can get my own stuff in. If I stack his boxes, I think it'll work."

Nick worked alongside him, their shoulders brushing, and the boxes piled up along the far wall quick and neatly. Light, most of them. Clothes, JK presumed, not least because the boxes carried the odor of cigarettes, both regular and menthol.

"Barton a smoker?"

"They both were," Nick said. "And they're big fans of chucking their butts in other people's yards. Ask them to stop and Barton gets in your face." He wrinkled his nose. "God, I really hate the smell of it."

"Those kind of neighbors, huh?" JK said.

"They sucked, excuse my French." Nick shrugged, a jerky motion. "He bullied her as well as everyone else."

JK shoved a box out of the way harder than he needed. Sometime he hated that regular people had all the opportunities in the world to connect with someone else and squandered it. Hated hearing that relationships could go bad. That someone who could touch freely abused that privilege.

His own relationships could be divided neatly into before and after with a seven-year abyss between. Before the accident, before the basement, he'd done the whole high school romance thing. He'd found the other boys on the football team who'd smile back and blush, who'd grind up against him behind the bleachers until they were breathless and sated.

After the accident, after the basement, there were the gloves. The secret. The lies. Relationships gave way to quickies in clubs when JK could escape his brother's over-protective tendencies.

JK said, "Did he bully the dogs, too? That kind of thing ends up pretty badly. Especially since they're big."

Nick nearly dropped the box he held, swore, caught it at the last minute and shoved it on top of the pile they were building. "The dogs? You know about the dogs?"

JK, kneeling to pick up the spilled items, glanced up at the tension in Nick's voice. He had to think about it. He'd heard dogs in the house, but... no, he had a better explanation than psychic slippage. "There's a damn big bag of dog food near the door. Large breed food."

Nick said, "Yeah. Barton has two. Ugly-tempered things. Shepherds. Took 'em with him when he moved out. They're probably the only things he does like."

"Weird that he didn't come back for his stuff."

"I guess." Nick sounded disinterested, but his shoulders were tense.

"I'd just hate to have him come back, expecting to find his stuff still here, you know?"

Nick rolled his shoulders. "Yeah, you and me both."

"You'd think he'd have taken the dog food when he took the dogs," JK said, eyeing the bag. "I mean, you said he liked them. Are they trained?"

"How should I know? It's not like I hung around drinking beers with the guy. I should go."

The change was abrupt. JK wanted to protest like a child who'd had a toy unexpectedly pulled away.

"Okay," he said, slowly, stretching the word.

"It's the cigarette smell," Nick said. "It's getting to me." Tossed off like it was the whole truth, and nothing but the truth, but it smacked of a man grasping at an excuse. JK knew that tone, had heard it from the people who found reasons to be elsewhere when they realized JK wore gloves everywhere he went. Inside or out. Night or day.

JK thought of responses—that he could set up a fan, air out the garage—but Nick's tone was uncompromising, closed off. JK decided not to force the issue. "All right."

"Sorry I can't help finish."

"No worries," JK said, though he wanted to know what had triggered the flight response in Nick. Talking about Barton? The dogs? "Thanks for saving my ass."

That brought a tiny smile back to Nick's face, there and gone, and he said, "That was my genuine pleasure."

JK felt a blush warm his cheeks, a smile tug at his lips. Nick paused in his walk away, and said, "Hey, let me make it up to you? Come to breakfast tomorrow."

"You sure you know what you're asking? I eat like a horse."

"I like a man with appetite," Nick said. "9:00. Don't be late."

JK watched Nick leave, and sighed twice. Once for the sight of Nick's broad shoulders and trim hips, the second time for the mess in the garage. Even with everything pushed over to one side, he still wouldn't have enough space to do more than set up his worktable—the garage just wasn't that big, a compact car size at best. If he was going to do any serious work, JK needed Barton's stuff gone. So he'd have to find out what time the city dump opened for trash drop-off, sort through the boxes first, and make sure they weren't filled full of hazardous materials that required special disposal.

In the meantime, he just needed enough space for the entertainment center. He could set up his worktable in the house for the start of the renovation, but as he progressed through the house—he shivered briefly, thinking of the house—the dust and debris thrown up by the saw would ensure JK spent twice as long on each task, cleaning up after himself. He wanted the rooms to be clean if Davis came to check.

Davis would come to check.

Maybe he could fit his table in if he stacked Barton's boxes higher, took out another row of them.

JK stacked them head high, bracing each box as best he could. The box towers sagged and bent while he built them. The final, lightest box slid and fell, bouncing away from his gloved hand as he tried to catch it.

The box broke open and its contents scattered like startled rats, spilling into every crevice between boxes, and down toward the concrete slab.

Something cracked and crashed at his feet, and he picked up a framed photo, now lacking its glass and brought it toward the light.

A man, presumably Barton, in desert camouflage, surrounded by a K9 unit. First Gulf War, given the man's age. Davis had said Mrs. Barton was in her fifties and Barton looked to be in his early thirties here. A brace of dogs sprawled about him, tongues lolling. Mine detectors.

Pinned in the corner of the frame, a gold medal. His service medal.

JK blinked.

This was junk?

Well, if Barton had left the medal behind when he left his wife, then maybe it meant nothing to him.

Still, the medals made JK uneasy, and when he bent to pick up the glass—gloves were good for that, at least—and came face to face with two metal dog bowls, he gave up on stacking and started searching.

Two hours later, JK had a pounding headache and a queasy feeling in his gut that had nothing to do with the heat or dust. Barton's belongings spread out around him like the remnants of a rummage sale. Fine dust and cardboard shavings fell from JK's suede gloves, and made him cough.

He had already annoyed his boss once today, but JK didn't see another option. He called Davis.

"Another problem, JK?"

He said, "I need Mrs. Barton's phone number."

"Why?"

"All her husband's stuff is here—"

"I warned you it would be. Call a charity or get a dumpster."

"It's all here. Clothes, checkbooks, credit cards, clothes, car title, shoes, house keys, dog bowls, leashes, everything. No one leaves this stuff behind on purpose."

Davis sighed. "It's not our problem. If it worries you, shred the financial stuff before you toss it."

"Just give me her number," JK said. "Let me double-check. Maybe she didn't mean to leave those boxes with the rest." Or maybe she had done it deliberately, a last act of spite toward a husband she hated. "I just don't want to get caught up in some type of domestic dispute. Or sued."

Davis groaned. "Why are you so goddamned stubborn? Fine, fine. If it'll get you back to doing the actual job I'm paying you to do."

Once JK had the woman's number in hand, he hesitated. He had hoped that once he told Davis what he'd found, his boss would take over for him and call Mrs. Barton. Davis had at least met her. JK would be dialing a total stranger.

He took a quick breath, then called.

Mrs. Barton answered, "Who is this?" and put him off balance instantly. She sounded as acid as a cracked battery.

"My name is JK Lassiter. I'm renovating your former house."

"Yeah? Good luck. You'll need it. That house isn't worth fixing."

"I found a bunch of your husband's things and needed to know where to send them."

"Straight to hell," Mrs. Barton said.

"There's a lot of personal items," JK said. "I don't feel comfortable—"

"Doesn't bother me any. I haven't seen that bastard since the night he walked out. I'm not missing him."

"Does he know you sold the house?" He'd have shown up for that.

"It's my house. My money. He hasn't called. Maybe he finally got a clue. I don't care. I told Davis I didn't want his shit. It's your problem now." She hung up on him.

JK stared at his phone in dismay, then shook off her hostility with a full body shudder, glad that Davis had dealt with Mrs. Barton during the sale. No wonder his boss hadn't volunteered to call her.

But now what? He eyed the credit cards, the checkbooks— the cards' expiration dates still months off, the checkbooks still with checks left—the dog collars, jingling as he moved them.

He could call Jesse.

Jesse might be able to help locate Barton.

JK slapped that idea right back down. He needed to be independent. That meant no calling his brother.

Jesse would be only too glad to help, to jump in and start telling JK what to do and how to do it. Bossy ran through his blood like rebar through new construction.

But it didn't seem right that Barton, no matter how ugly his breakup with his wife, would walk off without taking anything with him but the clothes on his back and his dogs. That horrible feeling in the house...

A shadow crossed in front of the garage and JK jolted, startled. The sun had been high overhead in a cloudless sky all afternoon, sun glare bearing into the garage. The shadow startled him. He stared, sun-dazzled, at the lean shape. It coughed once and said, "Come on out here." The man's voice, gravelly with age and heavy with command, seemed impossible to disobey. JK was moving before he'd meant to.

He found himself facing the old man who'd been pretend-reading across the street.

"Some of your trash blew onto my lawn," the old man said, holding up a scrap of familiar plastic—an emptied water bottle.

He said, "Sorry about that."

"What's your name?"

"JK."

The old man sighed, and scrubbed a calloused hand down the lines of his face. His stiff grey hair stood up like a brush, but one losing its bristles. It and the lines on his face were the only real signs of age. He held himself upright, his dark eyes were sharp and clear, and his forearms beneath his short-sleeved shirt were corded with muscle. A wedding band glinted bright and gold on his right hand. Widower?

Recent, if so, JK thought. His left hand still had a pale ring of skin that looked softer than the tanned and calloused rest.

"Um, JK Lassiter. Sir."

"What does JK stand for?"

The words *none of your business* crossed his mind, took a look at the old man in front of him, and retreated again. "Jasper Keely Lassiter. After my grandfather."

The old man nodded once, a motion that was less about agreement and more about the satisfaction of filing away new information. "I'm Ashford. Lieutenant Colonel Edwin Ashford."

After a moment, he grudgingly added, "Retired." Ashford held out his hand toward JK.

"Pleased to meet you, sir," JK said. He stuck out his hand for him to shake, grimacing internally.

"You're wearing gloves," Ashford said.

"I am." JK pulled his hand back, rocked onto his heels, wanting to escape. Nervousness flared in him. Ashford was the noticing type. Noticing and judging. JK wanted to fit in to this neighborhood, not stand out.

"There something wrong with your hands?" Ashford's gaze touched on his gloves, a heavier weight than Nick's light glances. Quick to pick out and distrust the different.

"I have sensitive skin," JK said. True enough and a lot easier than saying, *unless you want me to read your memories the moment we touch skin to skin—and you look like the type to have memories that I don't want to see.*

Ashford snorted. "Sensitive skin. What'd you do, cover them with gang tats when you were a teen?"

"No, sir," JK said. He relaxed; the guy couldn't be that perceptive if he thought JK was gang material.

"Got some kind of deformity?"

"No, sir," JK repeated. He'd heard worse guesses.

"I run the neighborhood watch."

"Good to know." JK put his hands behind his back. Casually.

"This is a nice neighborhood. We work hard to keep it that way. Look out for each other," Ashford said.

He pointed to the blue house on JK's right, the one with a kiddy pool. A stocky woman with a long dark braid waved as she checked her mail.

"That's the Sunitzes' house. They've got an autistic boy. He wanders. We all watch out for him. My wife Sofia used to babysit him before the cancer took her. The brick house with the flowers is the Martinellis'. They're a retired couple. Lou and Helen." He grimaced. Obviously, he didn't consider himself retired. "They putter and they garden. The house on my west side belongs to the Treanors. He's an accountant. She's a lawyer. Twin boys. Toddlers. They'll be back in three weeks. So will their dog. Bouvier. Nice dog, well-behaved. Sofia walked him sometimes. Not like Barton's ungovernable beasts."

Ashford went down the road, house by house, spilling facts. He was thorough in his information-gathering. "House at the closed end? That's college students. But they know better than to get loud late into the night. They're good girls. Brought Sofia Christmas cookies last year, when she couldn't bake them herself. Three of them. Amy Sheridan, Olivia Reed, and Inez Castillo. Amy delivers."

"Delivers what?"

"Groceries," Ashford said as if JK had been caught out not paying attention. "A boy like you probably lives on junk food. You should get Amy to bring you food. Good for you and her. She needs the money. She's paying for her own schooling and that doesn't leave her much. Graduate school. Her parents died in a car wreck a year ago."

JK nodded amiably, listening only half-heartedly to Ashford's rumbling voice, wondering if the girl with Inez had been Amy or Olivia. Amy, probably, given the money talk.

"... already met Nick Collier, of course, since he helped you unload your truck."

"What about Nick?"

Ashford's thick brows beetled in. His dark eyes gleamed. "Thought so. One of those sort, aren't you? Well, I'll tell you straight up. I don't approve, but it isn't my business to approve. Nick's had a damned hard year and he doesn't need any more grief."

JK's irritation faded. Questions burned on his tongue. Mindful of his own strangeness, JK bit them all back. He didn't want people gossiping about him, so he wouldn't encourage Ashford. He thought he saw a quick shine of satisfaction in Ashford's eyes, as if JK had passed some test by controlling his curiosity. Head of the neighborhood watch, his ass. Ashford was head of the whole damn neighborhood. Probably threw himself into it after his wife died.

"What are you doing?" Ashford said. "You've been in the garage for hours and you've still got stuff all over the front yard."

"Going through Barton's things," JK admitted. "He left so much behind. It just doesn't feel right."

"Let me see," Ashford said, his lips thinning. He strode into the garage, and began to flip through the essentials that JK had pulled out, neatly stacking each item back into a box as he went through them.

JK found himself waiting for the colonel's verdict.

"Nothing much here," Ashford said.

"His checkbook? The credit cards?"

Ashford let out a bark of laughter. "Not worth the paper they're printed on. Barton had a habit of writing bad checks, and I'd imagine the cards would be declined. Why do you think Mrs. Barton held the mortgage?"

"The medals?"

"The medals remind him of better days that he'll never see again. He threw them out once, only took 'em back when little Devi Sunitz found them and started playing with them. Didn't want them himself; but didn't want the kid to enjoy them. Barton is that kind of guy. Mean-spirited. We're well rid of him. Even leaving, he made an ass of himself. Staggering drunk into a friend's truck, shouting at the dogs to get their asses in the bed."

JK felt foolish; all his earlier concern was neatly explained away. He fidgeted and finally began helping Ashford box everything back up.

"You're young," Ashford said. "You think stuff is important. It isn't. It's just stuff. *People* are important. *Community's* important. But these boxes are obviously in your way. I'll call the local DAV and arrange for them to be picked up tomorrow if you get them down to the curb tonight. I'll take the financial stuff and run it through my shredder."

"Thanks," JK said.

Ashford said, "And in turn, you'll get all your stuff off the lawn and into the garage. This house has been a blight long enough. We're counting on you to make it better."

2

JK worked in the garage as long as he could stand it, even managing to get the brute entertainment center put away via judicious use of the dolly, furniture pads, and an excess of caution. But eventually, he had to face the interior again. He needed somewhere to sleep, and it was either the house or the U-Haul that he hadn't managed to return. With his abilities, motel rooms were the last place he'd turn to for rest: anything could have happened in them. Jesse had a wealth of grisly stories about crimes committed in anonymous rooms.

JK nudged the front door open, feeling his way in as cautiously as his cop brother would when answering a call of shots fired. He stepped into the house and—

Cooled air, cigarette smoke, wet dog, and shadows; a vibration flavored the rooms like the echoes of shouting and slamming doors.

Distinctly unpleasant, but nothing more.

JK let out a sigh of relief that almost sounded like a sob. He wasn't going to have to admit defeat. Wasn't going to have to call his boss and quit.

He took a careful, considering breath. The house stayed uncomfortable, but safe enough. Maybe Nick's idea of airing it out had been the right one. Maybe it was just the weeks sealed that had allowed all the bad that happened here to greet him so explosively.

JK worried the edge of his glove. That still didn't change the simple fact that this house felt familiar—not in its details, but in its atmosphere.

The last time he'd felt such a sensation, Davis had been hired to remodel an abandoned office building. JK had walked in, started work on the drywall in the furnace room and buckled under the weight of the drywall dust that blew violent memory into his face. He had bashed his head on Big Mike's hip belt and hammer as he went down, and missed all the real excitement. While he'd been outside, arguing with the EMTs that he didn't need a hospital trip, Raul and Rafael found the murdered girl's body wedged behind the boiler.

But if this house made him think about corpses, the question was: who had died? Mrs. Barton was alive and bitter. Barton's stuff had been left behind, but he'd been seen leaving the house.

Maybe it wasn't even one of the Bartons. The Bartons had been here for over twenty years, according to Davis. And in JK's experience atmospheric memories generally overwrote each other, the new over the old. But if something sufficiently violent happened before the Bartons had moved in, it could be possible.

JK deliberately stopped himself from going down this path.

Six months ago, exhilarated by the control he had gained over his visions, he'd chosen to confide in Ben Wilson, Jesse's good-looking colleague.

He'd been attracted to Ben and naively thought they would make a good team. He could provide insights into crime scenes that could make Ben's career and finally make himself useful.

In retrospect, JK should have seen the disaster coming. Ben was newly promoted to detective status, ambitious, and already dealing with the difficulty of being a gay cop in Texas. It made him... intolerant.

Ben flat-out hadn't believed JK, and worse, Ben had gone to Jesse's captain and complained that Jesse discussed his cases with his self-proclaimed psychic brother. A psychic on major antipsychotics, at that, because of course JK had to share every last secret he had. Psychic. Gloves. Medication.

Ben wanted Jesse fired, or at least, demoted.

JK had been on edge the whole time, worried he had ruined his brother's career. Even now, anxious fury roiled in his belly, made sweat break out along his hairline.

In the end, the captain had sided with Jesse, and Ben had transferred stations.

Ultimately, JK reminded himself, he didn't need to care, didn't need to get involved. He was here to remodel the house, and in doing so, he'd clear out the old atmosphere, the old house memories. Give the house—and himself—a new lease on life. The past could stay buried.

❊

That night in the upstairs bedroom, while listening to the pump chugging furiously to fill the air mattress, JK unrolled his sleeping bag. He was glad for the ruckus. The house felt empty with only his own breathing for company.

The silence made it too easy for him to give in to trepidation. Maybe the first force of the house had dissipated, but it wasn't gone. Just waiting to be rediscovered.

He'd been taking notes in the kitchen—remove linoleum, restore cabinetry if possible—when he realized that his shoulders were drawn up tight enough to hurt. Like he feared a blow.

His phone beeped, and JK twitched guiltily. One day on his own, and he'd almost forgotten to take his pills. He'd resented Jesse telling him to program the reminder into his phone, but his brother had a point. JK loved and loathed the pills equally. They made his life workable but, like wearing gloves twenty-four/seven, the pills marked him as different.

JK washed his pills down with a gulp of metallic-tasting tap water, and waited. Twenty minutes later, he'd found his shoulders easing, and grimaced. The house was still getting to him, just in a more subtle way.

Touching an object or a person without his gloves was a sure-fire way to get sucked into visions—all the pills in the world couldn't prevent that. His medication only muted his general sensitivity to the world, kept him from being overwhelmed by his environment. It wasn't working as well as usual.

If it kept up, he might have to ask Hannah about altering the dose. He would just have to invoke client privilege and hope she wouldn't tell Jesse.

Probably a vain hope.

The air pump shut off with a bang and JK jumped a mile, then laughed nervously. His voice sounded small and breathy in the dark and empty room.

JK had picked the master bedroom as his own, not just because it was nice to have space to move around, but as a matter of cleanliness.

The master bedroom at the top of the house had terrible old shag carpeting, and the layers of wallpaper smelled like menthol cigarettes, but the downstairs bedroom had been where the dogs lived. They had worried the carpet there ragged with their teeth and claws, tearing up great sections of it.

Barton had apparently staple-gunned down more layers of carpet on top of it as a fix. Brown, red, green, and patterned—obviously remnants, bought cheap. He'd had a heavy hand with the staples and when JK experimentally peeled up some of the brown carpet, then the builder's grade beige, he wasn't surprised to see that the old hardwood planks below were pocked and splintered.

No point in getting settled into a room where he needed to rip up the whole floor, JK thought. Instead, he'd take the slightly-too-warm aerie at the top of the stairs, which needed only cosmetic work.

He tested the air mattress, listened to the vinyl squeak loudly in the silence, and shuddered. Too damn quiet. The kind of silence that tempted his senses to stretch out and see what they could touch. Dangerous silence.

JK went back downstairs in the dark, careful of the frayed carpet on the stairs, and paused at the base. Had he heard dogs growling or the clinking of collars?

Nothing.

JK shook his head, shook away the jingling dog collars, realized that the noise came from the loose change in his pockets. He felt stupid, but he'd never heard such a silence. A low rumble teased at his ears, the echo of a snarling animal, and JK shook his head again. *No. No.*

He brought the iPod dock up the stairs, set it on the windowsill, and started playing television episodes, giving himself the comforting sounds of interaction without actual people. His lips curled as he heard his favorite character's rapid-fire and deadpan delivery of ridiculous lines and his long-suffering friends' responses. His tense shoulders eased.

JK stripped off his t-shirt, smelled it, winced, and threw the shirt across the room. It crumpled damply on the carpet. His cargo pants, stained at the knees and shins from crawling around on the dog-ruined flooring, came off next. JK looked at the bathroom longingly, thought about a shower, but exhaustion filled his spine like a lead weight. And no way was he getting into the shower before it had been bleached to hell and back. Bathtubs should be white, not mottled ivory and brown.

When people sold their houses, they fell into two categories: the ones who cleaned like maniacs, even if they'd never cleaned before, and the ones who just stopped bothering, figuring it would be someone else's problem. Mrs. Barton fell into the latter group. Usually Davis had his cleaning service come through right away, but this time JK figured that his boss saw no point in spending money on the same house twice. Once JK finished the renovation, *then* Davis would send in the service to scrub out any remaining dirt—the inevitable sanding dust, the little bits of spackle, paint drips, and the like.

JK crashed onto the air mattress in boxers and dirty gloves and let his eyes close, listened to the vinyl creak beneath his shifting weight.

His heart raced. His eyes popped open.

Too much in his head. Too much fear of the house, of the memories lurking in it. Even with the iPod playing, he couldn't relax enough to fall asleep.

JK was living alone for the first time ever. He'd gone from his parents' white-walled, windowless basement to sharing his brother's duplex to this solitary fixer-upper. But his life was getting back on track, going back to the way it should have been.

He could do the same for this house.

This bedroom had so much potential.

JK shifted on the mattress, and tried to imagine the windows shining and new, the wallpaper peeled off the plaster, the plaster smoothed out and painted some cheerful color. He pictured the carpet removed, and a polished hardwood floor gleaming beneath the long, narrow window that adorned the western wall facing the street. In the evening, sunlight would creep in, turning the old stained glass into a blaze of color on the bed and floor and wall. His own personal aurora.

After that—JK yawned—after that the downstairs bedroom needed the carpet pulled up and out. He'd sand the wood down, see how far the staple damage went. He might have to replace the floor. He hoped it would come to that. Replacing the floor would work to remove the house's lingering memories faster than almost anything else. JK could invite his coworkers over, have dinner for Jesse and Hannah—work on overwriting the house's bad memories with good ones of his own.

JK's lips curved, relaxing. Finally he allowed himself to fantasize about breakfast with Nick tomorrow. Potential to create good memories right there. He wondered if Nick would dress for breakfast, or if he'd let JK in, while still in his PJs, warm and sleepy and touchable...

JK sleep-jolted, awake all at once, heart racing. Gunshots? Had he heard gunshots? He lay there tensely, waiting, but finally sleep reclaimed him.

3

JK woke from agitated dreams when the sun lanced in through the dusty eastern window and burned into his eyes, making him curse his decision not to hang a sheet over the glass the previous night. But the backyard was a world of its own, a shadowy, dog-churned space of dirt and a single massive oak all hidden behind a tall privacy fence, and JK had been too tired to worry about squirrels getting an eyeful.

Now, he swore, and rocked his way off the air mattress, which, in the nature of all air mattresses, had inexplicably lost half its buoyancy in the night. It was a little like trying to climb out of a damp gummy bear's embrace.

He scrubbed at the patchy stubble on his jaw, smelled himself—stale sweat, lingering smoke—and nearly gagged. Shower. Now.

In the bathroom, JK took the precaution of spraying the stained tub and tiles down with tub scrub, then hit the sink first, giving the cleaner time to work. Brushing his teeth gave him an eye-opening taste of mint and chemicals and he made a quick job of it.

His electric razor buzzed erratically—JK stared at the plug and socket in exasperation. The Bartons had been damned rough on their possessions. The socket jiggled loosely in the wall, suggesting someone's habit of unplugging things by yanking the cord instead of the plug. An easy enough fix. He added it to his mental schedule.

He buzzed his stubble back, yawning and careless, thumping the socket as needed, and thought, *Good enough.* JK started the water running, rinsed the tub scrub away, leaving the enamel palely striped with the uneven concentration of cleaner.

After dropping his boxers, he opened the box of nitrile gloves that he bought by the hundreds, and carefully pulled off his right glove, the suede clinging to his skin, saturated with sweat and dirt from the day before. He'd have to wash them before he wore them again. He sniffed them.

Maybe he'd just throw them away.

It wasn't like JK didn't have boxes of the suede work gloves also. A portion of every paycheck went to keeping him in gloves: suede, nitrile, rubber, silk. His own tithe to sanity.

Right hand bare, air rushing over it, making his skin tingle with cold and adrenaline. What might he see if he let it brush the wall or the sink? He held his hand away from the counter, the walls, and himself, then peeled out the first pair of nitriles and rolled one over his bare skin. Then JK stripped off the other suede glove, let it fall, and used the gloved right hand to manipulate the sink and wash his left hand, touching nothing but the water and liquid soap. He waited for his skin to air-dry because nothing created frustration like trying to put nitrile gloves over wet hands.

Then gloved the left hand, peeled the right nitrile back off to wash that hand, and repeated the slow, familiar ritual. When both his hands were gloved and safe again, he sighed with mingled relief and sadness.

He was never going to be normal.

His stomach swooped, hunger and nerves mingling. Why had he said yes to Nick's offer of breakfast? He couldn't pull off normal if he tried, and this breakfast would just hasten the neighborhood gossip: JK, the new weird guy...

If he'd had Nick's number, he might have canceled. But he'd been raised too well to stand Nick up, so breakfast was a go. JK pushed back the worries, and focused on the bright spot. He'd get to see Nick at least once more.

The water pressure was good, and the temperature was set high, both things that went a long way to making up for the camo-patterned, tattered, plastic shower curtain and the complementing olive drab wallpaper. JK groaned in pleasure as the water sluiced over him. He craned his neck downward, scrunched his back down, ducking his head to get his hair under the stream. A long familiar woe. Ever since he broke the too-damn-tall mark of almost six and a half feet, he'd outstripped a lot of regular-sized items.

He still found it creepy, the sight of his own blue-gloved hands on his skin, but without the gloves, he could lose time just by touching his own skin. JK got lost in the memory of anything he touched, and everything and everyone had a lifetime of memories for him to explore. Including himself. Not only could he get trapped in his own past, but some of those memories were ones he wanted badly to forget.

It seemed a fair trade: the peculiarity of wearing gloves all the time so he couldn't even touch his own skin—versus reliving the cold horror of slipping through the ice, feeling himself speared by the impossible pain of freezing water, the drag of his heavy hockey skates, the agony in his lungs as he drank the water in, burning and drowning him at the same time. Who needed that as a wakeup call in the morning?

Especially when he had breakfast with Nick to look forward to.

JK dressed, realizing he hadn't unpacked his nicer clothes, only his workwear. He dug out a green t-shirt without holes, and found a pair of unstained jeans and a new pair of work gloves. Good to go.

❁

JK climbed Nick's front porch, studied the dark gloss of the well-cared-for wood, the two sturdy hooks in the blue-painted ceiling that suggested either potted plants or a swing had hung there recently, the shimmer of sunlight on the cut edges of the windows. Yeah. Leaded glass. Pretty stuff.

He stumbled over the sisal mat that declared him WELCOME. JK reached out to knock on Nick's door, saw his gloved hand curling into a fist, and hesitated. The damn gloves. Yesterday, wearing them had been unexceptional. In this circumstance?

No help for it, though.

He knocked, then waited, feeling exposed on the porch, his

back to the silent street—the new guy going to breakfast with his freaky gloves on.

From behind the door came a creak, a soft scuff of footsteps, a pause, and a shadow across the peephole as if Nick had stopped to use it. Unusual behavior for a six-foot guy in good health in a decent neighborhood. A moment later, a series of snaps and clicks, and Nick opened the door. He had on a pair of low-slung well-worn jeans, with another battered university t-shirt. His feet were bare. His sharp-edged jaw line was blurred with stubble. He held a pencil in his hand absent-mindedly. It looked like he'd been chewing on the end.

JK found himself grinning again. Nick squinted up at him, stepped back and gestured him in with a smile.

JK entered the dimly lit living room while Nick locked up. Two deadbolts and a chain. Shiny with newness in a sleepy neighborhood. Nick caught him looking at the locks. His shoulders stiffened, waiting for the obvious question: what was Nick afraid of?

He felt Nick's reciprocal curiosity, the other man's pale-eyed gaze on JK's gloves, but when JK looked up, Nick glanced back toward the front door. Toward the locks JK decided not to ask about.

"Morning," JK said, instead of asking. "What's for breakfast?"

"What are you in the mood for?" Nick's voice came out thick and gruff, a low rumble that did good things to JK's nerves.

"Everything," JK said.

Nick smiled, a slow, sleepy curve of his lips, and JK's hand twitched, wanting to touch that soft arc. His fingertips felt sensitized, scraping against the inside of his gloves, prisoners. "Let's start with coffee, huh?" Nick said.

JK took his time following Nick, admiring the house around him, taking mental notes. Where the Bartons' bungalow looked like demented patchwork, Nick's Craftsman could have come from any of the architectural design books JK had been mainlining to prepare for the remodel. Nick's house boasted plaster walls, which were creamy pale against the dark glossy hardwood floors, and natural wood box beam ceilings. An archway opened into a living room, while another arch beckoned up ahead, spilling sunlight across the floors.

The living room—JK lingered for a minute, studying it. There were built-ins along the living room wall between the heavily curtained windows, stuffed full of shadowed books, but Nick had added more bookshelves, turning the living room into something closer to a library. A nail-head leather sofa rested on an ornate floral rug that might be either a good reproduction or original to the twenties. If the curtains had been drawn back, he'd be able to see the Bartons' house... eyesore that it was. No wonder Nick had the windows draped even during the day.

A deep cabinet with stained glass doors sat on the wall facing the sofa—hid the television, JK thought. The whole room looked comfortable, welcoming, and as attractive as the man who owned it.

JK turned from admiring the room and found Nick watching him, idly tapping the pencil against his thigh.

"Sorry," JK said. If he'd been the type to blush, he might have. "It's great. Your house is great. I'm starting to get ideas."

"Always good to get ideas," Nick said. "I'll give you the tour later."

JK's senses woke up, pointed out that the smell curling itself through the house was coffee and good coffee at that.

The breakfast room was brighter than the living room; pale Roman shades lightly covered the row of windows, a distinct change from the blackout curtains that blanketed the street-facing rooms. JK found himself squinting in the brightness, and when his eyes adjusted, he found that the kitchen looked a hell of a lot more lived in than the other room, bookshelves notwithstanding. A large Mission-style table dominated the breakfast room, but in a friendly, laid-back fashion, like a large dog stretched out across a hearth.

Papers and a laptop took up one side of the table, books littered with flags on the pages. He asked Nick, "You prepping for a class?"

"Writing a book," Nick said.

"So you said. What's it a book on?"

"History," Nick said. "Specifically Texas border politics in the nineteenth century."

"That's specific," JK said. "You know a lot about the area? You grow up here?"

"Nah, I'm a California boy," Nick said. Sunlight touched his dark hair, lit the strong planes of his face, and cast a warm golden shade over his skin. Yeah, California. JK could see it.

The whole house smelled like percolating heaven and fresh toast.

JK's stomach, shameless, growled. Nick tossed his pencil onto his paperwork, and laughed.

"Didn't you eat dinner last night?" He moved on to the small open kitchen.

JK replied, "I didn't bring a lot of groceries with me. Just peanut butter and milk and bread and some of those orange cheese squares."

Nick sighed. "Now I know you're under thirty. Cholesterol doesn't actually mean anything to you, does it?"

"Like you're an old man."

"Sometimes I feel like it," Nick said. He shook his head. "Anyway. Coffee? Milk, cream, sugar?"

"If I say cream, are you going to break out the cholesterol talk again?"

"Imply a guest is being careless with his health? Never." Nick poured coffee into a mug the same faded blue as his jeans, added a generous spill of cream, and brought it to JK. JK reached out, his gloves wickedly conspicuous, and took the mug, shifting it so he could hold it from below. With the gloves, his fingers didn't fit beneath the handle.

JK felt Nick's attention on his gloves, but when JK looked up, Nick glanced back toward the front door. Toward the locks JK hadn't asked about. Nick sat down across from him with his own mug without asking any questions.

JK let out a shaky breath, then sipped his coffee and

groaned. "This is great. Let me guess—you were a barista."

"Had to pay my way through grad school somehow," Nick said.

JK stared at the pale swirl of coffee in the blue mug and said, "I didn't do college."

"Did you want to?" Nick sat down across from him with his own mug.

The coffee warmed his hands, even through the gloves—comforting. JK shifted a shoulder. He said, "I thought I would. But things got off track."

Nick rose, put a hand on JK's shoulder, thumb brushing his neck, the edges of his shaggy hair, and said, "Life can do that to you. I wanted to teach, so getting my degree was a necessary evil."

JK shivered when Nick took his hand away, and pivoted in the chair to watch Nick move about his kitchen with easy competence, collecting ingredients, bumping the fridge closed with an easy hip check. JK loved people who were good at things.

"Are you all right with *migas*?" Nick said. "Fancy southwest scramble. Eggs, tortillas, a lot of other things. Looks like crap, tastes like heaven."

"I'm in your hands." JK assessed the ingredients on the counter. Onion, tomato, peppers—bell and jalapeno—a block of white cheese. Sharp cheddar from the scent. At least half of them looked like they might need to be chopped. "Can I help?"

"Are those gloves the ones you wore yesterday, or clean?" Nick asked, matter-of-factly.

JK swallowed hard. "Clean this morning." He took a deep breath, and felt his heart thudding in his throat. "I have a lot of gloves."

Nick did another quick once-over, flicking from JK's strong wrists to the anxious expression JK knew twisted his face.

"All right, then." Nick passed him a knife. "Go for it."

JK did a little showing off—carefully; Nick's knives were wickedly sharp—but he wanted Nick to know that he retained dexterity.

"I saw you decided to put Barton's stuff out on the curb," Nick said.

"Yup," JK said. "I needed the garage space."

"Trash day's not for a few more days yet. You might get some grief from the neighbors."

"It's not for trash pickup. Colonel Ashford said he'd call the DAV. That they'd pick the boxes up today."

Nick stirred eggs into the sautéing vegetables and shredded tortillas, scrambling them together. It smelled wonderful.

"If he said they would, they will. Ashford's reliable as sunrise." Nick plated the meal, added the shredded cheese, and put a jar of salsa on the table.

JK fiddled with his fork, thinking about the boxes, about all the things Barton left behind. "Where *do* you think Barton went?" he asked.

"I don't know. He didn't tell anyone. Just took his dogs, his beer, and got a ride from some friend of his with a pickup in the middle of the night."

"Wasn't anybody surprised when he didn't come back?"

Nick shrugged. He said, "Only thing that surprised me was hearing he had a friend. Eat up. It'll get cold."

JK raised the forkful to his mouth and dug in.

"So what's your plan for the day?" Nick asked, while spooning salsa on his plate.

"The kitchen," JK mumbled through a glorious mouthful of cheese and spices. He swallowed, then added, "I need to get the appliances out and get the cabinets down. The shape of the room is good, so hopefully it won't require actual demolition. Just taking everything old and ugly out and putting restored stuff in."

The rumble of a heavy truck came from outside and JK found himself on his feet, feeling oddly panicky.

"You okay?" Nick asked.

"Just... it's the charity picking things up. Barton's stuff. Maybe

I should keep it after all... It just feels wrong that he left it all behind."

"He's not the kind of guy who makes good decisions," Nick said. "Serves him right if he regrets it later."

After they'd finished their meals down to scraps and JK had forked up the last little scrap of melted cheese, Nick turned on the radio—soft, slow jazz, good morning music—and started cleaning up. JK rose as well, dithering. Courtesy said he should offer to wash, but the gloves were suede...

"Sit," Nick said, making the decision for him. "Tell me a little about you."

"Right now," JK said, "I'm thinking I might have made a wrong turn career-wise. Your house is amazing. I'm supposed to make the Bartons' look something like this? Talk about the impossible dream."

"I got lucky," Nick said, hands deep in sudsy water. "Ridiculously lucky. I bought this house for a wish and a prayer. The previous owner worked at UT-Dallas, and loved the idea of a history teacher taking on the house. She made me swear on a stack of bibles as big as my head that I wouldn't modernize more than I had to. The mortgage is brutal though." He rinsed his hands, wiped them down with a dish towel, and refilled both their coffee mugs, a clear invitation for JK to linger.

JK sighed contentedly into his steaming mug.

Nick settled back down at the table, and said, "So where do you live when you're not flipping houses for your boss? Are you a local boy, or did you come to Dallas special to do this?"

JK turned his mug about in his hands. He said, "I was living with my brother and his wife. My brother Jesse, he thinks I'm a lunatic for even taking this project on. But he's a born pessimist."

"I got a buddy like that," Nick said. "Always assumes the worst." A quick roll of those pale blue eyes. "Sadly, he's right more often than he's wrong."

"You went to school with him?" JK asked. It sounded like a long-running relationship. He wondered, briefly, if "buddy" meant old boyfriend.

"Yeah. Undergrad together at K State, then graduate school here. He runs a local business, and I teach."

"Kansas," JK murmured. "How did that go?"

Nick leaned back, smiling. "You mean with me being gay? I won't lie. There was definitely tension. All those cowboys and me. But anyone gave me too much grief and I sicced Zeke— that's my friend—on them. I'm not one for fighting, but Zeke likes it just fine. Word got around. What about you?"

JK shrugged, uncomfortably. "I already told you, I didn't go to college."

"That's not what I was asking. You grew up..."

"Oh," JK said. "I grew up in the wildly liberal northeast. No serious trouble being a gay teen there."

"And I'm sure it had nothing to do with you being about nine feet tall and built like you are."

"Later development," JK said. "Always tall, but the muscle... That's good old construction for you. Two years plus of hauling heavy machinery and long hours."

"And you're not..." Nick hesitated, and JK frowned, wondering what he wasn't.

"Sorry," Nick continued, shaking his head. "Just trying to figure out a way to ask if you were beating off would-be boyfriends with a stick that didn't sound so... dirty."

JK laughed. "Construction work. I'm good with dirt. But no, all I've done for the past couple years is work." And that might not be the whole truth, but it was the majority of it. Most of the past two years had been spent either working his ass off for Davis and the crew, or wrestling with his abilities. "Though, I won't deny hitting up the clubs every so often for a night's company."

"Bet you don't have a lot of problems finding company," Nick said. He didn't look like the thought sat well with him.

"Finding the right company is always hard," JK said. "They're all about drinking and dancing, and sometimes you just want coffee and... pastry." He shied away at the last moment from *migas*; it felt too much like some type of declaration—and as cute and nice as Nick seemed to be, JK wasn't ready for any kind of declaration.

"Pastries are always good," Nick said after a pause, smiling.

They fell back to chatting. JK learned that Nick adored teaching, remembered his past students by name, and kept notes for when recommendations were needed.

Nick's love for history even showed itself in the movies he owned—anything with an historical bent got bought, even, Nick admitted, if the films had no more than a passing nod toward reality.

"So you're saying you were a big fan of The Mummy movies with Brendan Fraser?"

"More like *House of Flying Daggers*."

"Subtitles," JK said, grimacing.

"*The Mummy Returns* had subtitles," Nick pointed out.

"I knew you watched it," JK teased.

"Well, Brendan Fraser..."

In return, JK evaded, less than smoothly, a question about his parents and fielded a series of questions about what he'd done before he came to Dallas. JK said he'd done nothing much worth mentioning, that he'd been getting his act together, that kind of thing. Finally, he countered by asking about Nick's relationship state.

"Single," Nick said. "Sadly single."

"You've always got Zeke," JK pointed out and Nick howled with laughter until he had to wipe tears from his eyes.

"Oh, sure. Me and my attack dog. Who, by the way, is completely straight. Just so you know."

They ended up spending nearly two hours talking, sipping their way through a second pot of coffee, and it only took a few of JK's clumsy evasions for Nick to stop asking questions about his past. He never once asked about the gloves.

The whole morning felt like a gift.

JK only excused himself when Davis had texted him with a time for the delivery of the new appliances—before the end of the afternoon.

Nick invited him to come back any time and locked the door behind him.

JK breathed in deeply, taking in the quiet of the cul-de-sac. Distantly, traffic flowed. But here it was quiet, and on the breeze, he could smell the flowers the elderly couple—the Martinellis?—had put in yesterday. Heat shimmer started on the road, another scorcher coming up.

His phone rang, two tones at once—his pill reminder and an incoming call. His sister-in-law Hannah, ostensibly calling to see if he needed anything; more likely phoning to check up on him for Jesse the Worrier.

"I'm about to take my pill, relax," JK said, before she asked.

"Good for you, but I really did want to know how you were doing. Jesse's been nothing but doom and gloom about this—"

"Tell me about it. Does he think I'm going to electrocute myself or what?" JK did adore Hannah. She was kind, smart, and sensible; also, she managed to temper his brother's more smothering instincts. He wandered toward the house, noting that the DAV had been thorough. Barton's stuff was gone without even a mark left in the dirt.

He interrupted Hannah's defense of his brother; he'd heard it all before anyway. JK said, "If Jesse walked out on you, what would you do with his stuff?"

"What? Why would he do that?" she asked.

"So, the Bartons—the people who owned this house—he walked out, and she sold it. But she left his stuff behind. Would you do that?"

Hannah laughed, the sound as bright as her strawberry blond hair. "Honey, I've seen relationships that go so bad that one spouse locks the other out of the house and sells everything on eBay before the court orders come in."

"Her spite, I get that. But I mean, he left his credit cards and everything. Would you do that?"

Hannah said, thoughtfully, "Only if I was scared for my life. I've had clients running from abusive husbands, from abusive families." She stumbled over the last word, hastened past it. "Any sign of trouble like that? It would be unusual, but not unheard of, for the wife to be the abuser."

JK considered the quick vision he'd had, the woman with the hunched shoulders. He said, "I don't get the idea that she's a sweetheart, but no. From everything I've heard, he's a bully. The kind to make little kids cry. A soft spot for his dogs. You think it means anything that so far two people have told me he liked his dogs?"

Hannah said, "Yes. He had a hard time conveying affection to anything else."

JK opened the front door, and the weight of the house came down on him, making him gasp. He breathed it in—snarling dogs, a scrape and drag that made him turn quickly toward the living room, thinking someone stood waiting there—but he saw nothing. Heard nothing, except Hannah, saying his name with increasing concern.

"Nothing, it's nothing," JK said.

Hannah let the silence hum.

He said, "Something happened in this house. I'm... worried. It doesn't seem right."

"Want me to send Jesse?"

"No," JK said hastily. "Definitely not."

"The house... it's not giving you problems, is it? Are your pills working?"

"It's all good," JK said. He sought a new topic that would distract her. "Did I tell you about my next-door neighbor?"

"Aw, do you have a cute neighbor?" Hannah asked, taking the bait.

"And how," JK said. He found himself smiling. "Dark hair, pale eyes, looks like a movie star." That didn't really cover it, but as much as he loved Hannah, he didn't need to tell her about the way Nick's t-shirts pulled over his shoulders, the way the fabric clung to his waist. The way his pants outlined his thighs with devoted fidelity. The way his lashes swept down, sooty and thick, just before he said something teasing, then blinded you with the brightness beneath when Nick looked up, grinning. JK wanted to keep all that for himself.

"Just a pretty face?" she asked.

"He's a history professor." JK paused, closed the house door behind him as he edged around spilling secrets that weren't his. "He's kind of… cautious. He's thirty-three years old. No local family, but I guess there's some in California. Listens to blues. Makes a great cup of coffee and has a shitload of university memorabilia, so I guess he loves his job as much as he says he does."

All of it factual, none of it touching the warmth in his gut.

"He sounds nice," Hannah said. "Just remember…"

"What? To wear a condom? I'm not an idiot. Or a virgin."

"Defensive much?" Hannah chided. "I was going to say just remember that you have to live there until the reno's done. Don't jump into things. This isn't like the clubs."

"That's sort of the point," JK said. Some of his excitement leeched away, and he sighed. "I've got to get to work. I've got a kitchen to deal with. Plus appliance delivery. Tell Jesse I'm fine."

He disconnected, and leaned back against the door, trying to convince himself that he wasn't lying. The house felt unfriendly, but that didn't have to mean something bad had happened. Barton had just walked off, a bad-tempered man enacting a child's runaway, taking only his dogs.

JK took his pill, and scowled at the stove. His original plan for the day had been to get the bedroom scrubbed down, the wallpaper peeled off, and the walls prepped for painting. But he might want to offer Nick a meal himself, and that old electric stove looked like a fire hazard. A closer inspection proved him right: the wired connection between the coils and the power source had frayed in its casing. Not exactly something he could wait on.

First step, make sure he didn't electrocute himself. He headed for the breakers. If it sounded like dog toe nails clicking after him over the linoleum, the rough gust of panting at his calves…

JK ignored it. His pill would kick in and any residual ambiance would fade. He hoped.

He gave the medicine a head start by returning the U-Haul, and taxiing back to the house. An unexpected cost—both the late fee and the taxi fare—but worth it not to have to call Davis for help.

JK lost himself in labor, disconnecting the old range, and dragging it down to the curb. Mindful of Colonel Ashford's gaze—did the old man *live* on his front porch?—and his warning about the young neighborhood boy, JK removed the door to the oven, and stacked it separately. He did the same for the refrigerator, stacking the few foodstuffs he had brought with him on the counter.

A bad smell lingered somewhere, something rotten. He'd thought it was the aged refrigerator stuck with a bad memory of its own—a pound of hamburger turned so green that the lining of the fridge took on the scent, something like that—but even with the fridge outside, the odor stayed.

He'd find the source of the stink eventually. It might even be a dead mouse in an electrical socket. That happened disgustingly often.

A truck honked outside, and JK startled at the sound, flinching for no reason at all. The damned house still crept in around the edges, even with the pills. He needed to turn on the radio or something, anything to drown out the not-quite sounds he heard and felt.

The truck honked once more. Opening the door showed him that Davis himself had come to supervise delivery of the new appliances. And, no doubt, to see that JK had gotten something started. JK thought about the kitchen, only partially gutted. Thought about the downstairs bedroom, with its carpet only partially pulled up, and his workbench, still covered with a tarp. JK grimaced. Not his best foot forward.

4

Burned by Martin, Davis wouldn't rest until the new appliances had been installed and tested. He used the new oven to heat up a late lunch of Sonny Bryan's takeout ribs, then used the stovetop to warm the barbecue sauce, filling the house with the spicy sweet scent.

JK plugged in the new fridge, pressed it to make ice and keep the beer and potato salad cold. A dishwasher washed dishes that Davis had bought just for that purpose—JK had been fine with living on Styrofoam plates, plasticware, and paper coffee mugs. The washer and dryer had been started, washing JK's sheets. And they'd spent three brutal hours in the heat, yanking out the old air conditioning unit, and installing a new one.

The new AC filled the house with a welcome chill, which beat back that weird sour-sweet odor JK kept smelling around the edges of the back rooms.

Davis had taken a look at the exposed section of floorboards in the dog room. He'd shaken his head over the staple damage and said, "Yeah, you're right. You'd spend twice as long, and twice as much trying to restore the damaged boards. Go ahead and replace the hardwood. Figure out what'll match with the rest of the house and let me know."

Davis left a little past eight. On his heels, Jesse and Hannah arrived, bringing JK his pick-up truck, and a couple paper bags of groceries as their entry ticket.

Hannah rolled her eyes as Jesse lectured JK on home safety, and the need to lock his doors at all times, even in a nice neighborhood like this. JK would have rolled his eyes back in solidarity, but he knew why Jesse had hotfooted it over, right after work. Hannah had tattled.

"Doesn't look too bad inside," Jesse finished up. "Not nearly as bad as I thought. It could be a real nice house."

"Not subtle," JK said, glaring at them equally. "What did Hannah say?"

Hannah shrugged. "I was worried."

"She said there might be something wrong with the house."

"Yeah, it's ugly." JK crossed his arms over his chest. He all but dared Jesse to call him on his defensiveness.

"Play nice, boys," Hannah said, curiosity driving her deeper into the house. JK heard her poking into the kitchen, settling the grocery bags down—Whole Foods Market, nice to have a doctor's salary—then wandering upstairs.

"So what else is it... besides ugly?" Jesse asked. He held his jaw locked like he had a whole lot more he wanted to say.

"It's nothing much," JK said. "I can handle it."

They stared at each other, JK's arms tightening against his chest as he watched Jesse's jaw twitch. JK forced himself to lower his arms, to stop being so defensive. It made him feel younger, dumber, even more like someone who needed to be locked up for his own good. It didn't help that Jesse was his bigger brother in all ways. Taller, broader, classically handsome, and confident. In control of his own life.

Under the scrutiny JK caved. "It's just... impressions. A bad feeling."

Jesse scrubbed his hands over his face. "Maybe you're letting the stress get to you."

"What?" JK said.

"You need this job to work, and I think you're letting your worries take over."

"Barton—the husband—has gone *missing*," JK said, frustrated.

Jesse's expression closed off, both worried and angry. He said, "And so what? A moment ago you told me it was nothing much. Which is it, JK?"

Hannah came downstairs and hung back in the doorway,

watching them with careful neutrality as befit a psychiatrist. JK took a deep breath and lied to his brother. "I guess it's just a lot of bad feelings."

Jesse scowled. He said, "That sounded unconvincing. Try again."

Hannah stepped in. "Sweetie, stop playing bad cop with your brother. JK, stop glaring at me, you knew I'd tell him you were having some problems."

JK shrugged. He said, "They're my problems and they're manageable."

"Hannah, talk sense to him." Jesse snapped and stormed out to the car. He left the front door open after him, twilight crawling in through the gap.

Hannah sighed, and said, "I put the groceries in the fridge. And left a coffee maker on the counter for you. Just promise me you'll call if it gets too bad."

"Sure," JK said.

He moved to close the door and found Hannah in his arms instead, hugging him in a welter of light floral perfume and warmth. He closed his eyes and leaned into her. She said, quietly, "If this doesn't work. You can always come home—"

"No." JK stepped out of her grasp.

She studied him; he tried not to let the fear show. He couldn't go backwards, couldn't fail. If JK failed here, and had to retreat to Jesse's, what would stop him from failing there, and ending up all the way back where he'd started—a lunatic locked in a basement?

Hannah took a deep breath. "Okay. But listen, if the house gets too much, why don't you split the difference? Work outside. The yard looks a wreck."

It wasn't a bad idea. That rotting privacy fence needed to be torn down, and the siding scraped and repainted. "Yeah," he said, more loosely this time. Relaxing.

"Remember to take breaks." She smiled suddenly, glorious and wicked, and said, "And holy God, date the man next door.

You were not wrong." Her eyes were wide, and JK turned to see Nick doing a late night collection of his mail, the light over his porch illuminating the lines of his body.

"Yeah," JK said, admiring Nick all over again. "Definitely part of my plan."

✸

That night JK's dreams had lacked all color. First the walls of the house bleached white, closing about him and returning him to the basement. Then the basement floor opened beneath him. JK clawed at the walls, trying to hold on, but slid into the black earth beneath. Earth and insects covered him, drowning him in the earth—burying him alive. Belowground, the cold clay gnawed at his bones, made JK slow and heavy, made his bones ache.

He struggled upward, but dirt cracked like rotten ice beneath his desperate fingers and he sank back down, lungs aching, filling, the final spasm twitching out through his frozen limbs.

When he started awake, JK's stomach churned with misery, and he wasn't sure how much of it belonged to him. He popped his first pill six hours early and dry, before he even flailed off his mattress, and waited, breath tight in his chest, until the growling he heard faded into nothing more than a distant lawn mower.

JK ate leftover ribs and potato salad cold—tangier and tastier for the night spent steeping in the fridge—followed them up with a soda. Once he'd eaten, he arranged for a dumpster to be delivered.

The sooner this house was gutted, its memories overwritten, the better.

Davis had agreed about starting with the kitchen, said that it would set the style for the whole house redo. Then he told JK all design decisions were up to him, that he relied on JK's good taste. Another test. If he did this house well, then Davis would use him to flip others. An entire career path could be waiting for him.

JK took a deep breath, regretting it when that weird stink assailed him again. Not gone, then.

He spent the early hours of the morning prizing out the kitchen cabinetry, and trucking each piece out to the garage. He'd sand off the layers of paint, and see what showed beneath. If he were lucky, it would be the original wood—they'd been heavy enough to be the original wood—and he could refinish those easily enough.

Tearing out the linoleum was lonely work, even with music playing. JK missed his work crew—Big Mike's clumsiness and foul mouth, Sayid's off-key humming, the cousins who had joined up just last month who cursed like other people breathed—camaraderie without effort.

He took a break from the frustrating linoleum, scrubbed the grease from the kitchen walls, and got a first coat of primer on the walls. JK opened the kitchen window, cranked up the new AC and put it to the test. The rotten smell strengthened with the window open. The backyard, he thought. Those dogs. Before JK could resod the lawn, he'd have to look into treatments for tainted soil. That's what the smell had to be, he told himself, years of dog excrement sunk into the ground.

Around 10 a.m., he heard a tentative knock on the door. When he opened the door, Nick stood there, a mug of coffee in his hand; steam wafted upward. JK smiled. "That for me?"

"Nah, I thought I'd just come drink coffee in front of you." Nick passed JK the mug.

"Come on in," JK said. He took a sip. Closed his eyes in bliss at the fragrant, dark, richness.

"I don't want to interrupt." Despite his words, Nick's gaze lingered on JK's bare arms in a way that suggested he really, really did. "But you know, I'm open to the possibility."

"I'm tearing up linoleum," JK said, smiling. "I'm so bored I'm cutting it out in patterns. I'm working on the star of Texas, wanna see?"

Nick shrugged, tucked his hands into his pockets, and followed JK back to the kitchen. He said, "You weren't kidding."

"No. This project is making me crazy. I thought God, why would they keep this old horrible linoleum? Now I know. It's fucking cemented in place. It should have been an hour-long job, and I've been working on it for two and the bastard's still not done. Doesn't help that it's got all these tiny slits in it, so half the time, it just shreds."

"Dog claws," Nick said. He tangled his arm about his own waist, closing off. "Man, I hated those dogs."

"Hey, sorry for ranting."

"No, I get it," Nick said. "It's frustrating. My book's been fighting me this morning. Hell, all week."

"Then you should stay," JK said. "Give your brain a break. Join my battle against the world's ugliest floor."

Nick looked through the kitchen window, at his own house wall, his heavily curtained windows, and if anything, his posture grew more uncomfortable. "Weird to see it from this side," he breathed.

"So you didn't bring coffee to the Bartons?" JK said.

Nick laughed, but it lacked true amusement. "I am the last person the Bartons would have invited in. Barton would rather be in his grave than let me in his kitchen."

JK's turn to not-laugh as the casual words took on a surprise weight. "Do you think he could be dead?" he asked.

"Only if we're lucky," Nick said—then when JK didn't respond, he added, "Wait, seriously? You've been inhaling too many glue fumes."

"I just still think it's weird that he left all his stuff. I mean, he's supposed to be this big jackass, right?"

"Jackass might be mild—"

"But wouldn't a jackass be pissed when his wife sold the house? Wouldn't he be harassing her for money? She hasn't heard from him."

"Yeah? I bet she changed her number, made it unlisted, and didn't publish her address. That's what I wanted to do after I met him."

JK smiled, but it felt uneasy. The silence stretched, then Nick leaned against the counter and deliberately changed the subject. He said, "So, you have big decorating plans for the room or is white as far as you're going? Not particularly authentic if you're trying for period."

"Nah, man," JK said, accepting the conversational turn. He took another gulp of coffee, still fresh enough to be just the wrong side of too hot as it hit his throat. "I'm thinking charcoal counter-top, white cabinets, people like white cabinets, some of those tiles that mimic stone for the floor, and maybe some red and white tiling for the back-splash? I know Craftsman's supposed to be all about natural materials and colors, but statistically, white kitchens sell better."

"So, you're going burger joint?"

"It'll look sharp," JK protested.

"It'll look something," Nick said, but his lips were curling into a slow smile.

JK shoved him gently with his shoulder, his bare skin against the edge of Nick's t-shirt and a soft brush of flesh against flesh. Nick felt as warm as sunshine. JK shivered, glad he'd thrown on a tank instead of something with more coverage. He might not be able to touch Nick with his bare hands, but at least he could have this.

Skin hunger. Skin danger. In his life, they were inextricably linked.

"I should let you get back to work. Just thought I'd bring you coffee." Nick looked ready to leave —and the linoleum was still mocking JK and he might commit hara kiri if he had to fight with it any more.

"Hey, Nick—"

"Yeah?" he asked.

"Take me to your coffee shop."

Nick grimaced. He said, "Isn't it supposed to be *take me to your leader*?"

"That coffee you make is awesome. No way it's grocery store shit. I want the source."

"It's this little shop, Sabrina's, on the main drag past campus, about four miles from here. I can write—"

"I don't want directions," JK pushed. "I want you to take me there."

"Why?" Nick's face had shuttered, gone suspicious. "I do have work I should be—"

"You know coffee shops. They're cliquey. They like the regulars best. And you're a regular, right? At this place?"

"... yeah," Nick said.

"So, I just want an edge. I want them to know I know a regular, that you recommended them, so they won't think I'm some kinda freak." JK hadn't actually meant to say that last part. He tucked his gloved hands behind his back, and watched Nick track the movement.

The moment stretched, silent and embarrassing. Just when he was about to backtrack, pretend he hadn't asked, Nick caved.

"All right," Nick said. "It's a date."

"Our second, how nice," JK said.

Nick's tightly held mouth relaxed. "You a three-date kind of guy, JK?"

"I could be a one and done kind of guy," JK said. "If you like..."

"Flirt." Nick smiled but stepped back. "Coffee shop. But, man, shower first. You have linoleum glue in your hair."

"Deal," JK said.

A fast but thorough shower later, JK met Nick in his driveway, ducked his head, and compacted himself into Nick's silver Avalon.

"Thank God you don't have a Prius," JK said as he tucked his legs into the wheel well. His quip met with silence.

Nick sat behind the steering wheel, the key held in a shaking hand. Abruptly, JK realized he'd asked something big of Nick. He just wasn't sure what it was.

The coffee shop? The car?

He considered crying off, then Nick shook his head hard, shoved the key into the ignition and started the car with a coughing roar. The engine sputtered like he hadn't started it for at least a week. "Let's go."

❈

The coffee shop turned out to be in a strip mall just beyond the campus border, tucked neatly at the end. The rest of the mall marched on in a regimented array of grey concrete and orange awnings that housed an assortment of businesses from retail to office to other. JK saw a dojo tucked into the central space, the mats a splash of bright blue, shocking after all the orange.

But Sabrina's Coffee Shop broke the mold. It boasted a tiny brick deck with three small tables shaded by umbrellas in rainbow shades. Cars filled the small parking lot—students taking advantage of free parking in close proximity to the campus and the bus, judging by the number of UT-Dallas parking decals he saw.

Nick's lips tightened, but he slid his car down the street, entered the next lot, a few blocks south in front of an arcade, and parked. He gave a quick scan of the lot before he unlocked the doors, but JK only noted it and said nothing, preferring instead to clamber out of Nick's Toyota and stretch.

Nick folded his arms on the top of his car and watched him, a spark lighting his pale eyes. Appreciation. Hunger. JK scratched his belly where his shirt had ridden up, and Nick's eyes followed his gloved hand like it was a spotlight. The summer day got warmer.

JK shoved himself away from the car, and sauntered over to join Nick. If he put a little strut into his step, well, preening was natural enough when being admired.

Nick's lips quirked, mocking even while enjoying the show. He said, "You walk into the coffee shop like that and they're not even going to notice me."

"You can't tell me you're not the professor who has all the students following him around like baby ducklings."

A faint tint of color grew on Nick's cheeks, and JK said, "Oh yeah, I knew it."

"Ah, shut up," Nick said. "Coffee, remember."

JK ambled alongside Nick, shortening his stride, but only a bit. Nick, despite the fact that he had an indoor profession, took ground-eating strides, and they fell into easy sync.

Sabrina's adhered to the indie coffee shop template, being dim and filled with the sound of unobtrusive alt-rock. Bigger than he'd thought from their drive by; the interior held fifteen four-seat tables, a scattering of mismatched armchairs and ottomans, and a small stage.

"Poetry night?" JK asked.

"Live music," Nick said. "Do I look like the poetry type?"

"I don't know. History's full of poets, isn't it? Writing about war and... other historical... things?"

JK winced under the "are you shitting me" look Nick turned on him, but didn't have to defend himself because, at that moment, a petite redhead vaulted over the service counter as efficiently as a gymnast, and barreled into Nick's chest.

"Oh my God, you're here! We haven't seen you in here since— Oh my God, I have to call Zeke." She leaped out of his arms as fast as she'd landed in them, then planted three smacking kisses on Nick's cheeks. "We've missed you, you jerk."

Nick rubbed bright pink lipstick off his equally pink cheeks, and told JK, "That's Olivia. She actually lives—"

"In the yellow house down at the end of the street with two other students named Amy and Inez?"

"The colonel filled you in?" Nick said. Olivia gesticulated broadly while she chattered into the phone, as if her words needed winding up for her to spit them out at that speed.

"The colonel," JK agreed.

While the drama played out with Olivia, JK caught sight of a familiar brunette approaching, leaving her laptop unattended with the surety of long comfort with the shop. She seemed a lot more relaxed than she had when JK had first seen her. She looked a few years older than Olivia.

"I'm Amy Sheridan." She craned her head up, as if she had somehow missed JK's size before. "I bet you need a lot of groceries," she said. Something calculating crossed her face and she pressed a business card into his hand.

"Grocery deliveries," JK remembered aloud. He glanced at the card displaying her rates. "How does a person get into the grocery delivery business anyway?"

"Mr. Ashford—we all call him the colonel—suggested it," she replied. "I was doubtful, but it's working out just fine. You two should come sit with me. You have got to tell me how you got Nick out of the house."

"Amy," Nick said, his tone tight.

She wrinkled her freckled nose at him, curling a gentle hand around JK's forearm, bare skin against his. He flinched, nervous even though that touch should be safe, and her hand slid downward to catch on his glove. Amy blinked, staring down at it.

"You cold, or something?"

"Or something," JK said. He felt his shoulders draw closer together.

Nick said, "Amy," again in the exact same tone. Warning her off.

Before Amy could do more than repeat the nose-wrinkle, Olivia returned in a rush of coffee-scented air and vanilla perfume. She said, "Zeke's coming. He nearly choked when I made him guess who'd come in. What do you want to drink? The usual? Absolutely on the house. Be right back."

"Your best friend, Zeke?" JK said, once she'd sped off again. He wondered if she ever moved at anything slower than Mach 1.

"The one and only," Nick said. "He works a few doors down. Owns the dojo. Olivia's a brown belt there. And she's on the school soccer team. And does gymnastics in her spare time. High-energy girl. Very enthusiastic."

"I'll keep that in mind," JK said.

"Best do so. If you show the slightest interest in running, she'll be knocking on your door at dawn." Regret tinged Nick's voice and JK remembered the running sneakers. Nick used to run with Olivia? Didn't anymore? Olivia acted like she hadn't seen him for a while.

Olivia called over the counter to one of the watching staff, "Sabrina, I'm taking a break. Clock me out, would you?" Olivia ditched her apron and vaulted the counter again, landing precisely and neatly on the balls of her feet.

"Don't sweat it, kid, just stop treating my counter like a pommel horse," Sabrina said, her voice whiskey-deep.

Sabrina—presumably the owner—was in her late forties, but her long black hair was silver-free. She wiped her hands on her orange and pink apron that seemed to be the shop's nod to a uniform, and said, "Nick, glad to see you. Coffee's on the house today. For you and your friend."

"JK Lassiter," JK said. "I moved in next door to Nick."

Amy said, "Sabrina, he took the Bartons' house." A flicker of that previous tension crossed her face.

"Did he?" Sabrina said. "Nice to know Barton's really gone. I like you already, boy. But you need to stop blocking my doorway."

"Sorry." JK eased himself out of the way just as the bells over the door chimed and a man Nick's age pushed past, grinning like a maniac, all teeth and bright eyes.

He leaped at Nick's back and JK nearly shouted warning, but Nick had warning enough, apparently, in Olivia's widening smile. He only turned in the other man's embrace, and grinned back.

"Holy shit, never thought I'd see you in here again," the man said. His voice sounded raspy and rough, the scrape of a heavy smoker, but JK didn't smell anything of smoke on him. His stylish, dark hair was ruffled, as if he'd been rushing to the shop. As if he thought Nick might vanish before he got there.

"That's Zeke," Amy said, tugged JK toward a table. "They'll be a bit."

"All right," JK said. He couldn't help but let his eyes linger on the three of them; Olivia and Zeke and Nick, all of them touching each other with casual familiarity and fondness. Zeke threw back his head and laughed like a coyote, with sharp yelps of humor. Nick shoved him playfully. Olivia's hands flew as fast as her words, petting Nick's cheek, tugging Zeke's sleeve, poking Nick in the side.

"They've been friends forever," Amy said. "Zeke and Nick."

"Since K State," JK said.

"That's right. Then Olivia joined Zeke's dojo, ended up in class with Nick, and recognized him from the running path she took. She decided they should all be buds. And she's like a hurricane. The whole world's her friend."

"Must be nice," JK said. He ached for that kind of connection.

Perhaps sensing his melancholy, Amy touched JK's forearm with that same gentleness again, pointed him toward a chair and changed the subject.

"So, you getting settled in okay?" she asked.

"Yeah," JK said. "House needs a lot of work, but that's what I'm here for. I don't think the Bartons were much on upkeep."

"I don't guess they were," Amy said. "Especially not once he walked out. I tried to talk to her once, but she wouldn't open the door. Then she moved out."

"Where do you think he went?"

Amy shrugged. "Only thing I know is he took his dogs and left her."

She sounded sour, a little off. He could think of one reason off the top of his head. "Were they good customers of yours?"

"Ha! I delivered maybe once or twice to them. No more than that."

"They didn't tip?" JK asked.

She shrugged again. "They're gone. But you're here. So..." Amy made a complicated swirly sort of hand movement, and when he didn't respond, she said, "Tell me about your grocery delivery needs."

"I think I'm fine."

"Then tell me about you and Nick."

"What makes you think there's anything to tell?" JK asked.

"Oh, please," she said. "Neighborhood gossip says otherwise. Helping you unload for hours? Having breakfast together? Coming out for coffee?"

"Maybe he just believes in being neighborly."

"Not likely. I've got eyes. And a sixth sense for a budding romance." She cleared her laptop away, turned the "study desk" back into a table, and bussed her cold coffee, leaving a drift of hazelnut scent behind. Amy sank back down, smoothing her skirt around her thighs, kicked a cowboy boot-clad foot onto JK's chair rails. Her grey eyes dared him to call her a liar. "So spill."

Rather than fight her, JK went with it. He said, "What are my chances with him? According to your sixth sense."

"Nick's pretty easy-going," Amy said, then winced. "Or he used to be at any rate. Still, you should go for it. He deserves something good. Just be aware that Zeke is going to play guard dog."

JK looked at the close huddle of friends, at Nick lit up from inside, bright and joyous, and more—the way that Zeke and Olivia kept reaching out to touch him, as if Nick were a figment of their imaginations. "The colonel said Nick had a rough year."

It hadn't really been a request for information, just a reminder to himself, but Amy fidgeted in her seat, restless, then burst out, "Is it really sad inside the Bartons' place? I bet it is."

"It's definitely rough," JK said, accepting the change of subject warily. He'd gotten the impression she didn't want to talk about the Bartons. Maybe she just wanted to talk about Nick's bad year less.

He added, "Barton strike you as the kind of man to leave all his things behind? I found boxes and boxes of his stuff—"

"Yeah? Did you find a photograph of their baby? Did he leave that behind too? Did *she*?"

"I did, come to think of it. I didn't know it was their baby. They had a kid?" It had been a single picture, a child in a hospital nursery basket—a girl, given the pink trim on the blanket.

"Had, past tense," Amy said. "They lost her to child services." She leaned close, her grey eyes earnest, searching. "I just always wondered. I mean, they had pictures up all over the house, of his days in the war, of her and him, but never anything of the baby. Wouldn't you think they'd want one up? To remember her by? But they didn't even keep the picture when they left?" This close, her perfume smelled like watered-down lilies, sweet but light, and a little like tears.

"Maybe Barton meant to come back for it. For the rest of his stuff, too? I wonder where he is." JK leaned forward, tangling his legs around the chair legs, making room. His elbows rested comfortably on the table, slid over the wood like he'd been sitting here for years.

"Jail, maybe," Amy said. "Barton got laid off last winter, then he got real mean. Meaner than usual. Dangerous, drunken mean. He started harassing everybody."

"Neighborhood gossip?" Nick said, his shadow falling over them. "Sitting with a good-looking guy and all you can talk about is Barton?"

"Your good-looking guy," Amy said. "I've got one already."

"Yeah?" Nick said. "When'd that happen?"

"I wanted to wait to tell you face to face. When you were both around."

Nick eyed the shop curiously, scanning over the men in the room, then shook his head. Nick held two cups of coffee, passed one to JK.

"House specialty," he told JK. "Cinnamon mocha."

Nick found himself a chair, followed by Zeke and Olivia, and before JK could offer to drag over another chair to the four-seat table, Amy stood.

Zeke took her spot and Amy dropped back into his lap, nestling into him.

Nick nearly choked on his mouthful of coffee. "Zeke? You're dating *Zeke*?"

Amy wrapped Zeke's arms around her waist, grinned. "Well, you left us alone, Nicky, and once we got done talking about you, we started talking to each other."

"I guess I won't apologize for that," Nick said, ducking his head. "Anyway. JK Lassiter, Zeke Stuart, Olivia Reed. Y'all play nice, now."

Zeke eyed Amy, saw something that JK hadn't, and said, "You all right, hon?"

She replied, "We were talking about Barton."

Zeke's face closed off. "What do you want to talk about that jackass for?" he said.

Nick and Olivia shifted uncomfortably.

JK shrugged. "Just curious. He's vanished and no one seems to care."

"I sure don't," Zeke said. "So shut up about it, huh?"

"I said to play nice, Zeke," Nick snapped.

"Like you want to talk about him—"

"I'm Olivia," the redhead interrupted, stuck her hand across the table. "Thanks for getting Nick back in the shop. We missed him like crazy."

Nick groaned, embarrassed.

JK stuck out his hand, saw Zeke raise a brow at the glove, glancing questioningly toward Nick. Zeke got a tiny headshake in response. Olivia took JK's hand politely, but she released it as soon as possible.

Zeke said, "So I guess it's good to meet you. What do you do? You a student?" The others sat back to listen, content with Zeke taking the conversational lead.

JK said stiffly, "I work with Davis Construction. He hired me to reno the Bartons' house."

"Family local?"

"My brother is," JK said. He realized that Nick wasn't going to intervene between him and Zeke this time. In fact, given the way Nick settled back into his seat comfortably, JK got the feeling Nick approved of the interrogation. Nick's own pet pit bull, looking out for him. "Jesse's a cop."

"Dallas police? Or Fort Worth?" Zeke asked.

"Dallas."

Zeke subsided, then Amy patted Zeke's forearm, egging him on. Zeke took a deep breath and the interrogation began in earnest.

Why did he move here? Where did he come from? How long did he plan to stay?

JK gritted his teeth. He'd just wanted some more quiet time with Nick, not to have their date crashed by Nick's friends. He didn't think Nick had planned this hijacking, though, and the pleased smile lingering on Nick's lips made JK decide he'd just go with it. For the sake of harmony, and because Nick seemed so damned happy to be surrounded by his friends.

JK answered as nicely as he could. Moved for work, came from Maine, no plans to leave the city or state. Liked all sorts of music, liked all sorts of movies, was learning to love salsa on absolutely everything.

Zeke cut him off and said, "You're a big guy. Look strong."

JK didn't know how to answer that. It didn't even sound like a question, but one obviously lurked beneath. He shrugged. "Genetics."

"Yeah, but do you know how to use it, or are you one of those boys who folds in a fight?"

Fuck playing nice. JK leaned across the table and let the irritation he'd been stifling turn his voice to a low growl. "I don't like fighting. I think it's a dumb-ass way to solve a problem. Especially for grown men. But get on my bad side? Push me too far, and you'll find your doors nail-gunned shut and your vehicle full of wet concrete."

Nick laughed quietly, and JK's tension eased. Okay, so there was the line. He was allowed to play rough.

"Are you threatening me?" Zeke bristled.

"I'd rather just talk to you. Like normal people?"

"I'm not sure Zeke has more than a passing acquaintance with 'normal,'" Nick said. "Ease up, Zeke, yeah? We came here for coffee, not the third degree."

Zeke slumped back into his seat, jostling Amy, who shifted on his lap.

Silence fell over the table for a moment, a little uncomfortable, then Amy picked up the conversational baton.

"So why come all the way to Dallas to work construction?" she asked.

JK wondered what their expressions would look like if he said, *Well, my parents were desperate to keep me safe from myself and somehow that ended up translating into them sedating me twenty-four/seven and keeping me in the basement, and I needed to get away.*

He stretched his lips into a smile, and said, "Texas sounded nice, and I was sick of the cold."

"Well, that explains the gloves then," Zeke said. "Oh wait, it doesn't."

"Call them a personality quirk," JK said. "Or a fashion faux pas. Whatever you need to tell yourself."

Zeke raised a brow again—it seemed to be his default expression, skeptical of the world—then smiled, toothy and less than sincere. He said, "Touchy, aren't you? Well, welcome to the neighborhood, anyway."

"Y'all are total embarrassments," Nick muttered from behind his crossed arms.

"Hey," Olivia said. "I haven't been playing pick on the new boy."

Nick raised his head, smiling despite his tone. "That's only 'cause Zeke hasn't let anyone else get a word in edgewise. JK, they grow on you. That's all I can say in their defense." His eyes were fond as he surveyed the table.

"See, we're all sweethearts here," Zeke said, but his eyes were cool above his smile, lingering on JK's gloved hands.

Olivia rose, and came back with a plate full of brownies. "Here, Zeke, eat chocolate and chill out."

She thumped him on the head, and he snarled at her, but playfully. He sank his teeth into a brownie, but grinned afterward. "They're good. You didn't make 'em."

"Jerk," Olivia said. She turned to JK. "Burn one batch of cookies, and they never let you live it down."

"The fire department did have to make a trip out," Nick said. "Just putting that out there."

"Oh hush," Amy said. "She was tired. She fell asleep. Things happen."

"I'd come back from a marathon," Olivia told JK. "Starving. So I put the cookies in the oven, and passed right on out. Good thing Inez is big on keeping batteries in the smoke detectors."

"You do marathons often?" JK asked.

"As often as I can. Running's the best. Getting ready for the next Zombie Run."

Zeke grimaced. "I don't get the point of running while people jump out at you. Seems like a good way to get into a fight."

"That's because you have martial arts on the brain," Amy told him. "S'okay, I like you anyway." She kissed his cheek then scrubbed at the veneer of lip gloss she'd left behind.

"So how's the book going?" Zeke asked Nick. "You getting stuff done, or getting distracted..."

"Oh, the damn book," Nick said, and the conversation started running as smoothly as a well-oiled machine, folding JK into it.

A little later, JK, laughing so hard he wheezed over one of Olivia's stories, had to admit this wasn't so bad. Sure, he'd wanted Nick to himself, but this little gathering felt nice, like he might gain more than Nick's interest out of it: he might end up with some new friends.

The impromptu party broke up when JK's watch beeped, signaling pill-time for him, and, for the rest, a reminder of places they needed to be. Pill-time could be a mood-killer even when no one knew about it.

Olivia went back behind the counter, tying her apron on cheerfully. Amy packed up her laptop bag, and said, "Hey, Nick. You still on for groceries now that you're out and about again?"

"Please," Nick said.

Amy looked both relieved and guilty. Zeke bumped her shoulder with his, and her worried expression gave way to a shy smile. JK decided to add himself to Amy's deliveries. Helping her out might make Zeke nicer, and Amy might tell him more about the Bartons.

Besides, he hated grocery shopping. Wearing gloves made picking things off crowded shelves awkward, and people always stared and whispered to each other until he felt prickly with shame.

"You doing a grocery run, now?" Zeke asked. "'Cause I got a list."

"I can't get to it tonight," Amy said. "I've got a crapload of course work, and I have an afternoon appointment." Her voice wavered on the last word, and JK, sensitive to oncoming conflict, twitched.

Zeke's hands, pushing the chair back beneath the table, had stilled. "An appointment?" he asked.

Uh oh, JK thought, *argument brewing*.

"Don't tell me it's with that fucking psychic?" Zeke said.

JK twitched hard, nearly tipped his cup, but Nick was the only one who noticed.

Amy's chin tilted up, her shoulders taking on that brittle tension JK had seen before. She said, "Yes."

"She's screwing you over."

"I'm not an idiot, Zeke. She's the real thing."

"There isn't any real thing," Zeke snapped. "C'mon, babe, you're smarter than that..."

"Nick!" Amy said, her voice tight.

He said, "What, me? No..." Flustered looked good on Nick, too, JK noticed.

"You believe me, right? Believe in the possibility?" she asked him.

"I... don't know..."

Amy let loose an aggravated sigh. "Way to think for yourself, Nick." Her gaze flicked toward JK and he knew his face telegraphed his panic. His hands poured sweat.

"Fine," she said. "I don't care what you all think. I know. She lets me talk to them. That's worth it." Amy slung her laptop bag over her shoulder and pushed past Zeke. The outer door bells jangled in her wake.

"I could wring her fucking neck," Zeke muttered.

Nick shot him an appalled look, and Zeke said, "Not Amy! God, what do you take me for? I meant the so-called psychic bitch..." He trailed off, jaw knotting as he realized that didn't sound much better.

"Your temper is going to get you in a world of trouble," Nick warned.

"Oh, shut up," Zeke said. His exit jangled the bells on the door even louder than Amy's had.

Nick settled back into his seat, and sighed.

"That went south fast," JK ventured.

"Zeke's too damned protective," Nick said. "And Amy's hurting too much to be sensible. Her parents passed away unexpectedly. Hence the psychic. Amy sees her about three times a week."

"So you don't think psychics exist?" JK asked.

"I've never been given any reason to believe," Nick said. "You a believer?"

JK forced a casual shrug. A lie hovered, but... he wanted to be as honest as he could with Nick. Weren't you supposed to be honest with people you liked?

"Never had a reason not to believe," he said.

Nick studied him, then nodded. "Fair enough." He studied the streets outside, and leaned back, seemingly content to stay. JK bought a pound of freshly ground beans, got in on the lunch order when Olivia brought the delivery menus over to the table for Nick's opinion, and gave himself up to enjoying the afternoon.

When the mess of sandwich wrappers had been cleared away, the tables wiped down again, JK decided Nick was long past ready to leave. He kept glancing between the door and his watch. Yet each time JK rose to go, Nick sank more firmly into the seat.

Scared. The thought bloomed crystal clear in JK's mind, as painful as a vision. JK recognized that Nick bordered on agoraphobia and also suspected that Nick hadn't always been this way. His condition was new—something Nick's friends worried about, not dismissed as the status quo. Nick had taken a sabbatical, JK remembered. Last semester, Nick had been teaching classes. Leading a normal life. Going for runs with Olivia. Drinking coffee at his regular place.

But Nick hadn't been to Sabrina's since... Since what?

JK tried not to sound as clued-in as he felt. "Hey, not that I'm not enjoying myself. But I've got a kitchen to do battle with and it's nearly two."

Nick rose in stages. Out of the chair, his hands lingering on its arms. Tucking the chair in, his hands resting on the table, eyes darting toward the door. Just once. Just enough to betray him.

Outside, Nick seemed fine. The streets were busier now, so they walked slowly, close enough to each other that if it were a different setting, if JK had been coming out of a club with Nick walking so close beside him, radiating heat—JK would have taken it as a hint. He would have taken Nick's arm and ushered him someplace private to get off. Or private enough.

JK imagined them hidden in the shadow of a building, maybe the heavy, dark sandstone of the bookstore they were passing. Imagined Nick's weight pushing him hard against the rough wall, JK's shoulder blades scraping against the stone, their breath mingling in the tight space between their bodies, imagined the rocking of their hips...

JK forced his mind to behave, let himself enjoy just this: his skin reflecting Nick's closeness like a low-burning shimmer.

Halfway to Nick's car, a cluster of teens burst into furious argument, fighting over who had gotten them kicked out of some gaming store.

Nick shifted, sheltering against JK's body. It happened subtly; Nick's pace never altered; he didn't bump against JK. But the ebb and surge of his body heat steadied into a constant, tense presence by JK's side. Other people might not have noticed the new nearness, but JK tended toward hyperawareness of his space. Guarding his space had been essential in the dark days before Hannah's drug therapy had started working.

Things added up in JK's brain.

JK dropped a casual—protective—arm over Nick's shoulders, ready to remove it if Nick got offended. But Nick let out a tiny sigh, and his shoulders eased. His weight shifted just enough that his side landed against JK's and stayed there.

"I'm going to have a crippling new caffeine addiction, thanks to you," JK said. "I think I drank five cups there, sampling the specialties. And I'm pretty sure that none of them were decaf." Harmless blather to cover up how much he liked Nick pressed into him, how much he wanted to drag him the rest of the way into his arms and taste the rise of muscle at his shoulder and neck. Not the time.

Nick's voice was rough. "You're the one who asked me to bring you. Can't take the heat? Stay away from the espresso."

At the car, Nick slipped out of JK's grasp, fobbed open the doors, and let them both inside. Nick started the engine immediately, a gruff rumble of machinery, locked the doors, then sort of... folded over the steering wheel.

JK put a hand on his nape, felt Nick's shiver even through his gloves, and saw fine dark strands of his hair snag on the suede.

Locked doors. Blackout curtains. Agoraphobia. Hypervigilance. And the kids on the street. Loud and in a pack.

"Did you... you got jumped recently, didn't you?" JK asked him.

Nick coughed, then raised his face. He said, "That obvious?"

JK let out a breath. "Let's say I've been watching you pretty closely."

"Yeah? Close enough to see I'm a fucking mess?"

"Close enough to see you have little bits of green in your eyes, they're not pure blue. And that they get brighter when you smile."

Nick looked at him, expression blank.

"What? Too sappy?" JK shrugged. "I'm a construction worker. I could make comments about your ass instead. Believe me, I could make comments. Your jeans are—"

Nick made a sound that might have been a spluttered laugh. He thumped his forehead once, twice against the steering wheel. "You're a sweet guy, you know that? A really sweet guy."

Silence fell between them, comfortable enough, underscored by the rumble of the engine, of the people on the streets. The AC hadn't kicked in yet and the car interior quickly took on their scent; sun-warmed skin and coffee, Nick's cologne, and the lingering odor of linoleum glue on JK's clothes.

"I had a blind date," Nick said. "Here at Sabrina's. Low-key interaction, that kind of thing. I thought if we hit it off, we'd go get dinner. But, we didn't, you know? Chemistry's rare." A quick sidelong look—an acknowledgment of the fact that right now, in this car, the chemistry simmered between them.

JK twisted his hands in his lap, feeling the gloves slide around on his skin. One touch, and he could spare Nick this storytelling. One touch, and he'd have to explain everything to Nick. One touch, and he'd live through Nick's hell. JK kept his hands folded.

"So we came back to the lot, for our cars. There were these four kids with baseball bats. They were smashing headlights, and when we showed up..." Nick's throat closed, made his last words a bare breath. "Wrong time for us to wander by."

JK couldn't help himself; he reached out and hauled Nick toward him, over the gear shift, into his arms. "I'm sorry." The embrace was awkward; Nick's weight slid toward the wheel-well, JK had to brace against them being tipped over, and his skin prickled with awareness of the traffic outside, the people who might be watching.

Nick thumped his head against JK's shoulder, much as he had with the steering wheel, then pushed away after a second.

"They broke my arm, cracked three ribs. Broke Dylan's jaw, his hand. Concussed us both. They got arrested. Not exactly criminal masterminds. There's a security camera on the lot. Local police were already headed here because someone reported the vandalized headlights. Three of them went straight to juvie. The last one got eighteen months."

"That's something, isn't it?" JK said.

"Oh yeah," Nick said. He shifted in his seat, looked JK square on, serious. "It's not the kids that fucked me up, you know. It wasn't what broke me."

"Okay?"

"Fuckin' Barton broke me."

"Barton?" JK echoed.

"Why do you keep bringing him up, anyway?" Nick put the car in gear, and moved them out.

"I told you, it's weird—"

"Weird only goes so far," Nick said. "Aren't you supposed to be focused on the house reno anyway, not the people who lived there?"

"I am," JK said. "That's sort of the problem. The house... I think something bad happened there."

"Lots of bad things happened there."

"I think Barton's dead," JK blurted. He hadn't meant to. But something about Nick's stubborn skepticism maddened him. He wanted more from him.

"That wasn't funny this morning. It isn't funny now."

"I'm not joking."

"Then you're just crazy," Nick said.

"Thanks," JK said. "Never heard that before." He tightened his gloved hands around each other. Nick's gaze flicked downward, back to the road.

"Based on what?" Nick asked, after a long moment. They idled at the stoplight. The engine hummed. "Barton being dead. Convince me."

JK leaned back in his seat and shrugged, unwilling to lay himself bare. Not when Nick had already invoked "crazy". He replied, "Just a feeling."

When Nick stopped the car in his drive, they sat in silence. It felt like a void stretching between them. "Go on," Nick said. "You've got linoleum waiting."

"Yeah, all right," JK said. He got out of the car, tapped the hood, and said, "Thanks. For the coffee and the intros. For date two. We should go for three sometime. Just the two of us. We could... talk." Weak, but he wanted to salvage the day, wanted to bring them back to that simmering moment of connection.

Nick reached out over the hood, slid a fingertip beneath the cuff of JK's glove, snapped the elastic. JK twitched and jerked away.

"Seems to me, I just did all the talking," Nick said. "See you 'round, JK."

5

JK headed into the house, annoyed with himself, and annoyed with the world. With Zeke for being distrustful. With Amy for visiting some psychic. With Nick for being judgmental. He dropped his coffee off in the kitchen, and wondered what that bastard Barton had done to Nick. If Barton *was* dead, maybe he'd deserved it. Maybe if JK took off his gloves and touched, looked into the house's past, he would find the answers he wanted. He stripped one glove off, let his fingertips hover over the counter.

Taking off the gloves, risking his health. Risking everything to find out information that was none of his business.

Cramming the glove back on, JK tore into the linoleum again.

He got one strip done, and threw the scraper down. Frustration, irritation, and anger built in him like pain.

JK yanked his glove back off, and watched his hand tremble. For a moment, he saw his hand turn stub-fingered and nicotine-stained, curling into a fist...

He *had* to know. JK slapped a hand against the counter top before he could think better of it, fingers curling over the sink's steel edge, his wrists resting on the metal, touching the house.

The memory burst over him. Clearer than before. Uglier.

Bile in his throat and his head pounding, the taste of cheap alcohol burning in his gut, and fucking Collier... Jealousy, rage, disgust. A miasma of hatred—pounding his fists into the walls, the counter, without satisfaction.

JK jerked back, fell over the scraper and hissed as the metal bit into his shin. He welcomed the pain, as something all his and no one else's.

He staggered out of the kitchen—later, for that room. Just... later—and collapsed on the bottom stair, breathing harshly. It sounded like dogs panting, and he snapped his mouth shut, concentrated on his composure. His shin throbbed. He rolled up his jeans; the scraper blade hadn't penetrated through the thick denim, hadn't broken the skin, but a thin welt rose.

His breathing slowed; his shaking hands stilled.

All right.

The kitchen could wait.

JK could start another project. Two projects running at the same time might be messier than would be ideal, but it would still move him closer to completion. He spent the rest of the evening yanking up the carpeting piece by mismatched piece from the dog room, rolling the scraps tightly and carting the rolls into the garage. They were trash, but they were also full of staples and jagged edges. Just the kind of thing to endear him to the neighbors. He'd drag them out when the dumpster arrived. Not before.

JK crashed early, discontented with a day that had started out so promisingly. He'd screwed it up. Didn't talk. But what could he have said? He didn't want to talk about his visions. Didn't want to talk about the meds he took. Didn't want to talk about his past. What did that leave him?

Mute.

Alone.

Alone, at least until he fell asleep. Then it felt like some evil imp crouched behind him, shrieking glee as JK fired a weapon over and over at a dizzying array of targets—white glossy walls, at dark green siding, at a blue-eyed man, at howling dogs, at a looming dark shape. He wanted to let go of the gun, but his gloves were caught on the trigger, and every effort to release the gun only fired it. JK flailed off the air mattress, hit the floor hard, and just clung to it, relieved to be awake.

※

In the morning, JK turned his frustration to the damaged hardwood, prying it up with nothing but brute force and a lot of loud rock music as a soundtrack. He took a break for a late lunch, scarfing down three grilled cheeses, and garbling his way through a quick telephone conference with Davis—his boss had the new hardwood planks lined up and Big Mike ready to deliver them. JK would be at home this afternoon?

JK would definitely be at home, he thought. No coffee dates with Nick today. This morning, he traded self-pity for shreds of resentment.

Nick had chosen to confide in him. JK hadn't weaseled the story out of him, so if he regretted telling JK, it wasn't JK's fault.

Shaking his head, rubbing his too-hot hands against his jeans, he went back to work. Sometimes destruction was satisfying. Especially clean destruction. Not that sick frustration he had felt from Barton's kitchen.

This kind of destruction cleared the way for something better.

JK had all but the last boards levered off the joists, bracing himself carefully, when he heard the doorbell ringing and ringing. He reminded himself to replace that too. It had an angry buzz to it, instead of a pleasant chime. Checking his watch—4:30—had him frowning. It seemed early for the planks; JK thought Davis's question had been less about setting a time for delivery, and more about reminding JK to get to work. Big Mike would bring the planks by at the end of the workday.

Maybe it was Nick, JK thought, then stamped down on that hope. When he opened the door, he still managed to be disappointed that it wasn't Nick. Olivia and Inez stood there, eyeing him up and down.

"Well, you've been working hard," Inez said. She lounged in his doorway like a model—tall and lean, her makeup and glossy dark hair perfect—and as languid as if the word "work" would never occur to her. The lean muscles exposed by her sleeveless blouse and capri pants argued otherwise.

"Can we see?" Olivia said, slipping beneath JK's arm, as curious as a dog on scent.

"Sure," JK said. "Come on in," he told Olivia's back.

Inez grinned at him, sharp and fast, and JK found his brief spurt of anger fading. He thought he could really like Inez.

Olivia made a quick tour of the living room, and said, "You haven't done anything in here!" She sounded disappointed. JK blamed HGTV; all those extreme home makeover shows warped people's expectations.

"Kitchen," JK directed her, and she darted toward it.

Inez uncoiled herself from the doorway. "I gotta see, too. Gossip makes the world go 'round, you know."

JK wished he'd finished with the linoleum last night, watching the two girls inspecting his progress. He'd requested Davis bring him a heat gun along with the planks. But while he cringed over the unfinished linoleum, Olivia and Inez were exclaiming with pleasure over the freshly painted walls and the new appliances. Olivia said, "It's going to look nice!"

"Try not to sound surprised, Livvy," Inez said. "It's only the man's job..."

"Well, I'm used to thinking of it as a hovel." Olivia ran her fingers across the refrigerator, a quick brush against the shining silver. JK envied her. His glove had slipped while he and Davis were putting the refrigerator in. Even new, it had held memories. His brief hand-to-metal contact had fed him an argument between the men who'd been packaging it over a potential surface scrape.

"... isn't what you've been working on? We could hear you hammering."

JK tuned back in to find Olivia looking at him, waiting for an answer.

"Back bedroom," he said, then barred Olivia's dash toward it by stretching his arm across the doorway. "Be careful. There are a lot of nails, and there's only the joists to walk on."

She nodded, then petted his shoulder, and pulled her hand back a little too quickly for anything but disgust. "Ew. You need a shower. I wondered what smelled in here."

"Livvy!" Inez said.

"Well, I'm not saying he stinks, I mean, not usually. Just that he's been sweating today. And if he's coming with us, he needs a shower." Olivia nodded once, decisively, clearly certain she'd countered Inez's objection.

"Coming with you?" JK prompted. "Where?" He didn't know if he wanted to get swept up into any plan hatched between Olivia and Inez.

"Neighborhood barbecue," Inez said. "Starts at 5:00. At the Martinellis'. Didn't Nick tell you? He said he would."

"No," JK said. He wanted to ask when Nick had promised, if he'd simply forgotten to invite JK, or if he'd promised he would when he had no intentions of asking. A deliberate exclusion. JK had been popular in high school, but for a moment, he bet he knew what the unpopular kids had felt like.

"He's in a mood," Olivia said. "I thought... he went out with you, so... I thought he'd go running again, but he wouldn't even open the door to me."

"You knocked at 6 a.m.," Inez pointed out. "And he hasn't been running for months. He was just saving himself the pain."

"Anyway, JK. Go. Shower. Dress. We'll wait," Olivia said, as if the engagement had been decided.

JK raised a brow. "I've got work to do."

"You gotta eat," Olivia said. "At least come for an hour or so."

He did have an enormous amount of work to do, but JK gave in to temptation. Not least because he imagined giving in to Inez and Olivia was the only option. No wonder Ashford approved of them; they bossed people around nearly as well as he did.

"I don't have anything to bring," JK said. "Can we stop at the grocery—"

"I got you covered," Inez said. "You're bringing s'mores. With the good marshmallows."

JK couldn't do anything but nod and wonder, absently, how you could tell the difference between good and bad marshmallows.

✖

He might have felt awkward going through the Martinellis' front gate without ever having met them officially, but Olivia breezed on through and swept him in her wake. She was the anti-shy, he thought. He remembered what it had been like to be like that. Confident that people would like you.

JK tucked his gloved hands into his pockets, trying for discreet. He'd showered, scrubbed, and dressed in fifteen minutes, then spent another ten trying to figure out which gloves were the least weird. Suede work gloves kept him safest, but were so noticeable. His silk sleeping gloves were the lowest profile, but the least safe for him to wear in public. He'd compromised and chosen pale grey cotton with a layer of nitrile beneath.

"There you are," Mr. Martinelli said, descending from the front porch. His gaze skipped right on over the girls and landed on JK. "Lassiter, right? What do you have planned for the landscaping? If you don't know what you're doing, maybe you should leave the back alone. It's a mess, but it could get worse."

"I'm more concerned with the house right now," JK said.

Olivia and Inez rolled their eyes behind Mr. Martinelli's back. Inez slipped away toward the side garden, toward the sound of people talking and soft music playing.

Mr. Martinelli turned and caught Olivia mid-movement, and she froze. She said, "It's looking real nice in there, Mr. Martinelli. JK's doing good work."

Mr. Martinelli replied, "Be as that may. The season's getting on. It gets too hot to plant later—and then you've got dead plants, and—"

"Oh, leave the boy alone, Lou," Mrs. Martinelli said, coming from the side gardens. She reminded JK of a nurse in her white blouse, her no-nonsense short grey hair, her short fingernails. But green stains edged her nails, the knees of her khakis, and a pair of gardening shears hung off her belt loops. She eyed the bag hanging on JK's arm and said, "You've brought something. How nice of you." She patted his cheek, divested JK of the bag and disappeared back around the house. Olivia followed her, chattering amiably, weaving her way through the thickly planted side garden.

Mr. Martinelli said, "I'll make you a list of shrubs and annuals, and when to plant them. At least, you won't make things worse. But leave the back to a professional landscaper."

He said, "Like you?"

"Ha!" Mr. Martinelli said, tickled. "I'm an amateur. Took it up after retiring."

"What did you do before?" JK asked, curious. The man might be old, and creaky around the knees and spine, using a cane, but he seemed far from feeble.

"Oh, I was a troubleshooter. Here and there. For corporations. Nothing very interesting. Come on around, most everyone's in the back."

JK had thought the front and side gardens were fancy, full of well-behaved flowering shrubs and trees, a smooth grassy path winding between, but that didn't begin to compare to the backyard. He stopped and gaped. The Martinellis had the largest yard in the neighborhood, and they'd jammed it full of plants. A central courtyard, made of painted tile over concrete, held a built-in grill and a dining table that sat twelve. Around the dining area, the plants took over. Looping paths led through fancy beds.

He'd seen less elaborate landscaping in botanical gardens. On top of that, the whole yard smelled wonderful. Besides the smoky charcoal scent in the air, there were pungent herbs, sweet flowers, and a few fruit trees.

JK spotted most of the neighborhood through the greenery. Nick, head bent toward Amy, had a drink in his hand. Olivia and Mrs. Martinelli brought out trays, brushing through the rosy-pink masses of clematis. Inez joined a stocky woman with a long, greying braid, wearing a brightly embroidered tunic over her slacks. That would be Mrs. Sunitz, JK thought, identification spurred not only by the braid, but by the small boy at her side.

He seemed to be counting white rose petals on the grass. Ashford manned the grill, surveying the area like he was the host.

Nick turned and JK essayed a little wave. Nick nodded at him, but despite Amy's nudge, didn't move toward him. JK dropped his hand, feeling awkward. Unwelcome.

"Not too shabby, huh," Mr. Martinelli said. "A lot of work goes into keeping it like this. Full-time job, really." He bent, so suddenly that JK half-thought he'd fallen and leaned down with him. But Mr. Martinelli merely pinched a cigarette butt from the ground with a grimace. "Bastard's been gone months and I'm still finding his cigarettes."

"Barton?" JK guessed.

"He used to bring his dogs to the neighborhood get-togethers. Those damned animals pissed all over everything, knocked the kids down to get their food, growled at my wife. I put a stop to that. Smacked one of them with a shovel. Thought Barton might deck me for it, but Zeke intervened. Pity, really. I might be old, but I wield a mean shovel."

"So was that the last time he came?" JK asked.

"Last time we had a neighborhood party," Inez said, slipping back into their conversation neatly. "Barton didn't care if we invited him or not. He just came. Frankly, I think he liked playing the killjoy. Praised his dogs for being food-aggressive. It got so you couldn't reach down for fear of being snapped at."

"But he's gone now," Mrs. Sunitz said. JK chastised himself for expecting her to have an accent. "I'm Almira. This is my son, Devi. He's eight."

Small for his age, JK thought, and thin enough his bones showed at his joints. No wonder Ashford felt protective.

The boy blinked up at JK's height, then gazed at JK's hands.

"Gloves," the boy murmured, flexing his own small hands three times. Repeated the glance, the motion, the count. He smiled up at JK after that though, so JK figured he passed muster.

"Thank you for being considerate with your trash," Almira

continued. "Devi here gets into everything." She rested a hand on his dark curls, but he ducked after a moment of contact. Devi slipped away to stand behind Ashford.

Mrs. Martinelli reappeared on the scene, and beelined toward JK. "I'm glad the girls got you to come," she said. "It's been a long time since we've hosted a get-together and you'll get to meet most everyone this way."

"I think I already have," JK said. His eyes lingered on Nick, and Mrs. Martinelli laughed, a light, girlish sound.

"We are a nosy lot," she agreed. "It's why Barton was such a pill. He had all the nosy, but none of the good nature to go with it. We stopped the parties just so we didn't have to host him."

"Or her," Almira said. "You'd have thought that Kelly would like the chance to have pleasant conversation, but—"

"Kelly?" JK asked. It didn't seem like a likely name for that sour voice on the phone. Agnes, maybe. Bernice.

"Mrs. B.," Olivia confirmed, popping up in her usual jack-in-the-box manner. "Yeah. She wasn't big on mingling. She'd send her husband over and just stand in her driveway, chain-smoking, flicking the butts onto Nick's lawn, and watching. Watching until he got falling-down drunk, then she'd just go inside. The colonel—"

"Thank goodness for the colonel," Almira said in tandem with Mrs. Martinelli. They smiled at each other.

"Mr. Ashford," Olivia continued, "would drag Barton home."

Nick brought over a bottle of water, a hamburger, and passed them to JK with a nod. He said, "Olivia never remembers to feed her guests."

Ouch, JK thought, *I'm Olivia's guest. Not Nick's.*

"Good thing I've got you, then," JK said, poking at the sore spot. "I bet you know how to take care of a man." His words came out more teasing than he'd meant, and raised a quick hot blush across Nick's cheeks. It gave JK hope. He grinned at Nick, his mood lifting.

Nick might be running cold, but he sure wasn't indifferent.

JK took ruthless advantage of having Nick's attention, and said, "Hold this for me?" He pushed the plate back at him, making sure to brush against Nick's wrists.

JK stepped in close, watched Nick tilt his head back to keep meeting his eyes. Wary, but his breath hitched. JK could smell Nick's freshly applied cologne, sharp and bright, and while he wanted to chase that scent to its source, he focused on one thing—brushing tiny, fragrant petals from Nick's shoulder. The edge of his glove brushed against Nick's skin, and Nick shivered.

Just a little.

"What are you doing?" Nick said.

"Didn't think you wanted to rock the flower look," JK said. "Or maybe you do."

JK picked up another one, letting his gloves touch Nick's skin again. Another tiny shiver, another tiny dilation of Nick's eyes, blue drowned by his swelling pupils. JK bit his lip, excited by the idea of Nick liking the touch of the gloves on his skin.

JK blew the last few petals off his fingertips.

"There you go, all cleaned up," JK husked. "But maybe I should check more closely."

Nick swallowed, and took a step back. "JK... don't." Nick's eyes flickered, reminding JK they had an audience. "Take your food. Eat it. Don't you have work to be doing?" He shoved the hamburger back at him. "It's getting cold."

Brusque in content, not in tone.

"Don't I get to play at all?" JK asked him.

And there, he'd made some wrong word choice. Nick's expression hardened. He shook his head. "I'm not in the mood for playing games, JK. Just stop."

Almira's cautious smile faded as she looked between the two men. Mrs. Martinelli, with a hostess's sense for brewing trouble, slipped into the conversation.

"Is JK bothering you, Nick?" Her lips tightened. Her eyes grew steely. JK winced. He didn't want to be evicted. Even more than that, he didn't want Nick's answer to be "Yes."

"It's fine," Nick said, irritably.

"You said that about Barton in the beginning, too," Almira said, "and that man was very far from fine." She tucked Devi back against her side, tugging him away from JK.

Nick scowled. "I told you. JK's fine. I'm fine. And I don't need to be watched over like I'm a child."

Mrs. Martinelli put herself between JK and Nick, and said, "We are not going to let someone else like Barton—"

"I'm not like Barton," JK told her.

"You made Nick nervous," Almira said.

"He's hitting on me, not harassing me, ladies," Nick said, in exasperation. "Though admittedly, his lines could use some work."

JK said, "So I'm a little out of practice."

They were beginning to draw more of the guests' attention, and JK squirmed uncomfortably. The stranger in their midst. He could see the ranks closing.

"He doesn't look gay," Mrs. Martinelli said, and JK closed his eyes in resignation. He'd heard this a time or seven before.

Olivia laughed, bright and loud. "Trust me, Mrs. M., he is. He didn't even look at Inez more than once."

Nick rolled his eyes at all of them, and stomped off toward the grill.

"Really gay?" Mrs. Martinelli asked.

JK groaned. He wanted to follow Nick, cut him out of the neighborhood herd, and see if they could recover some of their earlier ease in each other's company. But Nick seemed content to be absorbed back into the neighborhood ranks, leaving JK at the mercy of Almira and Mrs. Martinelli's well-meant but ridiculous questions.

He got the impression they still didn't believe him, like until they saw him with his tongue down another man's throat, his orientation wouldn't count.

He'd have shown them, but somehow JK knew he wouldn't get the chance.

Nick moved quickly from one cluster of neighbors to another, talking school with Amy, and recipes with Olivia and Inez—trying to get them to cook some of the groceries Amy brought home. Inez ate a raw marshmallow, and said deadpan, "Oh no, how will I ever attract a man if I can't make a casserole?"

Mr. Martinelli traded places with his wife, who joined Ashford and Nick, back at the grill. Nick talked to everyone easily enough, while JK limped along in awkward conversation with Mr. Martinelli and Almira.

JK stuck around for another thirty minutes, but when he heard the familiar thunder rumble of Big Mike's behemoth Ford 450 coming down the narrow road to deliver his flooring, he made his excuses gladly. The truck bed rattled, stacked high with the hardwood plank boxes standing on end, wobbling even in their restraints. Big Mike had filled the rest of the space with two more pieces of Mission-style furniture. One looked like a china hutch. The other, JK couldn't begin to identify. A couch made entirely of wood?

He made his apologies to Mr. Martinelli, took the list of "essential" plants that the other man had managed to compile, and took a distinct pleasure in noticing that Nick had turned to watch him go.

✦

As JK crossed the lawn, he realized that Big Mike hadn't come alone. The bickering cousins—Raul and Rafael—leaned out of the extended cab, and the newest guy on the crew could be glimpsed behind the passenger window. Raul and Rafael were mostly good-natured, but Aidan had a lot of negative opinions and a habit of voicing them at full volume. Aidan was a fireplug of a guy, short and short-tempered.

Like cats, JK's coworkers scattered the minute they hit the house; investigating, poking, judging. Big Mike leaned back on his heels, grinned widely behind his beard and said, "Sorry. They wanted to come see what a shithole it is. Davis has been bitching about it all day."

JK said, "Even Aidan?"

"Eh, not him. I drafted him. He slacked on the job today, I figured he could carry some weight tonight."

"Speaking of weight, Mike... what the hell have you brought me now? I'm not ready for furniture in the house!"

"It's not furniture," Big Mike said. "Just a few things. A hutch. Davis brought you dishes, didn't he? Now you've got a place to put 'em."

JK contemplated the oak hutch. "It can go into the garage. Along with that couch thing."

"It's a glider," Big Mike said. "For your front porch."

He rocked back on his heels, studied JK's front porch. The whole five-foot space of it.

"Maybe it can go in the back," Big Mike said. "I'll build you a thing."

"No!" JK said. "No more furniture!" He knew they had an audience; the neighbors were all sloping down toward the closest edge of the Martinellis' garden, peering through foliage. JK sighed, then moderated his tone. "Run them by Davis first, okay?"

"Nice place," Raul said, popping out the front door. "Good lines. Not too much settling."

"*Looks* nice. You never look underneath," Rafael objected. "Your electricity, JK? How's that? Saw some substandard plugs. Your wiring old? You call me if you need help. You're not an electrician—"

"Neither are you," JK said.

"Eh, I get by," Rafael said.

"All new appliances?" Aidan said, following the cousins out, a sour expression on his face. "Guess Davis is paying you better than he is me."

JK just sighed. "It's not my house. I'm just working here so Davis can flip it."

Big Mike scruffed Aidan, dragged him back toward the idling truck in JK's drive. The planks and subflooring waited. Ten minutes' work for the five of them to get the truck off-loaded. Ten minutes where JK felt very conscious of the fact that Nick had also left the Martinellis' party early to watch from his porch.

Ashford appeared unexpectedly around the vast front of Big Mike's truck, which made JK jump. "You going to idle that truck all night long?" Ashford asked.

JK resisted checking his watch.

"We're almost done," JK said.

"We'd get done faster if you'd stop making nice with the neighbors and worked," Big Mike said. "Where do you want the planking? Garage?"

"Living room," JK said. "Garage is gonna be full. Of your furniture. 'Sides, I want to get the floor done as soon as I can. The boards'll need to adjust."

"I knew a house," Raul said. "Took up the subflooring. Underneath they found a whole nest of rattlesnakes."

"Not rattlesnakes," Rafael said. "Copperheads."

"Would you two fuckers shut the fuck up about snakes?" Aidan snapped.

Ashford's face tightened.

"Sorry, we'll be done real soon," JK told him. "I got the flooring up already. No snakes, boys, sorry."

"Want us to nail the subflooring in place?" Big Mike asked. "To get you started?"

"Where's your nail gun?" Raul asked, casting around as if he expected it to appear.

"Garage, I bet," Rafael said, opened it, observed the contents. "Holy fuck, JK. You even fit in there?"

Three hours later, they'd nailed the subflooring into place in the downstairs bedroom and moved the planking in on top of it. The air smelled of metal and sweat, plus the sharp tang and grease of the compressor, but JK could mark a task as done.

Big Mike dropped an arm over his shoulder. "So. Time for drinks. You're the designated driver, right?"

JK couldn't say no. Not with the reminder that here, among these guys, he fit in. A known quantity: gay JK and his weird gloves and the meds that meant he couldn't drink. Just JK. They weren't his friends, not quite, but they were close enough.

6

The next morning, JK wished he had said no, stayed home. Hell, even stayed at the oh-so-awkward neighborhood barbecue.

Sunlight forced its way through his mini-blinds with laser focus, going straight for his eyes; his air mattress had failed again, his entire body felt numbed, his head ached, stuffed full of nightmares, and someone was knocking at the door.

He peered at the clock. Seven a.m. Olivia? Nick? Probably Olivia.

Even if it were Nick, JK thought, he couldn't get out of bed. He dragged the pillow back over his head and sank back into the waiting nightmares. The knocking faded.

His phone woke him two hours later. Hannah.

"You're still in bed? You all right?" she asked.

"I'm fine," JK said. It was true. Mostly. "Went out with the guys to the bar. Paying for it."

"Are you hungover? JK..."

"I'm not stupid," he grumbled. "No drinking with the pills. Only one beer. I just... I had to take an extra pill." He hated to admit it, but Hannah should know.

"Why? Did you have an episode?"

JK groaned. "No. I just felt twitchy. Oversensitive. I got paranoid. Took an extra pill. Just in case."

"Because of the bar?" She managed to keep judgment out of her tone. But JK heard it anyway. Neither Hannah nor Jesse liked him going to places that crowded. That volatile.

"There were lots of people there," JK said. "Lots of skin."

It was easy to let the blame fall on the bar, no matter that they'd be more convinced than ever that bars were a bad idea. JK wasn't living with them. Didn't have to listen to their concerns.

The bar *had* been packed, and JK had been in short sleeves and his skin had felt like it could reach out to everyone there. His skin had tingled as if he could feel their memories like an electrical storm in the room. Aidan especially had rasped against JK's nerves. Big Mike had chosen their usual bar which had good cheap beer, decent music, and catered to a mix of people: blue-collar, white-collar, straight, gay, young, old—

Aidan, who'd missed the memo, didn't approve of the gay drinkers and spent the night telling all of the crew why in increasingly profane terms. He'd only stopped when Big Mike had finally said, "You shove that foot much further down your throat, and at least you'll choke yourself before JK decks you."

"What, you got a gay cousin or something, JK?"

"Or something," JK had said. "I have a gay boyfriend."

He'd said it just to see Aidan work that one out on four beers and a shot of Jack. But JK thought of Nick when he said boyfriend, and the idea heated his blood, gave his temper an edge. He'd always thought of Aidan as unpleasant but harmless. His bigotry meaningless. He wondered if Nick had thought that about Barton at first.

Aidan's discomfort had itched against JK's skin so strongly that JK thought if he just closed his eyes, if he just reached out a little... Let his fingers graze Aidan's elbow... He'd be deep in Aidan's memories, might even figure out what made Aidan's phobia work. Maybe he could say the right thing to adjust Aidan's opinion. His ability had to be good for something. Instead of just screwing up his life.

When the temptation to reach out and touch grew stronger, when Aidan's snarl made JK want to shove him from the booth, JK had called the night quits. He had driven the boys all home, then made his own way back, reeking of the liquor he hadn't drunk, the smokes he hadn't smoked, and staggered, exhausted, into his house under the sleepless gaze of Ashford's twitching curtains.

The house had been waiting for him. JK entered to a rushing, snarling mass of shadow that jerked his heart rate to rabbit-speed, made him flinch. The memory of the dogs faded, and left him shaking. He'd headed for that extra dose then and there.

Now, he groaned and tried to focus on Hannah worrying over the phone. "No, no, you don't need to come over. You've got clients. I'm fine. I'm going to drink a lot of coffee. A lot of water. It's good," JK said. "I'm good. Really."

"Call me first, next time," Hannah said. "I don't like you messing with your dosage. We're flying a little blind here, you know. Making it up as we go along. It's not like they cover psychics in psychiatry."

"Yeah. I remember." JK managed to get Hannah off the phone, get himself out of bed, and moving. Hannah wasn't wrong; that extra pill had put him into enough of a stupor that he hadn't even heard Big Mike reclaim his noisy truck this morning. He drank his coffee and brushed his teeth, and now stared down at the horrible linoleum, heat gun in hand.

Today, the linoleum was getting gone.

He dropped to his knees, knee pads taking the brunt of impact, and hit the trigger. Heat blasted back at JK, warmed his skin. The linoleum softened and he scraped it free. Slowly, but surely, he cleared the floor. He paused to wipe sweat out of his face, to peel off his shirt, and toss it out of the room. Heat guns were awful in the Texas summer.

JK figured if this took too long, he'd end up in his boxers, gloves, and boots.

The extra pill might have dulled his psychic senses, but it also dulled his reflexes; he brushed his forearm, singed the hair right off and scalded a tiny spot of his skin. He yelped, pushed away from the gun, rolling backwards. His back slid up against the cabinetry; his skull knocked against the edge of the counter. The linoleum began to bubble and darken where the gun rested. Automatically off, but still so hot.

JK winced, reached up toward the sink, and began to haul himself off the floor. His wrist pressed up against the edge of the sink, and the memories flashed back...

They'd been waiting.

A repeat at first.

Barton's fury—the emotion that had chased him away the first time—roared back.

"Deserve better, a real man, not like that pervert next door, teaching our kids, shaping their minds. He deserved to be mugged. Deserves worse."

Reaching for the .22 on the counter, acid in his veins and relief in every trigger pull—

Aiming at the house. Aiming at the man in it.

Imagining Collier in the crosshairs instead of the wood siding.

Whispering, "Bang, bang." The dogs howling with laughter, eagerness.

Take care of that bastard, make him run...

JK jerked back, tripped over the heat gun, gone cold now—how much time had he lost? He fisted his hands tighter, trying to rid himself of the feel of the .22 fitting snugly into his palm, the satisfaction in the shooting.

He wanted another pill. The house seemed to beat against his skin, Barton's malevolence—*Jesus, a gun?*—in the air itself.

Couldn't take another one. He had to live with Barton's old hatred.

JK traded his jeans for his cargo shorts, then his boots for old sneakers, and fled outside, where he stood in the sunny wreckage of the backyard. He couldn't work in the house today. But he couldn't leave it either. He felt like a raw nerve, exposed.

The whole world loomed like a raised fist.

He shivered gratefully in the heat, pry bar in hand, and attacked the fence. The slats of the fence came off with easy, angry tugs.

JK leveraged the first post loose and grunted as he yanked it up and out. Freeing it from the earth took longer than he'd expected. Eight feet, not seven, with a solid, heavy club of concrete at the end.

He nearly tipped himself over getting the post all the way out, then dragged it across the lawn down to the dumpster. Hefted it up and dropped it in with a resounding crash that made him wince.

He dragged the loose slats to the dumpster, giving himself a tiny break before tackling the next post. JK had the thing bruted over his shoulders, and started hauling it toward the dumpster when he realized he had an audience. Not just Ashford, disapproving of his noisiness, not just Devi Sunitz, skinny and staring from the very edge of his own driveway, but Nick, drawn out to his front porch.

JK, who'd been thinking about dropping the post and dragging it, never mind that he'd just have to lift it again when he got to the dumpster, stiffened his shoulders and soldiered on.

He dumped the post with a grateful groan, then rolled his shoulders, breathed without the weight on his lungs. Took a moment, then JK headed back for the yard.

"For God's sake, JK, it's getting dark. Call it a day," Nick burst out, like he couldn't help himself.

Twilight greyed out the world, blurring the edges. JK looked at the one small section he'd managed to clear, and Nick said, "Fine, don't listen to me. Keep working in the dark and throw out your back—"

JK detoured toward Nick's porch.

Nick didn't get up and close the door, but he looked like he wanted to. JK stopped at the two wooden steps up onto the porch, just short of inviting himself in.

"Barton *shot* at you?" he said.

It hadn't been what he meant to say, wasn't sure how it had slipped through his numb lips.

Nick reared back. "Who told you that?"

JK licked his lips, and threw Ashford under the bus. "The colonel."

Nick said, "He did not. Ashford doesn't tattle."

"Is it true?"

Nick's jaw tightened. "Barton shot at my *house*."

"And you didn't call the cops—"

"Jesus, JK, of course I did. It just didn't do any good. The cop gave Barton a ticket for discharging a firearm in a private place. It cost him cold hard cash, which just made him mad," Nick said. "After that I was too scared to try again, all right? Scared word would get out, wreck my reputation at the school, and scared that Barton would retaliate."

JK sat down, hard and heavy, on the lower steps to Nick's porch, his legs weird and rubbery. Barton had not merely *discharged a firearm in a private place*. He had picked up a gun and fired it in anger—JK shuddered, remembered the gun in his... *Barton's*... hands, his rage. "God, I'm so sorry."

Nick sighed, and settled down on the top step. JK turned sideways so his back wasn't to Nick. He pushed a pebble around with the heel of his sneaker.

"It's not actually your fault," Nick said. He sounded tired, looked tired, his face a collection of shadows and planes in the coming twilight. "You going to tell me who told you about it? Or you going to stick with Ashford?"

"The kitchen," JK said. "There were leftovers."

"Shells? Figures." Nick's mouth twisted.

JK took a deep breath. Now that he had Nick's attention... "Do I owe you an apology or something? You seem really pissed at me."

Nick flapped a hand, not dismissing the charge, not admitting it. "Call it confessor's remorse. I told you all that shit about me. Just dumped it on you, and I realized... I don't even know you. And you haven't told me anything much about yourself, and I felt dumb. And yes, kind of pissed. I learned more about you from Zeke questioning you than you told me in two days, and he didn't even ask the things I wanted to know."

JK asked, "What do you want to know?"

"Christ, I don't know. Something real. Something that I couldn't get by scanning your Facebook page. Not that you have one."

JK thought of all the things he could admit: that he had gone from being a high school student with a future to a psychic lunatic living in a basement for seven years. That he had expected to die there, and was still stunned he hadn't. Shame rolled the words up in his throat, and stuck them tight. JK coughed, tried to get even the simplest thing out.

Nick took his hands, bare fingers wrapped over gloved ones.

"I know it's not fair, I know that telling you about my low spots doesn't mean you have to tell me about yours. I just wish you felt like you could. You look like you've got everything going for you," Nick said, his gaze a weight on JK's skin. "But then there's the gloves, and when you aren't smiling, you look scared. And I really don't know why you keep asking and asking about Barton when he's a man you've never met. When he's a man you're lucky to have never met. Right now, you're nothing but question marks. I've had a rough year, JK. I can't do question marks."

JK said, "It's so fucking complicated."

Nick's fingers twitched against his, like he meant to pull away, and JK couldn't help himself. He tightened his grip. Nick sighed. "Olivia thinks germophobia, maybe with a side of OCD? Zeke thinks drugs—that you're shooting up between your fingers."

JK laughed. "Zeke's kind of an asshole, huh?"

"He does pride himself on it," Nick said.

"Ashford thinks I'm hiding gang tats."

Nick rolled his eyes. He said, "Amy thinks you burned them. That they need to be covered to protect the skin."

JK's slightly bitter laughter faded. "That's closest," he said. "The gloves protect me." He freed his hands, flexed his fingers within the thick suede.

Nick scratched at the scruff of forming stubble on his jaw. "Protect you from—"

"This... this thing happened to me," JK said, picking out words in brittle chunks. "I nearly died. I *did* die. Just for a moment. Everything changed." He shuddered, felt that chill race his bones again.

"You died?"

"I drowned. The EMTs brought me back," JK said. He shivered again. "I don't... I don't want to talk about it."

"Okay, okay," Nick said. "The gloves are part of that?"

"Yeah," JK said. He wished he could just tell Nick. But the ordeal with Jesse's colleague Ben had been so disastrous, it stifled him now.

"So, no questions about your past, no questions about your gloves. But you'll tell me when you can, right?"

JK nodded. Promises that came due "later" were easy to make.

Nick continued, "Can I ask you about your Barton obsession? 'Cause I know you want to make friends here, and I have to tell you, asking about Barton is no way to do it. The man is nothing but an asshole."

"Was an asshole," JK murmured. Content and calming with Nick's hands rubbing long, warm lines up and down his spine.

Nick paused. "Was?" he asked.

JK shifted on the step, tried to meet Nick's shadowed eyes. The twilight had crept up on them, over them, isolating them.

He said, "I keep telling you. Someone died in that house. Recently. Barton's the only one missing."

"He got a ride with a friend," Nick said absently. "Took his—"

"'Took his beer, took his dogs, got a ride with a friend, who knew he had one'. I've heard that a lot, same words, different people. Did you actually see him go?"

Nick licked his lips. Shook his head. "But dead?" he asked.

JK shivered. Nick's "safe" question led straight to JK's fragile core. He danced around the edge of it. "I get a bad feeling from the house."

"A feeling like someone died?"

"Yeah."

"Like a ghost? Like the house is haunted?"

"Sure," JK said, shrugging, like this all meant nothing. "Like a ghost. Or a memory." His hands knotted tight around his knees, held on.

"You really do believe in psychics, don't you?"

JK fiddled with his gloves.

Nick sighed. "I don't know what to say. Barton left. He's alive somewhere, being a dick to someone."

"I don't believe that," JK murmured. Nick leaned over him.

"Feelings like that are usually more about the person having them. I can't blame you," Nick hastened to add. "I don't know about murder, but that wasn't a happy house while they were living there, and that leaves signs. Like the shells you found."

"I didn't find any shells," JK admitted.

"Then how..."

JK said, "I told you, already. Leftovers."

"Physical cues that you pick up subconsciously," Nick decided. "Maybe not shells, but neglect and misery are in the walls. You've got your work cut out for you." He leaned forward, and JK felt the brush of heat, the puff of breath, the soft touch at the top of his spine. A kiss.

All the comfort in Nick's presence shifted to something more electric.

JK shuddered again—this time from pleasure.

"You know," Nick said. "Maybe you just need some company. Someone to get your mind off of things. How 'bout I come help you tomorrow? To keep you from crushing your spine carting those fence posts by yourself."

JK thought the offer might be partly out of pity, a polite way of saying: *you're making yourself crazy, and you need a keeper*. But with Nick's hands on him, and Nick's breath against his jaw as he turned, he thought he'd be crazy not to take Nick up on his offer to help.

Legs sliding, hip shifting, JK turned to get Nick's mouth on his own, tasting salt and heat, sighed into that closeness. Nick's dark hair brushed his cheek, tangled against his sweaty hair. Their hands—gloved and bare—knotted together, a flexing of careful, cautious hunger.

JK parted from Nick's mouth, and blurted, "My father's a plumber." Hardly romantic, but he remembered Nick wanting JK to share something real. JK flushed, not just from the kiss, but in belated embarrassment. He could have picked something more interesting. More relevant—

"Mine's a natural foods grocer," Nick said. His smile was small, but perfect.

"California," JK said.

"Holistic and healthy," Nick said, and drew JK close again.

He reached out and caught JK's wrist, the sensitive skin just above his glove. His thumb rubbed gently between JK's tendons, over the pulse.

JK couldn't stay worried, not while Nick's fingers were dipping beneath the edge of the glove, letting him anticipate the possibility of other, less chaste touches.

His hands flexed in his gloves. He snagged Nick's belt loops, urged him closer. Nick came, grinning, biting his lip. JK slid a gloved hand beneath the loose edge of Nick's t-shirt, watched those dark lashes flutter at the rough nap of the suede against his skin.

Maybe Nick didn't pity him at all.

"You're making me crazy, you know that?" Nick murmured. "I don't even... you make my brain shut down."

"That a bad thing?" JK said. Before Nick could answer, he leaned in and bit at that tempting stretch of Nick's throat, scraping his teeth gently over the corded muscle.

Nick groaned, and said, "Come here, come here." He tugged gently at JK's arms, ran his fingers from wrists to shoulders.

"Can't get closer," JK said.

"I bet you can," Nick said. "You're good at putting things together, right?"

JK rolled up to his knees, and even as he crept forward, Nick scooted back until he leaned against the wall, taking them into the deepest part of the porch. Here, twilight had given way to night, a shelter from prying eyes. And in this neighborhood, there were always eyes. If the ladies of the neighborhood were watching them now, they'd have no doubts at all where JK's interests lay.

JK let Nick guide him forward, and sank back down, straddling Nick's lap. JK's damned long legs, even folded, made his knees scratch across the siding, then onto the deck. His weight settled onto Nick's. Now, he was the one groaning. Nick's thigh muscles were tight and taut beneath his own, heated even through two layers of cloth.

Nick levered his knees up, just a little, set JK slipping that last inch until their hips met, pressed together. An entirely new line of heat scorched JK. He put his hand down, cupped that growing bulge under Nick's jeans. His own cargo shorts, loose as they were for work, felt uncomfortably snug. JK couldn't help the tiny jerk his hips made, and Nick sighed, put a hand into the small of JK's back, encouraged him closer.

JK bit at that sighing mouth, tiny teasing nips, and Nick put a hand to his jaw, gentling him, bringing him into a sweeter dueling. Nick's hips jerked beneath his, and JK leaned back, breathing harder, breathing faster.

"Where are you—" Nick protested. His cheeks were flushed, his lips swollen, his hands restless on JK's hips.

"Your shirt," JK muttered. He fumbled with the buttons, figured out the trick to finessing them with eager hands and thick gloves—if he'd known the night had this in store, he'd have picked a better pair—and bared Nick's chest. He spread his hands wide over Nick's pectorals, found them smoothly defined, and ruffled with dark hair. Nick hissed as JK ran his suede-covered fingers over his nipples. "You can keep doing that," Nick breathed.

"Yeah?" JK said.

"Yeah," Nick agreed, but then shifted position to lick a long stripe up JK's neck, to tug JK's sweaty and loose t-shirt off a shoulder. "Jesus, is there any part of you not solid as a rock?"

JK said, "Doesn't sound like a complaint." He ran his hands down to open those last few shirt buttons, and then, once he had the tails completely undone and untucked... since he was already down there, popped the button of Nick's jeans.

"Definitely not complaining," Nick said.

Nick wore Calvin Klein beneath his jeans, or so said the waistband JK exposed. JK wanted to find out if Nick liked briefs or boxer briefs, but he hesitated. Put his gloved hands over the jeans instead, over Nick's cloth-constrained cock, and stroked.

Nick jolted, gasping, pulling JK in, and the zipper on the worn jeans parted all on its own. JK kissed Nick again, pressed him back against the house. He could feel sweat trickling down his spine, felt Nick stroking that sweat back into his skin, and groaned. When had Nick gotten under his shirt?

A moth fluttered against the house, seeking the faint light behind the windows. JK tilted his head down, wished for better light. All he could see of Nick's skin was the dark glimmer of sweat springing to life, the sweep of where his gloved hands had been, like trails in the early morning grass.

He rested his hand over Nick's cock, pushing up through dark cotton, couldn't tell if Nick was leaking or not, not in the dark, not through the gloves, but the air trapped between their bodies had a familiar tang to it. The scent made his mouth water, his heart beat faster; his hips drove inward, and his grip tightened.

Nick moaned, muffled the sound in JK's throat, then scraped his teeth over JK's collarbone. An intimate, rough touch almost enough to send JK over the edge.

JK swallowed the shout that wanted to erupt from him, gritted his teeth. Nick's hips twitched in surges beneath him, pinned by JK's weight, and enjoying it. His cock grew more and more solid in JK's grip.

The moth fluttered down, brushed through JK's hair, and he broke their kiss to gasp, "Inside. We should take this inside."

Nick... hesitated, and JK froze. "No?" he asked.

Nick shook his head. "Too close. Moving would be... no. Just don't stop." He wrapped his hand around JK's gloved one, got him stroking again.

JK laughed, more relieved than he wanted to admit.

"Hey. Don't laugh." Nick breathed it out in discrete phrases. "Told you. Make me crazy. Your body. Your smile. Your... gloves. On my skin."

"Kinky," JK said, "if Ashford sees us. Your fault."

"Oh, I'm the one leading you astray," Nick said.

"Too much talking," JK said. His free hand tweaked Nick's nipple; Nick jerked upward; JK ground downward, forward. His ears were ringing. His spine tingled, his thighs trembled, protesting, loving the motion at the same time.

He shifted his grip on Nick's cock and Nick bit him in protest, but whimpered when JK peeled back the elastic on his briefs, and pressed his hand inside.

JK closed his eyes, heard the texture of crisp hair scritching against his glove, and admired the thick length of Nick's cock, so much closer to him now. The head brushed up against JK's wrist, a kiss of wet velvet, and JK stroked him, once, twice, and Nick came, breath hissing out, head thrown back, teeth clenched.

The spatter across JK's forearm scented the air, and that brought him over the edge, too, his thighs trembling, his breath ragged, his own cock all but untouched.

He rested his cheek against Nick's shoulder, listened to his breathing settle.

"My thighs are numb," Nick muttered finally, and JK shuffled back.

"That wasn't really a complaint," Nick said, smiling. "Just

thought I'd mention it."

"I'm just glad you sanded your porch or I'd have road rash on my knees," JK said.

Nick tidied himself away, watched JK rub his come off his arm with the edge of his t-shirt.

"So do you want to come in? Clean up a little?"

Nick sounded a little hesitant, and JK shrugged. "You haven't got clothes to fit me, so the walk of shame it is."

He replied, "Only shame here is that I didn't get my hands on you."

JK shivered pleasantly, and said, "You make me nuts, too. Just so we're on the same page."

"Next time, we'll try for stamina," Nick teased.

"And maybe some actual privacy," JK suggested. "Do you know what my brother would have said if he'd had to bail me out of jail on an indecency charge?"

Nick petted JK's shirt back into shape, not really a doable task with the way he'd been pulling on it. "Well, you still look... mauled."

JK stole another kiss, and Nick pulled him closer, and JK finally broke the kiss with a growl. "I've got work in the morning. Davis will kick my ass if I don't get moving."

"I'll help," Nick reminded him.

"Your help might kill me," JK said, and Nick kissed him again.

JK finally wandered back to his house in a sticky daze, looking forward to the next morning.

His nightmares were worse than ever.

❁

At 8 a.m., JK dragged the last of the linoleum scraps to the curb and caught Nick sleepily stumbling toward him, coffee mugs in hand, dressed for hard labor. Or dressed to make JK lose his mind. Worn jeans, gone threadbare at the knees and ass, shower-damp hair curling at the nape of his neck, a paint-smeared t-shirt worn so thin JK could see the shadows of Nick's body beneath.

They started with the fencing, tore off all the loose slats, and left the fence down to the uprights. The next day, when it dawned in the nineties and hit triple digits by 10 a.m., they fled indoors, and started painting the upper bedroom.

The work went slowly, hampered by the fact that the old plaster walls ate primer, and by the fact that if they worked too close together, work stopped while they pressed into each other—solid and warm in the close room—and traded slow, hungry kisses. Lazy, like they were teenagers and not adult men who knew what they wanted and how they wanted it. Like it was enough to share each other's breath and knot hands in worn cotton t-shirts and then pull away, grinning, only to fall into each other's orbit all over again.

JK wasn't sure which one of them was standing on the brakes; it might be both of them, he thought ruefully. Nick—waiting to hear JK's story. JK—waiting to tell it.

They were driven back outside by the paint fumes.

And JK cursed those brakes now as he hauled the last of the really big fence posts toward the dumpster, while Nick took a water break. He could think of more fun ways to work up a sweat. But he couldn't stay focused on his fantasies, too busy fending off the sensation that dogs moved in his wake, snarling heat against his legs, their hackles wet with blood he could almost smell.

JK rubbed sweat off his brow with the crook of his arm, smudged dirt off his chest, sticky with his sweat. His shoulders tightened; his spine ached, trying to hold back the atmosphere.

He decided, even if it got unbearably hot tomorrow, he'd keep working in the yard. Avoid the house. He'd call Hannah, see if he could up his dose, if that would help. He just had to get through this. One day at a time, and each day getting better.

He bent to pick up a rounded stone he kept nearly tripping on, and it turned out to be light and brittle in his grip; it crumbled in his hand, shedding teeth, shedding bone—a cat's skull—

Chased and cornered and killed, a thunder of snarling and teeth and pain.

JK flung it away from him, stumbled back, tripped over his own laces and hit the dirt. He grunted with pain, sprawled back on his elbows, and before he could try to get up, Barton's emotions roiled through him again.

Just emotions this time, formless and frantic. Hatred and fear and outrage.

"Jeez," Nick said. "Graceful much?" He set down his water bottle, laughing.

Nick was distant noise, buried beneath the great swell of blurred memories, of darkness and shouting and barking and gunshots like popped corks, yelping and pain, and the weight crushing him...

JK scrabbled for the house, trying to regain his feet, vaguely aware of Nick running toward him. Getting it. Getting that something was wrong.

So terribly wrong.

JK wanted another pill, wanted out of here. He couldn't think, couldn't figure out where the contaminating memories lurked.

In the house, the contamination made sense. Patterns of behavior etched into the walls. But outside, something triggered more memories, pushing them at JK beyond the ability of his pills to block out.

"JK!" Nick said, reaching for him, a helping hand.

JK eluded Nick's touch like a cat, a flex of bone and sinew, slipping beneath his outstretched hand. JK grabbed for the doorknob; his grip slid, his glove slick with sweat-laced dirt half gone to mud, and without thinking, wiped the glove off against his chest.

The dirt.

God damn it, the memories came from the dirt! The stinking *dirt*.

Too late for the knowledge to do him any good.

The great cresting wave of memory—shots, screams, rage, fear, pain, death—rolled out of the earth and yanked him beneath its poisonous undertow.

Someone was screaming, a litany of abuse in a voice gone hoarse with rage. Hands touching him, scalding hot on skin that burned with cold. He flailed, took in blue-green eyes wide with shock, and snarled, "My dogs will rip your throat out, faggot. Piss on your corpse." All that bitter hatred in him thrummed with pleasure when Collier jerked away, face gone white, let him drop back into the dirt.

Blank blackness—the dogs snarling, gunshots, rage, pain, fear, the *thump thump thump* of falling dirt—then more hands. Pulling him upright, the wail of sirens—

"God dammit, I said he doesn't need a hospital! Send it away!"

Two small bodies, clinging to each other, bruises—black and red and blue and yellow—quilting their ribs, their faces blank and swollen, and the taste of vomit in the back of his throat, the rage; he hated being a cop sometimes, but not as much as he hated people—

"He's having seizures—"

"Mind your own business, Collier."

A woman's voice, sharp. Familiar. "I'm a doctor; he's my patient."

A wizened, brittle woman in a hospital bed, the smell of sickness and despair, and her teeth pressing against her thin lips as she said, "I just wanted to not hurt anymore," rubbing her bandaged wrists. Then the ugly sensation of crying in a stairwell, choking sobs full of hidden self-doubt—she can't help everyone.

Dragging him like a corpse, like *the* corpse, weight hanging heavy between hard hands, dragging him through the yard.

Crashing through the back door—the dogs snarling and yelping, gunshots, shouting and the familiar rage, the gun warm in his hand, then dropping, his body jerking, the next gunshot loud as a broken bone, and the scream rising in his throat.

Another gunshot and all that rage splintering and spattering over the dirt—

A sting, distinct and sharp, an invading needle—

The ice cracked beneath his feet and he drowned.

❊

JK's shoulders cramped and he tried to stretch them out, but the jangle of metal prevented him, ringed around his wrists. He was cuffed to a bed frame.

Restrained.

Panic burst over him, and he jerked and twisted and fought. The cuffs rattled; the bed rocked, the frame creaked. A looming shadow came at him, and he flinched before his brain made sense of things: a scowling blond giant. His brother.

"JK." Jesse dropped onto the foot of the bed, said, "Come on, calm down. You'll hurt yourself. You gotta let me know you're in there." For a man who preached calm, every word vibrated with tension.

"Jesse?" JK sagged in the restraints, willing to hope things would be all right. After all, he wasn't in a hospital. Or in the basement. "What happened?" he asked.

"What do you remember?" Jesse asked him.

JK remembered—didn't remember—looking down at two murdered children, sickly sure that he could blame this on the family. It hadn't been his suicide attempt, leaving him scared and quiet in a hospital bed. Dogs hadn't savaged him. And JK definitely hadn't been shot and buried in his own backyard. Even if he remembered it all. None of that had been him. He was JK Lassiter, Jasper Keely Lassiter, and he was twenty-eight years old and... he finally admitted, "I guess I had an episode."

Jesse said, "You think?"

"What are you doing here? How'd you even know..."

"Hannah worries. She said you might be having troubles.

Guess she was right. Guess there's more to this house than ugliness, huh." Jesse's lips tightened until they went bloodless, until they looked like he had a hard time opening them again. "Torelli and I swung by and ended up following an ambulance down the street. Took years off my life realizing it was coming for you. I thought you were taking your pills."

"I *am*."

"How can I believe you? This just doesn't happen out of the blue—"

The words trembled on JK's tongue, words that would clear it all up, make Jesse understand... JK held them back. If he told Jesse what he suspected, what he'd learned, then he might as well give up on this job.

"Maybe I skipped one," JK said.

"Maybe you—" Jesse took a deep breath, and let it out. "I knew you weren't ready to be on your own."

"I am!" JK tried to sit up; the cuffs jangled and pinned him back. He fought them again, and Jesse swore.

Jesse said, "Hold still."

He flipped on the overhead light, and JK found a sick sense of relief that he was still in Barton's house. The bed... the bed was new though.

He said, "Did you put the bed here?"

"You were sleeping on an air mattress!" Jesse said.

"Because I need to rip up the carpet in here, damn it. You're making work for me, Jesse."

Jesse undid the cuffs. "I know you want this job, but... it's not worth losing everything you've gained. This is just the wrong house. I can get you out of your deal with Davis."

"No," JK said. "I know what I have to do. It'll be fine."

"What you *have* to do? I don't like the sound of that."

JK rubbed his wrists, gloves chafing flesh. "Take my pills. Keep to a regular schedule. Keep the gloves on."

Jesse frowned down at him, shadowed by the light behind him, shadowed by... bruising on his face. Jesse had a spectacular black eye, plus a split lip.

JK shrank back. "I did that?"

"You did," Jesse said. He sat down next to JK, his shoulders slumped. "It's not just that I worry about you. I get sick thinking how easily you can get hurt by these intangible things, and I worry that people will figure out what you can do and fear you. Or use you.

"But I also have to worry about *them*. JK, you're damn big and strong. You could hurt someone. You wouldn't want to, but—"

"I could," JK admitted. "If I get lost in the wrong memory."

As if acknowledging the possibility had brought it on, he had another leakage of memory. *Rage and hate and the gun in the kitchen, blaming everyone—"It's all their fault!"*—and reaching to hurt...

Another shuddering memory. Nick's frightened blue eyes as he tried to pull away from JK's brutal grip. Tight as a dog's bite on his wrists. He wanted that memory to be delusion, to be nightmare imagination. JK knew it wasn't. That crystal clear memory of spitting out Barton's threats to Nick—that wasn't house leftover, environmental memory. That had been *Nick's* memory that JK had channeled. Nick had been there. JK had touched him.

He'd blacked Jesse's eye, split his lip. What had he done to Nick?

JK folded his face into his gloves. "And Nick?" he asked.

Jesse grimaced. "I think he's more pissed at us than you."

JK struggled upright, fighting clothes and sheets and bedding. Blankets cocooned him; he found he'd been wrestled into sweatshirt and pants, socks, and gloves. The only skin bare was his face.

Hannah's work, he would bet. Trying to give him shields against the world, even if she smothered him doing so.

Someone knocked on the door, then opened it. JK winced, expecting Hannah's concerned face.

It was worse, though. Nick stepped in, slowing when he saw JK sitting up.

Jesse said, "I thought you went home. To think."

"I came back. I've been talking to Hannah," Nick said. He didn't look thrilled about it. His eyes flickered toward JK and that simple glance unblocked all the words tangling in JK's throat.

"I'm sorry, Nick. It wasn't me saying those things. I would never..." JK trailed off, trying to think of words to explain. Thinking he should have tried harder, earlier. Rejection would have hurt, but better his hurt than Nick's.

Nick braceleted his own wrist with his fingers, touching the swollen mark that edged toward black and blue. "That's what Hannah said." He didn't sound like he believed her.

"What do you want, Nick?" Jesse asked.

"To talk to JK," he said. "Without you standing over him." His voice tipped from flat toward angry.

"Fine," Jesse muttered, and slammed out of the room.

Nick closed the door and leaned against it. He said, "I think it's time for you to explain your 'complicated.'"

JK took a breath. "Yeah." He pulled at the edges of the sweatshirt, fought for the words. "I can read memories. Relive them. If I touch people. Sometimes things. I... read some bad things out there." He looked up from the pulled elastic, tried to meet Nick's gaze. "I'm so sorry."

"So you're psychic. Not psychotic."

JK flinched. "Definitely not psychotic."

"That's what your sister-in-law says, too. Psychic. The real deal."

"Do you believe us?"

Nick scrubbed his hand over his face, fast, like he was scared to take his attention off JK. "I don't know," he said. "There's a lot wrong here, JK. Not least that your sister-in-law is your doctor, and that your brother decided not to take you to the hospital after you suffered some sort of seizure."

"It wasn't a seizure," JK said.

"That's right. It was a psychic episode." Nick grimaced, waved a hand. "Sorry. I didn't mean to sound... dismissive. I just don't know what to think. After hearing Barton's exact words come out of your mouth... I never told anyone what he said to me. Not even Zeke." Nick shrugged, uncomfortable. "I pride myself on being open-minded. But I don't want to believe this."

"Try living it," JK said.

Nick sighed, finally left the shelter of the door, and sat at the foot of the bed. JK pulled his legs up, and gave Nick space.

He said, "I'm worried about your brother."

"About *Jesse*?" JK said.

"He fucking handcuffed you. He keeps talking about packing you up and taking you away like you're furniture."

JK shivered. "He won't. I won't let him."

Nick raised his eyes from his interlaced fingers and said, "You said some really disturbing things while you were out—"

"I'm so sorry—"

"Not to me, to Jesse. Begging him not to put you back in the basement. Whose memories are those, JK?"

JK felt the flush burn up his chest, up his cheeks. "It's fine. We're fine."

Nick studied him, and JK forced himself to relax. To look at ease. He wasn't. Nothing about this was easy.

"You said some other stuff, too. You said some bastard shot my dogs. What dogs?"

JK shuddered. The dogs. The words felt like an electric shock chained to the worst of the memories. He closed his eyes. All those bad feelings... he hadn't been wrong. The house felt like a murder site, because it had been one. Barton had died here. No, Barton had been murdered here. In the yard. Along with his dogs.

"Barton's dead," JK said. "In the yard."

"Barton moved out—"

"He never left the neighborhood," JK told Nick, too tired to even try to cover up his unwelcome new knowledge. For a moment, he remembered the taste of dirt and blood in his mouth.

Nick's expression darkened. "Are you sure—"

JK shoved sweaty hair out of his face, peeled out of the sweatshirt before he asphyxiated, and found, to his aggravation, a long-sleeve tee beneath. He said, "Let me get rid of my family. And I'll show you. I'll prove everything to you."

He dared to reach out, to brush Nick's bruised wrist. "I'm not crazy. Give me a chance. One more chance."

Nick studied JK, his gloves, and finally said, "All right."

❋

It took JK the better part of a night and day to evict Jesse and Hannah. Eighteen hours where Jesse grimly called in sick, moved the bed back out, and helped JK recarpet the bedroom. JK, still staggering with the massive dose of antipsychotics that Hannah had hit him with, was torn between gratitude and frustration. Episodes left him exhausted and groggy, inclined to do nothing more than sleep and be pampered. But the longer Jesse stuck around, the more likely he was to realize that JK had plans beyond renovation.

It wasn't like he wanted to lie to Jesse, but the few tentative sorties he'd made around the truth—Barton's absence—had elicited only a "Leave it alone, JK. Whatever Barton is up to is none of your business."

An even more delicate probe about the possibility of a murder had gotten the flat: "If I thought for one second that murder had been committed here, I'd yank you out of here, no matter what. I can do it."

"I'm twenty-eight, Jesse," JK had said. "How long are you going to be crazy protective?"

"Until you have a full year without an episode."

JK had decided then and there that he would do this without Jesse's help. No matter how strong the evidence was.

Hannah had tried to play peacemaker with the usual sort of results. By the time they left in the late evening, no one had been speaking to anyone. JK had been so wrung out from the arguing, the drugs, and the violent atmosphere lingering in the house that he'd sent Nick a two-word text. "Sorry. Tomorrow." He'd gone back to bed in a room that smelled like new carpet and fresh paint, with freshly washed sheets.

JK waited until nine o'clock to knock on Nick's door, and felt his heart leaping in his chest. Afraid. He could do this by himself. He just... he didn't want to.

It took a long time for Nick to open the door, though JK heard the first lock snap open a full minute before the second one did. Nick having doubts. JK backed up, leaned against the porch pillar.

It wasn't Nick that stepped out though, but Zeke. Zeke scowling and pissed, his arms crossing over his chest. He said, "You actually showed up this morning. I didn't think you would."

JK said, "I showed up." His heart sank. Zeke here so early, having obviously spent the night—it meant JK was a *problem* for Nick now. Something that needed talking about, talking over with his best friend.

Given the expression on Zeke's face, JK knew what Zeke's advice had been. *Stay the hell away from the crazy man.*

"What kind of bullshit you been filling Nick's head with? Psychic powers? Barton dead? I oughta kick your ass. Go near Amy and I swear to God I will put you in the ground. The last thing she needs is another person scamming her."

"Zeke," Nick spoke up, hoarse and uncertain. He edged past Zeke, and onto the porch. Nick held a shovel clenched in a white-knuckled fist.

"What?" Nick said at JK's surprise. "If Barton's dead, and you're going to prove it, I'm assuming there's a body. I figured you'd be needing this."

"Yeah," JK said.

"Oh, for Christ's sake," Zeke growled.

Nick pushed the shovel into JK's gloved hands.

The heft of the shovel silenced anything JK would have said. It wasn't an unfamiliar weight, or even an unfamiliar tool. It was just... a little too real. JK had used shovels for a dozen reasons or more, but this would be an unwelcome first.

"Second thoughts about your second sight?" Nick said, brittle.

"No," JK said. "Just... if I freak out again... get out of my way. Don't try to help me."

Zeke looked seriously unhappy, his brows folding down, his chin coming up. "You can bet he won't. You do anything sketchy and I'll put you down. I wanted him to press charges."

Nick said, "Zeke," again, this time more sharply. JK eyed the blackening bruises around Nick's wrist and decided Zeke couldn't be blamed for his hostility.

"This is bullshit," Zeke said, pushing past JK, stomping down the steps ahead of them. "So where is this supposed proof of yours? This... corpse."

"In the backyard," JK said. "He never left the neighborhood. No truck. No dogs. No friend."

"Ridiculous," Zeke said. "I don't want any part of this."

"So go away," JK said. He didn't want Zeke there, didn't like the anger he felt simmering in the man. He really didn't like the idea that Nick had spilled JK's deepest secret to Zeke. The sun rose hot and high, even early in the day, but the weight of Zeke's stare on his spine made JK's nerves prickle with cold.

"You'd like that, wouldn't you?" Zeke said. "Leave Nick to buy into your crap. Do you con artists have a newsletter or what?"

JK tossed the shovel into the backyard, took a deep breath, and hesitated. Anger churned in his gut. His own. He eased off a glove.

"Cold feet?" Zeke sniped.

JK spun and grabbed Zeke. He'd been aiming for his wrist, but got his hand instead. Zeke's muscles flexed beneath his own, and JK tightened his grip. Memories flashed into him, quick as hummingbirds, sharp as razors. JK rocked back, nearly fell.

"Ah, crap," JK muttered.

Zeke shook off JK's touch. "What, you going to tell me my future now? Give me your best shot." He sneered at JK, eagerness in his eyes, ready to dispute whatever JK said.

"Your past, actually," JK said. The memories moved like shadows within him, painful. He tried not to take them in, tried to keep them separate from his own sense of self. Not his memories, but Zeke's.

"Wow me, then," Zeke said.

JK glanced over at Nick. Nick had told Zeke his secret; did that make it fair for JK to tell Nick Zeke's most painful memory? He chose something less... volatile.

"You did thirty days for assault in Kansas," JK said. "For sucker-punching a guy in the back of the head after he insulted Nick..."

Zeke laughed, hard and mean. "That's all you've got? That's a matter of public record."

JK glanced Nick's way, but Nick evaded both their gazes.

Zeke said, "Go on then. Nick's not going to get you out of this. Tell me something more, some deep, dark secret you managed to dig out from a single touch. Prove to me that you're not a liar."

"Fine," JK said. His pulse beat hard in his throat. Zeke had asked for it. "When you were fifteen, you knocked up Rachel Burroughs. She was sixteen. Her parents didn't want her to get an abortion. Your parents didn't want you to marry her. You didn't want to marry her, either. You didn't even like her that much. She gave the child up for adoption—a boy with her brown eyes—then you transferred schools and never thought about your son again."

Zeke's face flushed dark red, panic in his eyes, and JK wanted to stop, but the words kept coming, erupting out of his throat, out of the darkness. "Except now you can't stop thinking about him because of Amy. *Amy's* adopted and she wants so badly to know why her birth parents gave her up and you won't tell her about your son because you're scared she'll hate you—"

In retrospect, the punch shouldn't have been surprising, but JK could see the past better than the future.

He staggered back, falling toward the ground, his bare hand stretching down... Barton's death waiting for him...

And Nick caught him about the waist, yanked him back to his feet. His face was sheet-white where Zeke's had gone red.

"Is that true?" he asked.

Neither JK nor Zeke answered, which seemed to be answer enough. Zeke turned his back to JK, his shoulders heaving with fury.

"Holy crap," Nick muttered, then stared wild-eyed at the backyard, as if seeing it for the first time. "You don't need to do this. We should just call the cops..."

"We should leave well enough alone!" Zeke snapped. "You know what? I don't care if Barton's there. He deserved anything he got."

"I care," JK said. Barton might have been a horrible man, but no one deserved to be written off like they didn't matter. Like they had barely ever existed.

JK jerked his glove back on, then hefted the shovel onto his shoulders, and took that first step into the backyard.

No monstrous memory lashed out at him. Not even when he found the spot and began to dig. Nick hovered, offering to take his turn; Zeke hovered, trying to keep himself between Nick and JK.

JK ignored both of them, concentrated on the shovel taking bites out of the dirt. The sound echoed oddly in his mind—the slice-scrape-thump of him pulling dirt out of the ground and the faint memory of the dirt moving in reverse—landing over the bodies. The yard... simmered to his senses, even covered head to toe in thick fabric, even with his gloves, his pills. He kept seeing tiny flashes of the past—the flip of dog tails chasing a cat, the crash of a beer bottle against the fence, the sullen fireflies of cigarette butts flung into the dark.

He thought finding the body would take longer, but it took him, at most, half an hour before the shovel brought up a clump of tangled and decaying matted dog hair. The grave hadn't been more than a few feet deep, nothing like the storied six feet down. JK shifted the stinking mass of fur, and unearthed Barton's decaying face.

Zeke gagged and fled for the front yard. Distantly, JK heard him retching.

Even knowing his memories had been right, JK still found himself feeling dully shocked. The shovel slipped in his loosening grip, carved a waxy path in Barton's dead flesh. JK shuddered, then dropped the shovel. His hands trembled. A new memory, this one purely his. This one... the feel of steel pushing through dead flesh... he couldn't ever let go. He'd given it to himself.

"JK, come away—" Nick said. "We'd better call the cops. Before Ashford does."

The mingled satisfaction and horror he'd been reeling under shifted, went cold. A splash of unwelcome reality.

This wasn't the end of the problem. Only the beginning.

8

As they rounded the edge of the house, JK heard Zeke on the phone, exasperation and stress in every exaggerated syllable. "... a body in the fucking yard, how many more times do I need... yes, send a car... God damn..." He shoved his phone back into his pocket, and kicked at the dirt.

Before JK or Nick could say anything, Zeke muttered "Aw, fuck," and headed across the street, moving to cut Ashford's approach off.

JK wondered how long the old man had been watching, judging, wondered if he'd seen Zeke punch JK before they all vanished around the back of the house. Seen Zeke stagger back and vomit—was that when Ashford had risen from his porch?

The only thing that could make this mess worse would be for the elderly colonel to have a heart attack. The neighborhood would never forgive JK for that. The colonel might be an old bastard, but they loved him.

Ashford pushed past Zeke, and into JK's backyard. The old man's face had greyed to the color of his hair, but his voice stayed steady. "Have you called the police?"

"First thing, man," Zeke said. "What do you take us for?"

"Someone who has no love for the police himself," Ashford said.

Zeke grimaced, but didn't deny it.

As if through some odd neighborhood telepathy, doors started opening up and down the street. Mr. Martinelli, garden shears in hand, stepped out, then turned their way. He dropped the shears.

Devi Sunitz wandered out, his mother on his heels, then she pulled him back inside, warned by some sixth sense of her own. Olivia pulled her car over and Amy rocketed out of it, slammed into Zeke when he intercepted her. "Don't go back there."

"What did you do?" she asked him, eyes enormous. "What's happened?"

"Barton's dead," Zeke said. "Murdered."

Amy startled JK by bursting into noisy tears, a wail ripping free from her lips. Zeke dragged her closer, muffled her cries in his shoulder. His hands on her hair and hip shook.

Nick grabbed JK's wrist and tugged him away from the yard, toward his own house. "Let's get you out of this mess," Nick said. His voice sounded tight and strained. But JK, all his senses firing, thought that Nick's agitation didn't feel like distress. It felt electrical, charged, felt like *excitement.*

JK wasn't sure how he felt, beyond vaguely ill. He kept feeling the shovel striking dead flesh. He focused on Nick's fingers trembling against his wrist, and let Nick tow him away from the scene. He couldn't stop thinking, wondering, should he have called his brother? But Jesse needed to solve that brutal case— those two murdered kids—and Jesse worked out of another precinct, so telling him would just make him crazy.

"We should wait for the police," JK murmured.

"They can find us next door, when they need us. It's not like we're fleeing the country," Nick said. "And we need to talk."

Nick's hand wrapped warm and tight around his arm, above his glove. The touch shouldn't have done anything to JK, not Nick's bare fingers on the safe area of his forearm, but JK burned with borrowed sensation. Not images, not memories, but bursts of intense emotion. Disbelief, a gasping weight in the pit of his stomach. Triumph, a quick syncopation to his heart. Terror, a swoop of vertigo, like the world dropping away beneath him. Happiness, relief, excitement, all pulsing through Nick's touch, translating into JK's blood and bone.

His body hummed on the edge of an adrenaline rush, like he'd just survived a life-threatening attack. All that energy... it had to go somewhere.

Nick tugged JK up the steps to his front door, glanced back, a wild light in his eyes. A surge of hunger through Nick's skin to his... JK's emotions narrowed to one single core of *want.*

Nick unlocked his door, one dead bolt after another un-latching, like clapping hands gaining momentum. Nick pushed JK's unresisting bulk through the door, and closed them in. JK felt an enormous tension spill out of his spine when Nick shut out the world.

He turned to say thanks, and Nick's mouth landed on his own. Nick pressed into him, hands knotting tight in JK's shirt, in his hair, and kissed him deeply, hungrily, voraciously.

"Should we really..." JK's voice felt raw already, scoured by desire.

"Yes," Nick said. "Definitely."

JK pushed back, pushing Nick against the door, pinned him and kissed him until he had to pull back to pant for breath against Nick's throat. "I told you. I'm *not* crazy," he said. "I *am* a psychic."

"You're not crazy, and Barton's dead and *I'm not*."

JK closed the tiny distance between them. Nick wrapped an arm around his neck, drawing him closer. Nick tasted like sugared coffee and cinnamon toothpaste, smelled like aftershave and sweat. JK wanted to devour him.

The brakes were off, and they were roaring downhill.

JK stroked down Nick's spine, felt each bump and jut of bone, even through the thick bulk of dirt-smeared suede, felt the way Nick pressed closer, slipping a thigh between JK's, bringing them together from knee upward.

Nick mouthed JK's jaw, bit at the stubble, breathed a warm track across his neck, and then followed that course with his lips. JK dragged his hand up Nick's back, and Nick's thin t-shirt stuck to his glove and rose with it. JK tried to get his other hand in on the action, and his glove stuck, tangled against the latches, the dangling keys. He jerked his hand past it, ignoring the fact that his glove had stayed behind. His hand ghosted over Nick's exposed flesh, bare fingertips against bare skin.

Sleek.

JK groaned.

Nick was sleek and warm and wonderful, the best thing JK had ever felt. He knew he should yank his hand away—that even the brush of bare fingertips was dangerous, but the tiny shifts of muscle beneath his skin were mesmerizing. JK pressed closer, dipped his fingers into the waistband of Nick's jeans, ignoring the visions flickering through him, pornographic fragments of heated breath and flesh pressing against flesh.

None of those visions compared to the real thing in his arms. His world dwindled to Nick's breath, the thump of Nick's heartbeat against his chest, the hard push of Nick's cock swelling against his own. JK groaned, and the memory slipped over him so easily that it melded with his own intentions.

Leaning back against a door, the sounds of a party behind him, distant, and Tony dropping to his knees before him, Tony's hands tightening on his hip bones, his hand curling into Tony's hair. Murmuring, "C'mon, cowboy."

JK popped the first button on Nick's jeans—*the same jeans. Ten years old, his favorite pair. His lucky pair*—and followed the zipper down.

Nick said, "JK," above him breathlessly, and JK thought, *JK, who's that*, and licked the damp head of his cock. Nick jolted against him, and JK pressed closer, put his cheek against Nick's bared hip and just breathed. Musk and soap and clean skin with sweat springing up.

"Not nice to tease," Nick whispered, stroking JK's hair.

"Who's teasing, baby?" JK wasn't sure if they were his words or pulled straight from Nick's memory, and Nick tensed against him for a moment, as if he too had sudden doubts. Then JK rolled his head, and sucked Nick down.

Salt and bitterness and heat and everything he'd been craving. The tension in his jaw, muscles working, the taste of controlled hunger. It seemed like he'd been wanting this contact forever. Easy to forget Barton's body, easy to ignore the rising sound of approaching sirens.

He curled his gloved hand around Nick's hip, slid the very

tips of his bare fingers across the other hip, greedily documenting each tiny shift and jerk of Nick's belly as he fought not to wreck JK's mouth.

JK's cock throbbed in sympathy, pressing eagerly against his cargo pants, but he ignored it.

JK looked up, saw Nick looking down, teeth pressed tight into a reddened lower lip. Only a thin ring of blue glimmered around Nick's blown pupils.

Next time, JK thought, he wanted Nick completely naked. He needed to see Nick's skin slicked with sweat, see how far the flush on his neck and jaw went, see the arc and tremble of tightening muscles.

The air in the room seemed overlaid with Nick's scent, hot and sharp and everything to JK. He wanted this to last, but Nick's breath rasped fast and rough, underlaid with a growl that JK *remembered* signaled close, very close.

Nick touched his hair, ran shaking fingers over JK's working jaw and said, "JK. Fuck."

JK slid his gloved hand—rough suede, gentle touch—between Nick's trembling thighs, the cage of denim, cupped the tightened balls, pressed his finger into the smooth skin just beyond, and Nick swore again, hard and harsh, and his hips jerked as he lost control.

JK swallowed, groaning, then pulled off and let his gloved fingers coax the last spurts out. He rested his face against Nick's fast moving abs, breathed out satisfaction. Nick shuddered as JK's breath ruffled the thin trail of hair into his splayed open jeans.

"Come here, come here, God, get up here," Nick said, tugging him up, jerking JK's pants down, wrapping his hand around JK's cock.

JK leaned into Nick's chest, and curled his arms over Nick's shoulders, letting Nick work him in sure, strong strokes. He mouthed at Nick's throat, bit, moaned, and was just drawing breath to admit he wasn't going to last when he came. His hands clenched hard, one on Nick's side, the other dangling in the air, fingertips scorched by Nick's skin, by the quick claiming of Nick's favorite sex memories.

He found himself sitting, bare-assed on the hallway floor, looking up at Nick, and laughing. "Holy shit, we can talk like that, anytime."

Nick slid down to join him, helping him straighten his clothes, and locating JK's other glove. "You touched me, bare-handed."

JK nodded. "I shouldn't have." He couldn't muster any regret, not while his body sang and tingled.

"Get anything out of it?"

JK couldn't read Nick's tone very well—sated, pleased... suspicious?

"A few tips," JK admitted.

"And here I was thinking you were a genius with that mouth of yours—" Nick stopped to kiss him again, and JK leaned into it, less frantic, lazy now, nipping at Nick's full lower lip as he pulled away—*always liked that, a little rough with the sweet. He'd kept Sebastian around for an extra month because Seb might have been a jerk, but awesome in bed made up for a lot.*

The front door opened, and Zeke stuck his head in. His worried expression went dumbfounded, then infuriated as he took in JK's swollen mouth, Nick's languor, the way they leaned into each other.

"Jesus Christ," Zeke spat. "There are cops wanting to talk to you and you wander off for a quickie? The fuck is wrong with you?" He directed the last toward JK, but Nick answered for them.

"Yeah," Nick said, smiling faintly. "We did."

"Well, I told them that you were feeling sick, Nicky, so you better get that grin off your face." Zeke opened the door, went out, left it open behind him. The world rushed back in.

"Probably not the best timing ever," JK said, looking out at the flashing lights.

"Regret it?" Nick asked.

"No." JK pushed himself to his feet, tugged Nick back to his. They walked out to face the chaos—a sea of uniforms and two plainclothes women with hard faces. He should have regretted it, maybe. It was disrespectful, bad timing, and as Jesse would say, just plain dumb, but JK couldn't regret the interlude. It felt like the start of something more. Something good out of bad.

❂

JK didn't recognize either of the detectives who immediately migrated toward them, but Jesse tried to keep JK away from the police as much as possible; Hannah might go to the police shindigs, but JK didn't get the invite. JK had no interest in fighting Jesse's restriction: even setting aside the disaster that had been JK's short-lived relationship, cops teemed with violent and terrible memories.

They introduced themselves—Detectives Gunnarson and Conroy, the former a brisk tall blond woman with clothes as crisp as her manners. The latter woman was dark, bird-thin, and watchful.

"Which one of you is Lassiter?" Conroy asked, her eyes darting between them.

"Me," JK admitted; he felt obscurely guilty. Conroy had the cop expression down pat. She jerked her head at him, and he followed her toward the Barton house. His stomach knotted, hoping she wasn't going to make him go back in the yard. He looked back, expecting to see Nick following, but he was being herded back to his own house by Gunnarson.

Conroy ushered JK in first, then looked taken aback by the empty rooms, the lack of furniture. Besides JK's bed upstairs, there wasn't a single place to sit and talk. She looked around, then chose privacy over comfort. She pulled out a tablet and a stylus. The uniformed officer who'd followed them both stood by the open front door, keeping an eye inside and out.

JK leaned against the kitchen wall, and the thump of his shoulder blades hitting plaster reminded him of Nick falling back against his closed door, hips canting up into JK's hands. He felt his lips curling up.

Conroy asked, "Something funny?"

"No, not at all," JK said, banishing the smile.

She eyed him sidelong, bird-like again, and he kept his expression still with an effort. His hands sweated gently within his gloves. He could smell himself. Sweat and dirt and rot and sex. He hoped Conroy couldn't.

"Tell me what happened," she said.

"I dug up a body," JK said.

She waved her stylus at him. "Big picture, Mr. Lassiter. Big picture. Why were you digging a hole?"

"I'm renovating the house for my boss."

Conroy said, "The yard is not the house."

"It's part and parcel. Landscaping, you know? I was going to plant a tree."

Her pen stopped moving. "You were going to plant a tree?" she asked.

"Yeah," he said. JK knew almost immediately he'd given the wrong answer, but didn't know why, or how to fix it when he couldn't tell the truth.

"And your neighbor was helping?"

"Keeping me company."

"You moved in when?" She took him over his arrival timetable, questioned him as to whether he'd been here before, known the neighbors, and the like. JK's lack of history with the neighborhood made her frown ease, made him feel less like a rat pinned beneath an owl's gaze.

"So you didn't know the deceased?" Conroy asked him.

"No," he said.

"You have any idea of who he is?"

JK's foot, propping him against the wall, slipped, landed with a thunk. "I thought it was Mr. Barton, the previous homeowner. Isn't it?"

"Why do you think that?"

JK hated the way the police refused to answer any questions, but at least living with Jesse had gotten him used to it. "A couple of things. The dead dogs," he said. "Everyone told me that Mr. Barton had two big dogs. Also..." he paused, throat working.

"Also?"

"I saw a picture of him. The guy in the ground's all coming apart..." JK shuddered. "But it looked like the same guy."

"Hmm. You have any problems with the neighbors? Anyone strike you as violent?"

"No," JK said.

"No?" Conroy repeated.

Another wrong answer. His phone rang, shrill in his pocket and she shook her head slightly. He let it ring.

"Mr. Ashford said that you took a punch today from Zeke Stuart. You've got a bruise coming up on your jaw."

JK touched the spot, and winced. "I deserved the hit."

"You *deserved* it?" Her lips tightened. "Why?"

"Personal disagreement that got ugly. No big," he said.

Conroy tapped her stylus against the edge of the tablet, and said, "All right, then. What picture?"

"Sorry?"

"You had a picture of Barton. Why?"

JK ducked his head, and her attention sharpened. Conroy said, "Mr. Lassiter, if there's something you need to tell me—"

"He left all his stuff behind," JK said. "Just piled in the garage. I thought that seemed weird."

"Weird?"

"Worrying," he admitted.

"What did you do?"

"I got rid of it."

"Where?"

He told her, and she made note of it, then said, "So you were worried, but you didn't do anything about it?"

"I called his wife," JK said. "*She* told me to get rid of it. My *boss* told me to get rid of it. Everyone told me it wasn't important.

And I figured they knew what they were talking about, only now it turns out he's dead." The words rushed out of him, despite his attempts to call them back.

She tapped her stylus twice more, once he'd fallen silent. Conroy looked at him, and he dropped his arms from across his chest, let them hang naturally. Easily. As if he had nothing to hide. His phone rang again and JK jumped.

After the ringing stopped, Conroy said, "Look, this is the situation, kid. You moved in a few days ago, didn't know the deceased, didn't know anyone before you moved in. That right?"

"Yeah," JK said.

"And you were digging a hole for a tree."

JK nodded.

She sighed. "Your friend told my partner that you were digging a hole for a water feature." She waved the tablet at him gently, the texts from her partner bright oblongs on its face.

That made more sense, JK thought. Maybe he and Nick should have talked instead of...

"You don't have any trees to plant," she said. "What were you digging for, JK?"

His arms folded across his chest without his volition. JK said, "What do you want? I've told you all I know. What I was doing. And you know what I found."

Conroy looked at her tablet screen again, and JK wondered what it told her, what her partner told her in digital silence. What Nick might be saying. Nick knew all his secrets, now. His stomach felt tight, and from the living room, he heard dogs snarling, a woman—a *young* woman—crying. He wanted to cover his ears, but it wouldn't do any good.

"Lassiter, JK!" she said, and he snapped back to attention.

"I feel sick," he told her. "Can I go now?"

Her dark eyes were fixed on his face. "A couple more questions," she said.

JK closed his eyes, tried to close off his senses, tried to press himself further into his freshly painted kitchen wall—all the memories erased from it. "Fine."

"Any ideas who hated Barton?"

"Everyone who met him," JK said. "Do I know anyone who would actually have killed him? No."

"Why were you digging in the yard?" she asked again.

"Trees," he said.

She took a deep, pained breath. "You're Jesse Lassiter's brother, aren't you?"

JK nodded, warily. No good came from cop questions that seemed irrelevant.

Another deep breath. Conroy said, "The psychic one."

JK flinched.

"Never underestimate a police station's capacity for gossip," she said.

"What do you want?" JK asked.

Something about the way she looked at him seemed... calculating. Like she was doing math in her head, adding things up.

"I'd think your brother would have a higher solve rate, if you really are psychic. Although Lassiter's never been one to mix family and the job." Conroy leaned forward. "But you know what? A psychic might be exactly the type to *stumble* on a body, and come up with a poorly thought-out cover story. A psychic might be able to give me a tip toward the killer." Her gaze met his, fell, lingered on his gloves, and rose to meet his eyes again.

"I can't help you with anything," JK said, turning away. Staring out through the kitchen window didn't provide an escape. It only showed him men toiling to bring the bodies out of the dirt. In the front, through the opened door, he could hear the neighbors chattering.

"No?"

"No," JK said.

Conroy tapped her tablet off, tucked it into her pocket. Came up with a card. She handed it to him, raising an eyebrow when he fumbled the thin paper with a gloved hand. "Wouldn't it be easier to take those off indoors?" She answered her own question. "Let me guess. 'No.' Is that how it works? Through touch?"

JK put her card in his pocket, intending to throw it out as soon as he could. "Can I go now?"

"Please," she said. "Keep your eyes open. Any of your... eyes. Someone in this neighborhood's getting away with murder."

JK shook his head. "No," he said. "It had to be someone from the outside."

Conroy's black eyes went as hard as obsidian. "Are you that naive?" She gripped his arm, and urged him toward the front door. "Look out there. Look."

The neighborhood crowded the street, all the homeowners out and watching. Nick caught JK's attention; the long line of his back telegraphed distress. Gunnarson kept talking to him. Talking *at* him. Beside them, Zeke glared at the detective; Amy had a restraining hand on his arm.

"You've been here a few days," Conroy said. "Had a few visitors that at least four of your neighbors told me about. Your brother; your sister-in-law; a big man with a small voice; your friends in the big truck. They noticed, and they remembered enough to describe them to me. Do you really think a stranger managed to get onto this street, kill him, *bury* him, all without being noticed?

"Look, you seem like a nice young man, so let me tell you this. You think it's all over. That getting Barton's body out of the yard is the end of your problem. I'll tell you what your brother would. Be careful. Don't trust these people. One of them's a killer."

❋

Watched over by the uniformed officer, JK packed up a bag of his clothes, all his necessities. "How long is the house going to be a crime scene?" he asked. "I've got a deadline."

The uniform said, "You have Conroy's card. Ask her."

Not helpful, JK thought. He added another shirt to the pile, a mixed box of his gloves—nitrile, suede, silk—just in case. He took his pills out of the bathroom, noticed the uniform's eyes landing on the orange bottle.

"Those prescription?" he asked JK.

"Yup." He tucked them into a shirt pocket, buttoned it closed. "What are they for?"

"For me to take," JK said.

"You always wear gloves?" the cop asked, trying a different approach. He wasn't any older than JK, a rookie, but already he'd earned hard lines around his eyes.

"Yeah," JK said.

"Got something to hide?"

"Conroy talked to me," JK said. "Ask her." He slung his bag over his shoulder. "I'm done."

The rookie cop looked like he wanted to keep asking JK questions, trying to run his own investigation. He hadn't gotten the memo. Conroy wouldn't leave a rookie alone with JK, if JK were a suspect. Not when JK could have made two of the wiry young man.

JK moved toward the stairs, down them, expecting the cop to call him back and demand answers to ill-thought questions. But the uniform stayed behind; JK heard the rustle of his stuff being moved and he sighed. He stopped by Conroy, now conferring in person with her partner, to say, "Your uniform is snooping through my things without a warrant."

Gunnarson swore, and stalked back toward the house. JK's phone ringing saved him from another conversation with Conroy. He answered it, and got Jesse in a temper.

"What the fuck did you do?" Jesse said. "Torelli said there was a call-out to your place."

"Dug up Barton's body," JK said. "Conroy and Gunnarson are here."

Jesse swore again, this time with a vicious edge to it that made JK's heart race.

"What?" JK asked him.

"Don't talk to them."

"It's not like I'm a suspect, Jesse."

"Kate Conroy is Ben Wilson's cousin. You remember Ben."

"Aw, fuck," JK muttered. No wonder she'd heard the rumors

about his abilities—Ben would have told her directly. But she seemed to believe in them. JK couldn't figure if her belief made things worse or not. "Look, it's done. She was nice enough."

"That's her shtick," Jesse said; he sighed. "If she comes to ask you anything else, even if it's what you take in your coffee, you say nothing without me present."

"You're not a lawyer. And I'm not a suspect," JK said. "I think you're missing the point."

"I'm trying not to dwell," Jesse said. "You lied to me, deliberately. Why couldn't you just leave it alone?"

"What, Barton's body?" JK heard his voice rise, wincing when he felt attention turning his way. "It's not like I meant to find him. I was just digging a hole for a tree."

Jesse said, "Oh, Christ, tell me that's not what you told Conroy."

JK let the silence answer him. Nick moved toward him, blue-green eyes intent, focused on the phone.

"Conroy's family runs a nursery. She's all about planting times and trees and soil loads."

"Oh," JK said. He really should have taken the time to find out what Nick's story was going to be. Water feature looked better as an excuse all the time.

Nick indicated the phone, mouthing, "Your brother?"

JK nodded. Nick's jaw hardened. He reached out and took JK's duffel, slung it over his own shoulder.

"I've got a shitload more hours of work here; sweating the kids' uncle, I know he did it," Jesse said. "But Hannah's off in an hour. She'll come get you. Bring you home. The house is a crime scene. You can't stay there."

"I'm staying with Nick," JK said tentatively, looking at his duffel in Nick's grip. Nick nodded.

Jesse said, "The fuck you are. You're not a suspect, but he's right at the heart of it."

"Jesse, shut up!" JK said. "I need to be here. I need to keep an eye on the house. It's my job."

"You need to get away from that house. As soon as possible. It's not safe—"

JK glanced warily around for eavesdroppers, and when he saw that Gunnarson and Conroy were occupied dressing down the uniform who'd been poking through JK's stuff, he said, "It's a lot safer now that the body's gone."

✵

JK brushed his teeth with a spare toothbrush Nick produced, then lingered in Nick's tidy bathroom, feeling awkward. It had been easy to say yes when Nick asked him to stay.

But JK hadn't done the sleepover thing in years. This slow deliberation before bed, stripping down to his boxers, changing his gloves, brushing his teeth, washing his face... knowing Nick was doing the same? It felt alien, a social mechanism he hadn't had the chance to learn. In high school, his sleepovers had stopped when he'd come out to his parents: they hadn't been comfortable with boys staying overnight. After the basement, there'd been hookups in bars, rushed encounters where gloves could be quirky or kinky and not really worthy of comment.

Even sex with Nick had been all about impulse and hunger, the discharge of relief and excitement. An unexpected indulgence. Nothing more out of the ordinary than a charged bar hookup.

Now, JK looked into the mirror and saw only confusion. Nick tapped on the door frame, leaned into the room.

He said, "Hey. You need me to make up the guest bed?"

"No," JK said.

Nick smiled, came up beside him and kissed him. JK watched Nick's lashes flutter closed, kept his open to see the blurry relaxation and hunger on Nick's face. Nick pulled back, left his fingers threading gently through JK's hair, rubbing his nape. "Want to come to my bed? Get the bad taste out of the day?"

"Yes," JK whispered.

It was as easy as that, after all. He linked hands with Nick—

thin white silk gloves against Nick's smooth skin. JK let Nick draw him into the bedroom, into bed, to breathe apologies into his bruised jaw until JK couldn't even remember who or what Nick was apologizing for.

JK's body ached in strange places—his shoulders and his forearm from his frantic digging, bruises on his elbows and knees from falling during his episode, and the bruise Zeke had left on his jaw. Nick seemed to intuit his exhaustion, and their lovemaking turned sweet and simple. They pressed chest to chest, tangled their legs together from thigh to ankle. Nick just reached between them, clasped both of their cocks in his hands, and stroked them off, his breath fast and fluttering against JK's throat, JK groaning, his teeth scraping Nick's freckled shoulder.

JK rolled away, drew in some air that wasn't superheated by their bodies, and sighed.

Nick twined his fingers into JK's gloved hand, raised it up above them both, looking at the white-gloved fingers woven between his tanned fingers. "So, even in bed?"

"Especially in bed," JK said.

"That sensitive?" he asked.

"Some memories are easy to be overwhelmed by."

"You picked up some stuff earlier. About me, I mean. And you didn't seem overwhelmed."

"The moments sort of meshed," JK admitted. This conversation made him twitchy. Even with Jesse and Hannah, they didn't talk about his abilities this way. Their conversations were all about how to control it, to keep the memories out. Jesse and Hannah didn't ask him questions about how his abilities worked.

"Can I ask what you saw..."

"They were your memories," JK said. "You already know them."

Nick kissed JK's wrist, and let his hand go, catching JK's tone, the discomfort seeping through his veins. JK bit his lip, and gave in. He said, "When I was touching you. Bare-handed. We were..."

"I remember what we were doing," Nick said. That soft smile touched his mouth again.

"It's like category searches. You were thinking about sex. And comparing me to—"

"Hey, no, I wasn't—"

"You were. It's okay," JK said. "It's not really at a conscious level. It's a deep down thing. It's not like comparison shopping, just your body thinking *oh yeah, this is awesome,* and dredging up similar experiences. Which started the boyfriend parade in the memory banks." His cheeks felt stupidly hot, flushed with his own memories.

"That's how it works?"

"With people, yeah," JK said. "Like... like Zeke." He touched his bruised jaw. It ached, but dully. "He was focused on me, on revealing my secrets to you—trying to prove me a liar. It meant his own secrets were close to the surface."

"So you can't just..."

"Just what?" JK said, warned by the interest in Nick's voice. "Touch things or people until I find out who killed Barton?"

Nick propped himself up on his elbows, crooked a knee for comfort, and said, "You can't be surprised I'm asking. I'm a researcher. You give me one fact, I'll turn it into others. My entire career is built on finding things out."

"My sanity depends on *not* finding things out," JK said. "Do you think that I enjoyed that episode in the yard any more than you did?"

Nick frowned, rubbing at his bruised wrist. "You said that wasn't usual."

"It could be. If I started touching things. Touching people." A spurt of alarm ran his veins. He didn't want to talk about it. It seemed... unfair. Nick already knew the biggest of his secrets, and he wanted more?

"How bad does it get?" Nick asked.

JK said, "Bad."

"But if you take your pills, if you—"

"You don't get it," JK snapped.

"Then tell me."

"They're *my* memories now. I told you I died once."

"I know," Nick said. "I looked you up. You were playing hockey. You were the farthest out when it cracked. You *drowned*."

JK shivered, wrapped his arms around himself, brushed skin against skin, their crossed calves rubbing together, bony ankles bumping. *The lake water, gelid in his lungs, filling him up, scouring him out. Leaving him burned out and empty.* "I remember."

"Researcher," Nick said again, an apology of sorts. He stroked the long line of JK's spine.

"I remember dying five times now," JK said. He bent his head, spoke into his knees. Nick's stroking paused.

"My own death," JK said. "Death by drowning. The hospital bed they put me in. A man had a fatal heart attack there. I had a fatal attack there." *Crushing leaden pain, dragged down by the black hole his heart had become. Without even a breath to protest. Never see his kids again.* "A boy who ran away and got hit by a car." *Heat and agony and terror.* "The woman whose body I found at a construction site." *Strangled, his hands tight on her neck, vision going bloody as her eyes hemorrhaged. Clawing at him, fighting so hard. Losing.*

"And Barton—" Nick sounded sick. "Shot and buried. You felt that?"

"Buried alive," JK said. "Not for very long. But long enough." *The struggle for air, blind with pain, and his dogs crushing the last breath from him.*

"So you *saw* who—"

"Jesus," JK snapped, and surged away from Nick, stumbling over his shoes, stumbling toward the door.

"JK!" Nick started to follow, then sank back into the bed. "It's okay. I won't push."

"I *don't* know," JK said. "I don't. I only got the gist, from the ground. His pain so bad it stained the dirt... You want to know how bad it can get? Nonstop episodes, me screaming and thrashing until I'm sedated. Locked in a basement so the world can't get to me, sedated for days at a time. To keep me safe from myself. Clawing at the walls, my own skin, screaming my throat bloody. Nothing but other people's nightmares. That's how bad it gets." His tight breathing savaged his vocal cords, made his words as ragged as if he'd been shouting.

"I've been there, been that lunatic *thing*," he whispered.

"Did Jesse do that to you?" Nick's response, though low, vibrated with fury.

"My parents," JK said. "Jesse got me out. They were trying to keep me safe. It just snowballed. By the time I realized I was in trouble, I couldn't get out from under it."

Nick let out his breath, smoothed the tangled sheets with hands that shook. JK leaned back against the door jamb, waiting for Nick to... what? Show him to the guest room under the guise of giving him space? Get himself away from JK's crazy?

Instead, Nick took a breath. "Okay. So Jesse's a good guy, and your sister-in-law... she's treating you? Prescribing for you?"

"Yeah," JK said.

"Is that ethical?" he asked.

"For her? No. For me it's better than the basement. Better than losing my mind, my sense of self, my life." JK tried to keep the anger out of his voice. Abstractly, he understood Nick's concerns. But his life wasn't an abstract.

"Okay, okay," Nick said. "Come back here. Come on. I promise. No more questions. I just wanted to know." He patted the sheets. "Your turn to ask questions if you want, how about that?"

JK said, "So you and your parents had a falling out."

Nick sighed. He said, "Right for the jugular, huh?"

JK rejoined Nick on the bed. "You weren't shy about going for my weak spot."

"I didn't know it was one." Nick shrugged, twitched the sheets smooth around them, and rubbed the length of JK's spine beneath the cool cotton. "My family disowned me. But it wasn't the gay thing. My parents are liberals. Dad's a hippie."

"Natural foods," JK recalled.

"He and Mom had this store, always on the edge of bankruptcy. Big dreams. No business sense. My sister and I worked in the store after school. But when it came time for college, they needed our savings to keep the store going. They wanted my tuition money."

JK said, "You said no?" That surprised him. But then, no one got to be a professor of history without loving the subject.

"I said yes," Nick admitted. "They promised I'd go to school, just... later. My grandmother had a fit. If they were liberals, she was old-school conservative. All about education. Lots of fighting and Deb and I just trying to keep out of it. Earning our minimum wage.

"But a year later, Grandma died and left me money for college."

JK said, "You went this time."

"Kansas State. First place that would take me. I almost missed going then, too. Mom asked me for the money again. It's hard to say no to your parents."

JK nodded, thinking of his father saying, *"We made a safe space for you. In the basement."*

Nick said, "I found out they'd had more than a dozen offers to buy the business, good deals. Ones which left my parents in control of pretty much everything but budget and marketing. They preferred to take money from their kids. I left. They didn't forgive me. Neither did my sister."

"I didn't talk to Jesse for nearly seven years," JK said. "I wanted to. I just... couldn't. Every time he tried to visit, I lost it. All that death around him. Everything horrible that stuck with him. Gave him sleepless nights. I absorbed it all."

Nick tugged the blanket up higher, wrapped it around JK's shoulders. "And now there's Barton."

"A horror show all my own," JK said. He shut his eyes, breathed in Nick's scent. Warm. Welcoming. Restful. He leaned closer, tried to absorb that warmth. "Let Barton be the cops' problem. Please."

"Okay," Nick said, soothingly. "Okay. None of our business anymore."

9

First thing in the morning, someone started pounding on Nick's door. JK's phone started ringing shrilly at the same time, and finished off JK's sleep haze. JK answered, and Davis shouted, "I'm at the door. Why aren't you awake? It's seven o'clock."

"I'm awake, I'm awake. Stop knocking!" JK snapped. He tugged on a clean pair of cargo pants, juggling his phone in the slippery silk gloves. "I'll be right out."

"Bring me coffee." Davis hung up, and JK savored the silence. He let his heart return to a more regular beat from the tap dance Davis's knocking had started.

"Who the hell was that?" Nick mumbled.

"My boss."

"He's horrible." Nick rolled over and put a pillow over his head.

JK said, "He is, and I'm going to give him your coffee."

"Horrible," Nick mumbled again, before going back to sleep.

Ten minutes later, JK joined Davis outside the Barton house, passing him a cup of just-brewed coffee. He said, "Don't lose the mug, it's not mine."

Davis eyed the UT-Dallas mug and said, "Yeah, I can see how this would be hard to replace."

"Sarcasm this early might be a reason to call OSHA," JK said.

Davis's sour expression shifted to a near grin. "Yeah, all right. Tell me about yesterday."

JK hopped up to sit on the bed of Davis's truck, watched the crime scene tape flutter in the wind. "I'm sick of that story."

"JK. This coffee bought you a few minutes' grace. Use them wisely. Nobody wants a murder house. My investment just plummeted in value."

"Actually," JK said. "I've been thinking about that. This is the best time for the discovery."

Davis rocked back on his heels, then peered up at JK against the early morning sun. He said, "Explain."

"Finding the body now, when the reno's still new... gives people time to forget."

"And if the news takes a picture? There's the house, easily searchable."

"No news crew yet. This is nothing crime by their standards," JK said. "A man was murdered and it's nothing. Which in this case," he hurried on, "is a good thing for us. And even if the news crews show up and take a picture, I'll be fixing the outside too. The house won't be recognizable. If you sell now, trying to get out of it, you'll never recoup. If you hold on, you might."

"Depending on how good a job you do," Davis said. "So far, you've been less than impressive."

JK swallowed some of his coffee to ease the nervous dryness in his throat. Murder or not, he still needed this job. "I'm trying."

Davis sighed. "Try harder." He handed JK the keys that Conroy had taken from him yesterday. "The house is no longer a crime scene. The yard—stay out of it for seventy-two hours. Don't mess with the crime scene tape. The cops are going to be asking questions of the neighbors today. Don't get distracted. Don't get involved."

JK nodded, a knot in his chest easing. He said, "Thanks for finding that out. I didn't get a clear answer from the cops."

Davis tapped JK's knee. "You need to stand up for yourself and your rights more. Don't let people push you around. Now get to work." His boss shrugged, apparently well-aware of the contradiction in his words.

❈

With Nick's help, JK tore out the downstairs carpet, rolling it in big chunks and dragging it out to the dumpster. They did an awkward bobbed-head acknowledgment each time one of the crime scene techs, now working in the back, passed by. JK looked at the hole torn out of his backyard and winced. The pit yawned three times the size it had originally been, and twice as deep. He added "new soil and sod" to his endless list of housing needs.

But the hole made him remember Ashford's cautions, and he went to the edge of the tape. The tech nearest the tape said, "You need to stay back."

"No problem," JK said. "I just... There's a neighborhood kid who explores. Make sure you don't leave it—"

"Uncovered or unguarded or little Devi Sunitz will fall in and break his neck," the tech said.

"Colonel Ashford?" Nick said.

"Oh yeah," the tech said. "He's been keeping a close eye on us. Questioning everything we do. Trying to get a look at everything we find. And the other old guy—he just keeps complaining about the body ruining the soil. Irritating old geezer." The second tech wandered up and bent his head toward his younger assistant, saying something too quiet to overhear. But the young tech's friendliness closed off. "Go on. Back away from the crime scene."

Suspicion, JK thought, vaguely nauseated. JK was okay. Not a suspect. Just the renovator. But Nick earned suspicion. JK guessed it made sense. If he didn't know Nick, and knew how much Barton had harassed him, JK might be suspicious, too.

Nick's cheeks were redder than their exertion merited. He said, "Come on, JK. Let's get the rest of the carpet up and out."

JK nodded, and let Nick lead him back in. The stiff set to Nick's shoulders suggested that any attempt at reassurance would be unwelcome, so JK settled for brushing too close past him, leaving a kiss in the ruffled edge of his hair.

Once the carpet was torn out, they sprawled on the exposed hardwood, JK studying it closely, Nick poking blankly at the old varnish. "So what color are you going to paint these rooms?" he said finally. "Not white."

"White is for basements," JK murmured.

"Definitely not white," Nick said.

"Maybe a dark red?"

"You're planning on flipping the house, right? Not red."

"I like red," JK protested. "It makes me think of old libraries. Sort of impressive and peaceful at once."

"This is an American bungalow, not a library," Nick replied. "Besides, it's Texas. Red is for bordellos."

"Point taken," JK said.

"What about sage? Neutral, but not dull."

JK frowned. "I'm not actually sure what color sage is."

Nick sighed. "You are woefully unprepared."

"I don't need to know the names of paint colors to pick them out at the store," JK said. "I'm not stupid; don't treat me like I'm dumb—" Irritation jangled through him.

"Just teasing," Nick said. "Sorry." He didn't sound sorry. He sounded... concerned.

"Whatever," JK said.

A shadow moved in his peripheral vision, close to the floor—a dark shovel blade, scraping the carpet deeply enough that the pile bent behind it. JK reached out to touch that mark, the shadow moving slowly, heavily through the room, dragging darkness behind it, and Nick's voice crashed over him like a slap.

"JK! Stop it!"

JK jerked his hand away. The mark disappeared, left his gloved fingers tracing the smooth hardwood. "What?"

Nick studied his gloved hands, and JK twitched them behind his back, breaking Nick's focus. They looked at each other for a long, silent moment, then Nick said, "Are you... picking up memory?"

"No," JK snapped.

"Only, you're pretty much biting my head off for no reason, and you're watching something that isn't there."

JK wanted to argue that Nick was the one being overcritical, but Nick's worried frown made him reassess. Then JK realized his dominant emotions weren't irritation and anger, but hunger.

He wanted to kiss that wrinkled line between Nick's brows, kiss softness into that tightly held mouth.

"Maybe I am," JK said.

"How 'bout we take a sanity break," Nick said. "Let things air out before you get hold of the sander."

JK pushed down a surge of annoyance, the impulse to snap that he didn't need to be managed, didn't need a break. "All right."

Nick got him outside, back to Nick's front porch, with an icy soft drink, cold enough for the temperature to seep through JK's thick suede gloves. It cooled his temper. Not *his* temper.

"Fucking Barton," he muttered. JK would clean out the house. JK would win.

Nick sat down beside him, tapped his water bottle against JK's soda. "I'll drink to that."

JK leaned in and kissed Nick, pulling away only when a shadow fell over them, coughing in a show of feigned politeness. Nick stiffened first, and JK opened his eyes to find Detective Gunnarson standing there at the foot of the stairs.

She said, "Mr. Collier. I have a few follow-up questions."

"Have a seat," Nick said, waving a casual hand toward the steps. JK felt him shiver against his side, though, and leaned closer. Reassurance.

"We'll stand, thank you," she said. Ice queen polite.

"We?" Nick asked.

"We," Gunnarson said, nodding toward JK's house where Detective Conroy spoke with the crime scene techs.

Nick paled, and JK found himself missing some of Barton's easy anger. He felt helpless.

Conroy joined them, gifted JK with a brief smile, and said, "How goes the renovation?"

"Got the carpet up and out," he said.

"Anything I should know about under the carpet?"

"Nope," JK said. "Plain ol' carpet pad."

"Mr. Collier, you left out quite a lot of information when I spoke to you yesterday," Gunnarson said.

Nick leaned into JK, and said, "I can't think of anything relevant."

Conroy rested a hand on the railing and leaned in, her dark eyes crow curious. "Not even the fact that Barton was harassing you?" she said.

JK put his hand on Nick's bruised wrist, a warning to watch his words.

Nick said, "He moved. Or I thought he moved. The problem solved itself."

"You didn't report him?" Gunnarson asked. JK distrusted the mild way she asked Nick that question.

"You know I did. Once. It didn't do any good. Your uniform came out, didn't make things better. I learned my lesson."

"So after that, you just gave up?" she asked.

"I'm a quick learner," Nick said. A flash of temper bloomed like a match in his blue eyes.

"So, when reporting Barton didn't work, you had your martial-arts friend, Zeke Stuart, assault him?"

JK twitched—Nick had done that?—and Conroy, damn her quick eyes, noticed.

Nick explained to JK, ignoring the cops. "Zeke lost his temper, popped Barton one. I didn't ask him to do anything."

No, JK thought. *Nick wouldn't have needed to ask.*

"Do you own a gun?" Conroy asked.

"No," Nick said, his temper still quick. "I'm a California transplant. I believe in gun control. Un-American of me, I know. And downright embarrassing for a Texan."

"Maybe you didn't bother reporting his harassment because you had a plan to get rid of him," Gunnarson said. "No need to report him if you're going to kill him. Less of a paper trail."

"Does he need a lawyer?" JK asked. Less of a real question, more of a forced pause in the conversation.

"We're not at the station. He hasn't been Mirandized. We're just talking," Gunnarson told JK. "You don't need to be here. Your brother wouldn't approve." Her expression suggested she didn't approve either. Though JK got the impression Gunnarson didn't approve of much. Her icy demeanor and white blond hair made JK think of ice-covered mountains.

"Where were you when Barton was killed?" Conroy asked. She tilted her head, her sleek cap of dark hair unmoving, and fixed her dark eyes on Nick's face, ready and willing to catch him in a lie.

Nick licked his lips. "I'm afraid I can't answer that. I don't know when it happened."

"About the same time he 'moved,'" Gunnarson said. "Three months ago. Around the same time you said he got a ride with a friend."

"That's what we all thought," Nick said. "I'm hardly the only one who took it for bible truth."

"Did you start that rumor? Get him out of the way—make sure no one looks for him? You live next door, hard to imagine you saw or heard nothing."

"Nick, seriously. Lawyer up," JK said. "Or tell them to leave."

Nick squeezed his hand. "JK, it's fine. I don't have anything to hide." He looked up at the two women, and said, "Three months ago, my arm was broken. I was on painkillers. I was probably asleep."

"A broken arm wouldn't have stopped you from shooting him," Gunnarson said.

JK sucked in a breath, but at least with Gunnarson's overt accusation, Nick finally shut up.

He said, "You know what? JK's right. We're done talking."

"Actually, we aren't," Conroy said, almost apologetically. "Let's go to the station."

JK said, "Are you charging him with anything?"

"We're just asking questions."

"Then he doesn't have to go," JK said.

"I think I do want a lawyer," Nick said, awkwardly, as if he had never considered needing one.

"Fine," Gunnarson said. "Go ahead and call one. He can meet you at the station."

JK said, "Nick doesn't have to—"

"We could arrest him, hold him for forty-eight hours," Conroy pointed out. "Right now, we're just talking."

Nick pulled his phone out of his pocket, made the call. "Lourdes," he said. "Can you meet me at the police station? Yeah, soon as possible." When he hung up, he said, "Will you let me drive myself?"

"Parking's expensive," Gunnarson said. "Let us save you that cost."

Nick handed JK the keys, flipped through them. He said, "This is my house key. Stay there while I'm gone, hey? Take the rest of the day off."

"Davis won't like that," JK said.

"You know I didn't do this, right?" Nick said, a bare whisper in JK's ear. A kiss of breath on his cheek.

"I know," JK said. Absent-minded agreement. He didn't know. Not really. He couldn't imagine Nick killing anyone, but Gunnarson and Conroy obviously thought it possible. He bit his lip; Hannah and Jesse said that anyone could be driven to murder, if the situation warranted it.

"Stay out of the house," Nick said again. "You shouldn't be in there alone."

"I'll be fine."

Nick looked more worried than ever as Gunnarson urged him toward their car.

Once they'd driven off, JK turned back, looked between the two houses—Nick's, less welcoming without its owner, and the Bartons' house. A tiny worm of doubt crept through his mind; was Nick worried about JK working on the house? Or worried about what he might see?

JK shook the doubt off. It tasted like Barton's loathing and suspicion of Nick, not any doubt of JK's own. He might not have known Nick for long, but he'd touched him. Bare-fingered. Right after the body had been found. If Nick had anything to do with the murder, JK would have seen it.

Probably.

※※

A quick call to Jesse accomplished nothing, first dumping JK into voice mail, then when he called back, to Jesse's impatient platitudes. "If he's innocent, he'll be fine, JK, you know that."

He replied, "Yet you tell *me* never to talk to cops without a lawyer."

"I'm hanging up, JK."

"C'mon, Jesse. You gotta give me something."

"It's not my case."

JK paced tight circles around Nick's living room, layering in a memory no one else would ever sense: fear and concern and a whole lot of freaked-out.

"Fine," Jesse said. "I doubt they'll hold him, or even charge him. The murder was committed with a small caliber weapon, a .22. To kill two attacking dogs and a man without taking injury himself? It took someone good with a gun."

JK said, "And Nick had a compound fracture of his dominant arm—"

"Ah, fuck, what are you even worrying for?" Jesse said.

"Because they were making noise like they thought he had someone do it for him."

When Jesse said, "It'll be fine, JK," it lacked the conviction JK wanted to hear.

After hanging up, JK tried to shake off some of his nervous energy, thought briefly of Nick's method of corralling his own adrenaline rush, and had to sigh. His tight pacing eased, and he started looking at the bookshelves in the living room instead of passing them every fifteen steps.

Maybe built-in bookshelves would be nice in the Barton

house; the building must have had them once. His gaze caught on a gouge that marred the edge of one shelf. Ice ran through his veins: it looked like a bullet scar.

JK slipped off his glove, wanting to know, needing to know how close it had come, how dangerous Barton had been. Wanted reassurance that Nick hadn't been in the room when the bullet entered.

The moment he touched the shelf, he realized his mistake.

The gouge went the wrong way...

Then he fell into memory, unerringly drawn to pain.

The shot, oddly muffled by all the books, by the thick shelves, made his heart lurch, shoving through the house—the sound inside and Nick inside and Barton?

Finding Nick looking up at him, staggering drunk and miserable, his face yellow and black with faded bruising, his arm out of the sling, swollen. The gun dangling from his hand.

"It went off," Nick says.

A spurt of terror through Zeke's spine. Nick was barely conscious. Zeke caught him, his skin fever hot against his callouses.

"Jesus, Nicky, why do you even have that, what were you thinking? Is that my gun? Did you sneak that from my truck? What the fuck are you thinking?"

And the dogs bursting out barking next door and Nick dropping the beer, the last dregs of it surging out and foaming. Dropping the gun... Zeke snatching it up.

The dogs howling and Nick flinching.

Looking beyond Nick, taking in the wreckage of the room.

"What the hell have you been up to?"

Books all over the floor, the bookshelves shoved across the room, blocking the windows. Nick's arm cradled close and the pain on his face.

"Oh you fucking idiot, what the hell did you do? You're gonna make your arm worse."

The dogs barking and snarling, fighting each other, the world.

"I went to get my mail. He sicced the dogs on me, tore my

shirt," *Nick's voice raspy, ruined. "He called them off and laughed...*
I just want him gone. I want him dead!"

Twin jolts of mingled rage and terror—so strong he's tasting
blood.

"You want him dead, Nicky?"

"I want him as afraid as I am." Nick's voice so close to tears.

Dogs howling and barking from the next door, Nick flinching
with every cry, sliding off the chair to the floor. Zeke wrapping him
up, holding him while he shook. Putting him to bed.

Hands moving, quick and tender, brushing the curling hair
out of Nick's eyes, and Nick whispering, "Leave me the gun?" be-
fore passing out.

JK pulled out of the memories, sick at heart, and wondering
if Zeke had done what Nick asked. If he'd left the gun for Nick
to use.

Feeling every bit as invasive and prying as the rookie cop
didn't stop JK from going through Nick's house, room by room,
checking for the gun. He didn't know if he'd feel better or worse
if he found it.

In the end, he came up with nothing at all. Not even answers.

10

JK skipped lunch, steadfastly browsing paint samples on his phone, hiding away in Nick's bright kitchen, and trying not to suspect Nick. When someone knocked on the front door, he jumped in his seat, nearly overturning the chair when his legs tangled in the rungs. He thought, *Nick's back, the police cleared him.*

Relief made his steps quick, his heart light, then he opened the door, and found Zeke scowling at him, Amy a nervy shadow at his side.

Zeke said, "What are you doing here? Where's Nick? Amy said the cops were here, saw their car outside. He's not answering his phone..."

"They took him to the station," JK said.

"Did he call Lourdes?"

"He called his lawyer—"

Zeke's scowl eased a bit. "Well, thank God for that. Lourdes is a shark. She'll get him out. Did they arrest him?" he asked.

"Not that I saw," JK said.

"What, with your freaky psychic powers?"

"Wait... what?" Amy said.

"With my eyes," JK snapped.

Zeke made a sound more like a growl than speech. He said, "Don't you dare get pissy with me. This whole fucking mess is your fault."

"I didn't kill Barton."

"No, you just kicked over the hornet's nest. Why the hell couldn't you leave it alone?"

"It was making me crazy."

"From what I can tell you *started* at crazy," Zeke said. "You should have taken it as a sign, and quit. The neighborhood would have been better for it."

"You don't even live in it!" JK said.

"Like you do? At best, you're a squatter, living on your boss's leavings. Is that any job for a grown man? And now, you're doing what, living with Nick? What do you want with him?"

"You need a diagram?" JK said.

"Zeke," Amy said. Her face screwed up tight. Distressed. "Zeke, stop it. You said we were just checking on Nick."

Zeke ignored her completely. "Moving pretty damn fast. Maybe that's your speed, but Nick's a slower sort."

"How the hell would you know? Nick *gave* me the keys. He *told* me to stay." JK's temper spun between hurt and anger. Zeke was Nick's best and oldest friend... who had already punched him in the face. JK outmassed Zeke, and had reach on him; Zeke had his black belt skills and attitude, liked to hit and hit hard. A fight between them would end ugly. Better to just avoid the whole mess.

JK took a cautionary step back.

Zeke closed the gap and Amy said, "Zeke!" again.

JK said, "What's your problem, Zeke? Because you obviously have one. I'm into him, he likes me. I had nothing to do with the cops taking him for questioning."

Zeke pinched his mouth tight, then said, "If this goes bad? It's not like breaking up with someone you'll never see again. You're his neighbor for as long as it takes for you to sell this house. Nick's had enough bad luck with neighbors—"

"I'm not Barton."

"You could be worse. Using your... thing to get inside his head, seeing all his secrets. Using them to get to him."

"Screw you. I wouldn't do that," JK said.

"Wouldn't you?" Zeke simmered with tension.

"I like Nick. He likes me. That's all it is."

"Nick thinks with his heart, always has."

"Better than thinking with his fists," JK said. His own hands curled within his gloves, picking up on Zeke's rage and the protectiveness that fed it. If Nick had gone through hell, Zeke had been at his side.

Zeke said, "You got him arrested, smart ass! You and your insistence on digging Barton up!"

JK's senses were in overdrive; this much stress, and his pills had to work extra hard to keep the atmosphere from pouring over him. He stepped away from Zeke, took a deep breath, let it out, tried for another. JK had to calm down. Before he lost control.

"Don't walk away from me," Zeke growled. He seized JK's bare arm, pulled him back. "You're not good for Nick. You're not good for this neighborhood..."

Amy shouted, "Zeke, what are you..."

JK couldn't hear the rest of her protest, drowned beneath his own bellow. "Stop *touching* me!" he shouted.

Zeke's eyes flared wide with shock and horror as he realized what he was doing. He jerked away as if JK were radioactive, but it was too late. The vision slammed down hard and fast.

JK staggered and fell, barely aware of Zeke pushing past him. Fleeing. Didn't matter. JK was living Zeke's memory.

Stepping out of Nick's house at dawn, the morning sunlight casting strange shadows over Nick's driveway... Frowning, staring, and all the previous night's distress roaring back. Nick's tires slashed, not just a single slice or puncture, but turned to ribbons.

A spurt of pure terror. The car so close to the house and Barton creeping up, so furious, getting crazier and crazier by the day. The time it had to have taken to ruin the tires. The sustained hatred... the danger growing.

His hand in his pocket, pure instinct, pulling the gun free. Not leaving it with Nick, no way, no how, he'd shoot himself, drunk or despairing—bile in the back of his throat, the thought that Nick—his friend, his brother, his family—could...

I want him as afraid as I am. I just want him gone. I want him dead!

The gun nestled in his palm like the solution to the problem. No one would miss the bastard. Not even his wife.

Nick's front door gaped, then slammed shut so hard it had bounced off the latch. The echo lingered in JK's mind, the slamming door, Zeke's brusque apologies as he fled, Amy swept along with him. He rolled himself to his feet, shut the door, and—thinking about Zeke and guns and rage—threw all the bolts.

JK let himself out onto Nick's back deck, shaking, grateful for the afternoon heat. He welcomed the sun, a bright contrast to his dark thoughts. Zeke's determination still made his hands shake with the desire to hurt, to kill, but the rest of him churned with despair. Nick's best friend, a murderer?

It felt like betraying Nick to even consider calling the cops, but a man was dead...

A man who deserved worse.

Killed and buried alive in his own backyard, no one to miss him.

He'd harassed Nick to the point of madness and for what? To soothe his own bitter dissatisfaction, his life so unfair, so full of unfairness.

JK clutched his head. It felt like Zeke and Barton were arguing it out in front of him. No. Arguing inside of him. At war with himself and the memories of others that lived like parasites within him.

He wasn't Zeke, certain that Barton deserved to die.

He wasn't Barton, striking out at a target who deserved everything he could dish out.

He was JK Lassiter, renovator. JK Lassiter, brother to a cop. JK Lassiter, who believed in right and wrong.

His breathing steadied. The invasive memories slowly subsided.

The deck creaked beneath JK as he paced, trying to outrun the basic problem while going nowhere. Nick was in police custody for something he hadn't done. Zeke had taken the gun with him, after all. And Zeke had tried to stop JK from digging. Nick had handed him the shovel.

JK didn't think about it, couldn't think about it and do it; he just did it. Went back through Nick's house, back into the bedroom, found Conroy's card, bent in half, dumped in the wastebasket, and dialed her.

"Conroy," she said, a little muffled.

He hadn't expected her to answer, somehow. Maybe because he'd been imagining them sweating Nick in some locked room. Instead, she sounded like he'd caught her eating a late lunch, the squeak of forks on Styrofoam, the hasty sipping of a drink to clear her throat.

"Who is this?" Conroy said.

"Zeke Stuart has a .22," JK said, ripping the Band-Aid off.

"JK?" He had her attention now, sharp and fierce even through the phone.

"Yeah," he admitted. "I just thought you should know. Though you've probably checked gun records already, I guess."

"Don't hang up," Conroy said. "How often is Zeke in the neighborhood? Often enough to go unremarked?"

The phone felt slippery in his grip, like the nervous sweat on his palms had seeped through the suede. "He's dating Amy Sheridan. He and Nick go back a long way. The colonel knows him by name."

"So that would be a 'yes,'" she said. "And he's violent. He assaulted Barton, a man twenty years his senior."

"Zeke's protective of Nick," JK said. It made him feel disloyal even to admit that much.

"And you saw his gun?"

"… I know he has one." God, JK hoped Nick hadn't taken the gun back. "He keeps it in his truck's glove compartment."

Conroy paused. "I see. Anything else you can tell me? You said he's protective of Nick. Would you say he'd kill for him?" Her gentle tone made his nerves prickle with awareness of all the issues they were skirting. JK's psychic abilities. The fact that he was accusing Zeke of murder—

JK's stomach roiled. "I can't, I need to go."

"Wait!" she said. "Thank you for calling. I'll look into it.

And JK? You can call me any time, all right? About anything. Not just Barton, if you understand me. I'm always glad to hear what you have to say."

"Your cousin thought I was crazy. A liar." He swallowed hard; weird to be talking about it, especially to someone he didn't trust or even particularly like.

Conroy sighed. "Ben likes his world black and white. Me, I know there are a lot of different ways to look at things. Call me. But let's keep it between you and me. Don't tell Jesse."

JK disconnected. He felt like a playground snitch, tattling on another kid. But the sickening swoop in his belly reminded him this was far more serious than who let the class hamster escape... this was murder.

Another sickening swoop of realization. Texas had the death penalty.

JK hung his head between his knees. He hadn't given anything to Conroy that she wouldn't have figured on her own. He just... accelerated the process.

The self-justification sat sourly in his brain. He couldn't dress it up like that: Zeke Stuart had scared him enough to make JK think him capable of murder. Barton should have been in jail for what he did to Nick. Not dead.

❁

Trying to escape the guilt he felt, JK fled the neighborhood in favor of the Builders Surplus. He needed tiles for the kitchen floor, needed to focus on something other than Barton, other than the tangle he'd created for himself the minute he called Conroy. He couldn't even run to Hannah, spill his guts to her— she'd freak out about Conroy not only believing in JK's ability, but attempting to recruit him.

It had been recruitment, hadn't it?

Thankfully, buying tile ended up being far more complex than he had expected and took his mind off murder. Color and thickness and hardiness and shape and deciding to lay in a pattern or not, and grout had colors all of its own to worry about... JK charged it all to Davis's account, and headed home.

Ashford greeted him as he loaded the first boxes of tile onto the small dolly.

"Has Collier been arrested?" No small talk, not even a hello. Just the sharp question. His voice carried in the slow, hot afternoon air, and the crime scene techs, packing up, stopped to watch.

"No!" JK snapped. "Just talking to the cops. He'll be back, any minute."

Ashford asked, "Did he call his lawyer? Collier can be too trusting..."

JK winced. "He called her."

"You need some help with those boxes?"

"I got it. Thanks."

"None of my business, I know, but... are you sure you should be working by yourself? You had some sort of seizure. Collier called the EMTs—"

"I'm fine," JK said. Heat flooded his face; heat he couldn't blame on lifting heavy boxes of tile under the full sun. Of course, Ashford had witnessed JK's episode. The old man saw everything.

"Are you epileptic?"

"No," JK said, shortly.

Ashford eyed him in silence. The crime scene techs backed their van out and drove away. JK envied them.

"Is it drugs? Did you OD?" Ashford's mouth twisted in disapproval.

"Jesus Christ, no," JK snapped. "I'm not a drug addict. I'm not an epileptic. I'm not sick. And I don't owe you an explanation."

Unexpectedly, Ashford grinned at him. He said, "Got some spine to you. All right. I'll mind my own business. Keeping in mind that this neighborhood is my business. Don't give me reasons to ask questions and I won't. Fair enough?"

"Deal," JK said.

Ashford said, "Shake on it?"

JK eyed him warily, but stuck out a gloved hand. Ashford shook JK's hand with a grip that, even through the gloves, felt like a tangle of high-tension wires.

"Let me know if Collier needs help," Ashford said. "I can be a character witness for him if he needs it."

Ashford retreated to his porch, picked up his ever-present book, and settled down to "read", his gaze already tracking toward the end of the road where Olivia and another girl were jogging toward the campus.

JK sighed. The man probably wasn't even admiring the view. Just playing shepherd.

He got the tile into the Bartons' house, piled neatly just outside the kitchen, and got a ping on his phone of an incoming text. He lunged for it, hoping it was Nick.

The message came from Davis—a terse, but approving, "Good choice on tiles," in response to the picture he'd sent.

JK should have felt a spurt of relief that he'd chosen well; instead, all he felt was watched. It made him... edgy. Defensive. Not a good way to start out feeling in the Bartons' house where that touchiness moved so easily toward rage.

He dragged out the new stove, the new fridge, and started scrubbing the underflooring as clean and even as he could get it. Scraping out old memory. He was removing the last little bits of grit when he realized he had an audience.

JK jerked to his feet, heart in his throat; Amy jumped in helpless twitch-response.

"Sorry, sorry," she gasped. "I didn't mean to scare you."

"Ditto," he breathed. He slapped dust off his gloves, and said, "What's up, Amy?"

JK expected her to apologize for Zeke; she seemed like the type who wanted people to get along, the kind who went around trying to smooth ruffled feathers. He didn't expect her to wring her hands briefly and say, "You're psychic?"

JK felt every muscle in his body freeze.

"Zeke said you were..."

"Zeke doesn't believe in psychics," JK reminded her. She didn't bite.

"I heard him, JK. He believed. He's scared to death of you. Of what you might see."

"Okay," he said.

"Is it true?" Her eyes were hot, red-edged. "Tell me it's true. I know psychics exist. Marietta's real. So you might be, too."

"Marietta?"

"My psychic advisor," Amy said. She sidled into the room, assessed the floor, and boosted herself onto his countertop. "She keeps me in contact with my parents."

"Okay," he said again. JK desperately wanted Nick back, and not just for Nick's own sake. He felt like he had stepped into a minefield.

"Do you believe in curses?" Amy asked.

"What? No," JK said. "Like *real* curses? Black magic? No." Even when he muttered about his abilities being a curse, he never really meant it. Not the way it sounded like she meant.

"My parents were criminal attorneys," Amy said. "They made lots of enemies. Marietta said they were killed."

"I thought..." JK couldn't remember who had said it, probably Ashford, but hadn't her parents died in a car crash? "It was an accident."

"Or supposed to look like one. Marietta—"

"What does Marietta say?" He toed the trash bag gently, when he wanted to kick it. Ben Wilson had been a skeptic, and why not. There were a whole lot of fakes out there.

Amy read his tone and got defensive. "She's a real psychic! I thought you'd understand. I mean, she knows so much. She knows what CD they were listening to, what paperwork my mother was working on in the passenger seat. Even what they were wearing, that my dad had put his wedding ring in the cup holder... Mom always made him take it off when he drove because he tapped it against the wheel and drove her nuts..."

JK closed his eyes. "Amy," he said. "All of that would be in the police report."

Amy swallowed. "But she hasn't read the police report. I haven't even seen it."

"People can get hold of them more easily than they should," JK said.

"She says the curse is on *me*, now. That everyone around me will suffer. And Barton's dead."

"How does she do it?" JK asked.

She replied, "Lift the curse? I don't know. She doesn't even know if she can, but she's willing to try."

JK bet Marietta would charge for the attempt, too. "I meant the psychic part," JK said. "Does she read your cards, your palm, your aura?"

"She touches people and just knows..."

"Guess she's got a lot of gloves, too," JK said.

"No, why would she..." Amy's gaze dropped to his gloved hands, the gloves he never took off. Her chin came up. "She talks to the spirits, too."

JK got a bottle of water out of the fridge, got one for her, too, and passed it over.

"You think she's a fake," Amy whispered.

"What does she charge?"

"Not as much as I would pay."

"She's trying to take money from you to solve a problem that you didn't know existed until she told you it did?" JK tried not to sound judgmental. He was pretty sure he failed.

Her response came fast, frantic. "My parents died. They shouldn't have died. There was no reason! If someone killed them, or cursed them..."

"You'd have someone to blame." JK got that. He'd spent enough time trying to remember whose idea it had been to go out on the ice that day. He never could bring that memory back, and in the end, he was glad not to have someone to blame—someone to hate.

Amy cracked the bottle open, took a sip. She picked at the label.

"I've seen a lot of crap," JK said abruptly. "Touching people. But they're only memories. Bits and pieces left behind. No spirits. No curses."

"But you might be wrong." She didn't look at him, but she wasn't crying anymore, and she wasn't asking him to use his abilities.

"Nothing's completely certain," he said.

Amy set down her bottle, and slid off the counter. She reached the door, then turned back. "Would you go with me on my next appointment? To see Marietta? See for yourself."

JK looked at her, at the quiet desperation in her eyes—grief kept raw, and fear for the future—and couldn't say no.

He had finished tiling the first third of the kitchen floor, and was trying not to notice how the light through the window dimmed, how the shadows lengthened across his chalk grid. Nick had been at the station for hours now. The better part of a workday. JK began to wonder if Nick had actually been arrested and charged. He harbored no illusion that he would be Nick's one phone call, and Zeke wouldn't be in any hurry to share his troubles.

Maybe Nick had gotten the gun back from Zeke after all. Maybe he'd used it. Or maybe, he just wouldn't cooperate with the police, knew that Zeke had done it, and was trying to cover for him. A lot of other things were unclear in JK's borrowed memories, but not the way Zeke and Nick defended each other. JK wondered what had made them so close; Jesse and his partner Torelli had that kind of bond and they worked in the line of fire together.

JK gnawed at his lip, thought about calling Jesse for at least the sixth time in as many hours. He pushed it off again.

The doorbell rang, and JK dropped a tile, chipping the corner. "It's open," he called, his voice scratchy with nervousness.

The front door opened, footsteps on the bare floor and JK's heart leaped. He knew those steps. He headed out toward the living room. "Nick! You're out!" JK said. He felt like a weight had come off his shoulders. If the police had released him, then obviously they were convinced that Nick was blameless. JK sighed. He'd let himself get worked up over nothing. Saying you wanted someone dead didn't mean you went out and killed them.

"Thank God, I was worried." He scanned Nick head to toe, checking him over.

"Me, too," Nick said, with a pained grimace. He ran a hand through his hair, as if he could shake out police-station dust. "Hey, I thought you were going to stay out of here."

"Can't hide from the house forever," JK said. "Got too much to do. What did the Ice Queen and Curious Conroy have to say?" If his voice faltered on the last, he hoped Nick took it for dust-roughened vocal cords. Not resurfacing guilt.

"They got a new lead, apparently. Conroy got all hot about it. Lourdes said it wouldn't have mattered, that they've got nothing against me but my bad feelings for Barton and that I didn't hear the shots fired. I tell you, though, I wasn't feeling so sure. Gunnarson is terrifying." He made a face, and JK gave in to his urge to hug him.

Nick leaned in against him, breath a little uneven against his throat. He pushed off of JK's chest, and said, "Come on. I'm making dinner for us. Get-out-of-jail-free lasagna."

JK hesitated, and Nick said, "No? You hate lasagna? You're... tired of my company?"

"No," JK said. "Lasagna's great. You're great." He shook his head. He should tell Nick what he'd done, warn him that things weren't over, but couldn't get the words out.

"All right then," Nick said. "Come on. You can change your gloves and help me cook."

❀

Nick's kitchen was a welcoming space. Calming. Though neither of them, JK thought, were particularly calm. Nick moved about his familiar environment touching everything, reconnecting with it, fidgeting. Nervy. A near agoraphobe dragged from his comfort zone, and for such a hostile reason. His preparations betrayed a hectic edge, a pot banged down a little too roughly, a cutting board that slid across the counter when he let it go.

Maybe scared at how close he came to being arrested. How close he'd come to being caught...

JK bent his head, and grated crumbly mozzarella like his life depended on it. Nick didn't have it in him to kill someone. JK clutched that thought close, shored it up with memories stolen from other people. If Zeke had done it... Nick wasn't to blame.

"You're quiet," Nick said, after he'd started layering the pasta.

"Been a long day," JK said. It seemed eternal, his times spent worrying about Nick, confronting Zeke, ratting Zeke out, talking to Ashford about his "condition", dealing with the weight of Amy's troubles.

"Tell me about it," Nick said. He rolled his shoulders. "I feel like shit. I was happy Barton was dead and those two women wouldn't let me forget it. Guess they wanted to make me feel guilty. It worked." He laid the last layer of pasta down, spread the cheese across the top. "I don't want to be that guy. You know. The one who delights in other people suffering."

"You've got a long way to go before you fit that type," JK said.

Nick flashed a sudden bright grin. "Ask my students around finals week and they'd give you a different answer."

JK had to smile back, but couldn't hold it. Nick wiped his hands off on a towel, chucked it toward the washing machine, and said, "Are you all right? You just seem—"

"Zeke came by," JK said. "We kinda got into it again. Plus, he told Amy that I'm a psychic." A spurt of resentment. He really wished that Nick had kept his mouth shut, never let Zeke in on JK's abilities.

"Aw, fuck," Nick said. "He really is a great guy."

"How'd you meet him anyway?"

"College," Nick said, shrugging.

"Oh, there's more to it than that, I bet," JK said.

"There is," Nick said, "but it's not my story to tell."

"You told him I was a psychic," JK pointed out, a little bitterly.

Nick paused, turned that over, and said, "Sorry. Look, I helped him out during a bad time; he helped me out in return. We got into the habit. He's a good man who lacks coping mechanisms. He gets stuck in that stupid macho posturing he gets into."

"Is it only posturing?" JK asked.

Nick stilled, hand resting on the oven timer. "What do you mean?"

"He hated Barton. He had a gun."

Nick sucked in a tight breath, an audible rasp of air in his throat, as he put two and two together as neatly as he had his lasagna layers. His jaw went white.

He said, "You called the cops on Zeke? *That's* their new lead?"

JK said, "Earlier you wanted me to help."

"Yeah, I thought you might be able to name Barton's killer, not put Zeke in the frame. He's not a killer! He doesn't even have a gun. I have his gun."

"You told the police you didn't have one," JK said.

"Well, it's not mine, technically. But I do have it."

"Show me."

Nick stalked into the living room, JK on his heels, and yanked open the bottom drawer of the entertainment center. He rummaged around in a pile of electrical cords and old DVDs with increasing urgency. He slammed the drawer shut finally, and went back to the kitchen.

"I must have mislaid it, somewhere," he said, after a moment.

"It's gone, Nick. He took it back. You were drunk and scared and hurt, and he wanted the man dead—"

Nick jabbed at the buttons carelessly, racking up minutes, his head ducked. Then he turned and said, "What are you talking about, JK?"

"I told you. You asked Zeke to kill him. Zeke wanted Barton dead. And hey, look at that, Barton's dead."

"It wasn't Zeke," Nick said. "You don't know him. And you had no right to look through my things. To look through my memories... you took your gloves off? Touched my things?"

"There's a bullet scar on your bookshelf. Once I saw that... I had to touch it. That's how I found out Zeke has a gun," JK said. "I'm not saying he's a bad guy, Nick. Just... he's got a temper, and he hated Barton, and he's your best friend, and he had a gun."

"You think he's a murderer, you called the cops, but you don't want me to think you don't like Zeke? Is that really what you're telling me? Jesus Christ, JK, you don't even know him—"

"I know he doesn't like me, and he hurts people he doesn't like. I saw his memories, Nick. I saw—"

"*What*, exactly. What did you see? Do you even really know? You saw a single moment out of time. And you extrapolated an entire murder from it." Nick shoved the lasagna pan into the oven, let the door close with a bang. He said, "Well, guess what. You were wrong. The night you're talking about wasn't the same night Barton disappeared. He went over, called Barton out, and punched him in the teeth. The cops were called. You just saw a random terrible night, not *the* terrible night."

"It didn't have to be the same night. I felt what he felt. His hatred—" JK shuddered. Felt it scouring his veins again, bitter gall behind his teeth, metal beneath his tongue, the spasm of rage in his hands.

Nick took a deep breath, his blue eyes stormy. "And if I had your power, if I touched you, can you honestly tell me I'd never find a moment where you hated someone to the point of wishing them dead?

"You're scared of Zeke. You don't like him. Fair enough. He hasn't put his best foot forward with you, that's for damn sure. But own up to your own intentions, JK. He punched you and that's why you suspect him."

JK's breath went out of him as if Nick had hit him. "You really think that I'd do that?" His face burned hot; his eyes stung.

"I don't know, JK. I can't just magically see your weak spots, the way you can see mine," Nick said. Bitterness edged his voice, and ugly humiliation. "But I can jump to conclusions of my own."

"Fine," JK said. It wasn't fine, nothing was fine, but "fine" could get him the hell out of there. "Fine. You made your point. I overstepped. You wanted me to use my abilities as long as it didn't implicate your asshole friend. You want me to keep my gloves on in your house, but read every single thing at the Bartons'. Good to know the rules."

He fled the kitchen, the bright brassy light that felt like he'd been stripped bare beneath judging eyes.

JK grabbed his bag from Nick's bedroom; he'd repacked his things this morning, trying to be tidy while in Nick's space, but now, as he snatched the bag up, he wondered if he'd seen this moment coming.

"Where are you going?" Nick said, framed by the opened door.

"Where do you think?" he replied.

"The Bartons' house isn't safe—"

"You know what?" JK said. "Right now, it's better than here."

He headed for the door; Nick bobbled in his path, then stepped aside. JK refused to look back as he closed Nick's front door behind him, refused to listen. He didn't want to hear the locks all snapping shut like the final words in the argument.

Stepping into the Bartons' house, riled up and edgy, was probably one of his least favorite moments in recent history and that was saying something. The house hit JK like the car-crash body slam of the first day again.

Misery.

Rage.

Frustration.

Along with the dogs lunging and surging through the shadows.

"You're all dead. Go the hell away," JK snapped at them. He took refuge in the kitchen, where his work had lessened the memories soaking into the walls. He leaned against the counter and looked out through the window at Nick's house. If only he could go back in time thirty minutes and start that whole conversation over.

He still didn't know if he'd done something unforgivable or if he'd done what needed to be done. Forget going back thirty minutes; maybe he could go back far enough to undo Nick finding out about his abilities, then Nick couldn't ask him to use them, and be angry when he did.

Of course, if JK was undoing pieces of his life, why not start at the fucked-up foundation? Why not wish he had never had anything in his life change from the ordinary? Maybe then, he'd know how to navigate relationships. He'd have the tools he needed.

But people couldn't be remodeled. Couldn't be torn down and rebuilt to a new template. JK had his cross to bear—not only his ungovernable ability, but what it had shown him time and time again: that love was conditional. People reached out to each other... and found that doing so hurt.

His parents, locking him away until he wanted to die for the loneliness of it, drugging him until he didn't know if it were day or night, all in the name of love. Jesse, who had come to save JK, but nearly drowned him beneath the weight of things Jesse had seen—the husbands who killed their wives, the mothers who killed their children, the kids who killed their friends. Murder on murder, violence and more violence, where there should have been love.

And he couldn't escape it. Everywhere JK looked, people hurt each other.

A woman's memory shrieked in the house, from the midst of snarling dogs, and JK's hands clenched until they ached.

He'd had enough.

JK took his evening pill, dry-swallowed, on his way to the garage. He mixed up more cement, ignored his stomach complaining, and went back to tiling. The work soothed him; the precision needed kept his focus on nothing more complex than lines and squares. The corrugated slide and scrape of the trowel through the thin set soothed his nerves as neatly as raking a Zen garden. He had the kitchen floor laid by midnight, and stifled his hunger with a few granola bars. The grouting could go in tomorrow. JK figured he'd have plenty of time on his own now.

The thought twinged, equal parts hurt and anger. He couldn't help but chalk it up to another loss, another chance that his damned abilities had cost him. Another failure of normal. Nick's distrust had just taken longer than usual to surface.

JK's bed smelled cold, like clay—the scent of all that churned earth outside seeping upward, the lingering spatters of thin set on his clothes—but he fell into it gratefully enough, not tired so much as just ready for the day to be over. He lay twitching in his sheets, hands scrabbling at the cotton through his gloves, listening to the sounds the house made, dog collars jingling, growling, the scrabble of dogs racing up the stairs, the arguments permeating the walls, one voice shrill, one gruff, the pop of gunshots, the scrape of a shovel dragging through the house...

He rolled over, pressed a pillow to his head, and tried to focus on the other sounds. The regular sort of sounds—creaking and settling of old joists, the whisper of the oak leaves outside, the distant barking of a dog. The growling echoes inside the house continued.

His hands fisted, but JK couldn't fight his own senses.

The night passed, but it did so slowly, and dawn found him bleary and sluggish, spilling his coffee over his chin and gloved hands when he tried to take the first scalding sip.

He couldn't keep himself from glancing through the kitchen window to Nick's house. But the siding gave him nothing back—no glimpses at Nick, no suggestions that Nick had suffered a sleepless night also.

JK put his mug in the bathroom sink, took his pills, made himself a peanut butter sandwich and called breakfast done. He couldn't do too much more with the kitchen right now; the tiles needed to set more before he grouted them. But he could sand down the hardwood floors.

Using the sander calmed him; it wasn't the kind of tool you could use angry, no matter what Nick feared. It required set up—hanging plastic sheeting so the sanding dust didn't take over the house. It required prepping the floor, pounding in or removing any jutting nails. Running the sander required a steady touch, a meditative smoothness to the diagonals he drew.

He had just managed one full pass of the living room when the dust in the room eddied about him, and sunlight spilled across the floor. JK turned, shut off the machine, and pushed his goggles off his face.

Amy stood hesitantly in the open doorway. "I knocked this time, but..."

"Okay," JK said. He wasn't sure what else to say.

"So..." She shifted from foot to foot. "You said you'd go with me. To see Marietta," she added, like he might have forgotten overnight.

"Now?" he asked. It wasn't a nice response. But he'd been hoping Amy would change her mind.

She squirmed; he saw politeness warring on her face with urgency.

"Give me twenty to shower and change," he said.

Her shoulders slumped with relief. "JK. Thank you."

He nodded. "You can stick around and wait, just don't walk in the kitchen. Tile's setting."

❊

When he came back downstairs, he found Amy pretty much exactly where he'd left her, hands held tight behind her back like a nervous child told not to touch.

JK had a weird butterfly sensation in his own belly and chest. What if Marietta *was* the real thing? What if she could tell him how to cope? What if he *wasn't* alone in this world with this ability?

Hope and skepticism burned evenly in his chest. They stepped outside, and he looked at Amy's little Matchbox Car, and grimaced. "How about we take my truck?"

She eyed his long legs, and nodded, a smile flickering over her lips. It couldn't stick though; she was too keyed up for that.

Amy directed him out of the neighborhood and onto the interstate; JK merged his truck, engine whining, into traffic and nearly got sideswiped by a blaze yellow DART bus changing lanes on a dime.

They passed monster apartment complexes, brutally modernist concrete architecture along the Telecom Corridor, a flash of green—a glimpse of a park in a city slowly being swallowed by concrete.

Amy fiddled with his radio, shifting between NPR and the college station. Most of the time, JK liked Texas, was grateful as fuck to be here, and not still trapped at home. But he missed winter, which disguised gloves so easily, and he missed the smaller, older landscape of his Maine hometown.

The megalopolis of Dallas-Fort Worth, and the small cities it had engulfed, could be used as a lesson in overwriting history.

As they passed building after building, concrete and glass, and one that looked iridescently scaled in the morning sunlight, it seemed harder and harder to believe that any psychic could exist here.

"Take the frontage road," Amy directed.

He peeled off and found himself driving past a series of nearly identical strip malls—coffee shops, little BBQ restaurants, cheap clothing stores, cell phone stores, and college-related bookstores.

JK pulled into a lot that looked the same as the others—sparsely inhabited at this midmorning hour. Too late for the coffee shops to be picking up commuter business, too early for the restaurants to get the lunch rush.

He parked too soon, which left them five or six shops down from where they needed to be, but Amy's impatience echoed his. She dropped out of the truck, and he joined her. Amy waited for him, and after a wary look, took his arm. JK wasn't sure if she wanted the support, or if she thought he might back out. He couldn't. The need to know burned in him.

He knew Marietta had to be a con artist, but there might be a chance she was for real, wasn't there? His skills existed. There might be others like him. A tiny smidgeon of hope roused in his chest that Marietta would be able to offer him more advice than Jesse's *try not to touch anything.*

Amy leaned up against him. "Thank you," she said. "You'll see. I think you'll see."

So friendly. Trusting. A renewed surge of guilt touched him. How long before Nick told Zeke that JK had ratted him out to Conroy? How long before Zeke told Amy? Nick had already shut him out. The neighborhood would be fast enough to follow suit.

For the first time, his summer-long remodel plan seemed like a terribly long time. His steps dragged.

"C'mon," Amy urged. "She doesn't see people if they come late."

JK's hopes veered back toward skepticism, added a tinge of dislike. He imagined Marietta as a petty tyrant, establishing dominance. Making it so Amy leaped to do as Marietta said. He didn't need Hannah's psychiatry classes to understand that much. Get people used to jumping, keep them off their feet, and you could own them.

The shop was more tasteful than he'd expected—no neon *"Readings"* in the window, no New Age-style stagecraft of dangling crystals or staring mystic eyes. Instead, the entry of the shop looked more like a doctor's waiting room. It contained a few comfortable end chairs and a nice side-table. The side-table held an artful spread of magazines—*TIME, Vanity Fair, Vogue, Parents, Money,* and *Sports Illustrated*—an entire gamut just waiting to reveal something about the person who picked one up. There were some carefully angled mirrors that JK thought might conceal cameras.

His hopes, faltering, took a nose dive. Would a real psychic need all this stuff? The inner door opened, and a woman came out, tear-stained, clutching tissues.

Amy and the woman did a strange little dance, stepping out of each others' way while trying not to look at each other... a weird clutching at privacy. JK found himself dropping his gaze, studying the woman's sneakers as she left the office, old white leather, scuffed and well-worn. Comfort shoes.

JK's mouth tightened; given her tears, he doubted that she found comfort here.

He missed Marietta's entrance, only felt Amy's fingers tighten on his forearm, but raised his head just as she said, "I see you have finally brought Zeke. He may stay, but only if he listens."

Her mistake burst like a shock wave in the room. JK felt it travel through them. Amy's hand on his arm trembled.

Absolutely not a psychic, JK thought. His crushed hope ached, no matter how small that hope had been. "I'm not Zeke," he got out.

"He's a friend," Amy said.

Marietta looked less like a con artist than he'd expected. She dressed well but without overt luxury. No fancy jewelry, no fancy clothes; a dark green blouse over a pair of grey slacks. Her eyes were sharp; her lipstick glossy. She raised a perfect brow, and said, "A friend? He wants more than that from you."

Trying to cover her misstep, JK thought. Trying to explain without explaining, and more, trying to sow doubt in Amy, to make her distrust her *friend* and his motives.

Another failure. Amy knew where JK's romantic interests lay. Her breath let out in a gasp, too quiet for Marietta to notice.

"Come in," Marietta said. "But be aware, skeptics make poor listeners."

"Only when we're listening to lies," JK said. "If you're not a liar, I'm willing to listen."

Marietta's eyes flickered up to his. Contemptuous. Confident of her abilities. He swallowed nervousness. He hadn't thought this through—too much hoping that she would be the real deal, even though he had known better.

"JK," Amy said. "Please."

The inner room smelled good, like vanilla and fresh coffee and apples, and JK felt his tension ease almost against his will. Fake psychic, con artist or whatever, she knew how to set a mood. This felt more like Hannah's office, a comfortable space to release secrets and burdens; JK knew how many designers Hannah had consulted to get that effect.

Bookshelves, comfortable chairs arranged to let people chat. A couple of small end tables. A vase or two of flowers—artificial, no scent.

Amy tucked herself into a small loveseat, Marietta settled gracefully into the wing chair nearest her and extended her hand over the end table. Amy took it. JK stood, awkward and lanky in the room.

"Please sit," Marietta said, barely looking away from Amy.

"I'm good," JK said. Choosing any of the other chairs wouldn't let him keep an eye on Marietta and her grip on Amy's wrist.

Marietta shrugged. "If he upsets the spirits, Amy, we may not find out what we most need to. Who cursed you..."

"Cursed Amy?" JK said. "I thought her parents were cursed. Not her."

Marietta didn't even look his way. "There are bad things still happening around you, aren't there? You're at the center of it. Your parents, and now Barton..." She licked her lips, a flash of a gesture, there and gone, but JK saw it, recognized the savor in it.

His rare temper surged. He couldn't watch this. Couldn't wait. He ripped off his glove, tossed it into Amy's lap, and took Marietta's wrist before she could do more than shriek in surprise.

"Let go of me! I'll call for help—" Her words faded out; her memories poured through his skin, burned into his blood, pounded their way into his brain in hateful surges. His vision greyed. Vaguely, he heard Amy jumping to her feet, spilling things to the floor.

JK said, "Your name isn't Marietta Contreras. It's Eleanor Marie Guthrie, and you're wanted for securities fraud in Florida. You skated out on four warrants with your clients' money, and you washed up here. Renamed yourself. Gave yourself an offshore account—" and then the numbers tumbled off his lips.

Marietta—or was it Eleanor?—grabbed the artificial flowers and hurled them at him. He let the vase bounce off his shoulder, a shower of dust and plastic. JK continued, "And your password's the name and birth date of your first husband. The one your sister stole."

Marietta shoved him. She was a small woman, and he was a big guy; she did nothing more than make him rock in place. The touch swamped JK with remembered misery—*crying, clutching her wedding ring, the note. Bobbi took everything! She always did!*—but years of smug satisfaction at her thievery and scams overrode that sympathy. JK had a strange dizzying moment where Marietta gloated over what an easy mark her earlier self would have been, and ended up guttering out in self-disgust.

"What the hell are you?" she asked.

"I'm the real thing," JK said, exhausted. He reached for his dropped glove, staggered, and decided it could stay on the floor, just a little longer. "And if you don't want me to share everything I've learned with the police, you'll give Amy's money back."

Amy bit her lip, then picked up his glove, and passed it to him.

Misery, shame, loss.

Marietta glowered at him. She said, "It's your word against mine."

"My brother's a cop," JK said. "Whose word do you think will count?"

Her mouth twisted. "Will you take a check?" Marietta asked him.

"What do you think?"

"I don't keep cash—"

"The safe is in the cabinet above the microwave. I already know the combination. I just wanted to give you the opportunity to play nice."

"Fuck you," Marietta spat, but headed toward the safe.

JK hadn't felt like a bully until he glanced over and saw Amy's face. Tears slicked her cheeks, misery showing in every slumped line of her body. JK's heart sank. He had done it wrong. Somehow, he'd done it all wrong. He'd wanted to free Amy from Marietta, not hurt her further. But his own disappointment had made him harsh, even brutal in ripping the veils off.

Marietta came back a minute later with a handful of cash. "Take it. Seven thousand dollars."

Amy clutched the money to her chest. "You weren't really talking to them?"

"Get out. And don't even think about coming back," Marietta said.

This time they went, and Amy got to the curb before she spoke again. "She was lying to me. All this time. And I fell for it. I'm so *stupid.*"

JK shook his head. He said, "She's scammed a lot of people, Amy. She's a pro. Can you drive a truck?"

"What?"

JK sat down suddenly on the curb, his knees folding without his permission. "'Cause I feel pretty damn sick."

"JK!"

At least Amy wasn't crying anymore, he thought. He shivered, trying to sort through Marietta/Eleanor's memories, trying to wall them off. Her scouring contempt for her clients sat like a brick against his heart, pressing down. Tainting everything.

He looked up at Amy and God, she had been *stupid*, and so *easy*... a few half-sentences, a few facts culled here and there, and Amy had fallen hook, line, and sinker, hearing what she wanted to hear. She wanted her parents' spirits to be warning her about curses. It was better than being alone.

Amy collapsed beside him, leaning up against his shoulder—still seeking comfort from all the wrong people.

JK shook her off. He said, "You shouldn't touch me." Brittle.

"Do you think there are real spirit-talkers out there?"

"You're going to try *again*?"

Amy flinched at his tone. "No! I mean, no, I just wondered."

"Don't," he said. Still rude. But if he'd gone through all this, and she wandered off to find another fake, he'd... well, he'd be frustrated.

"I can't drive stick," she said. "You want me to call someone?"

"No," JK said. Who would he call? Jesse? Nick? Zeke? He scowled at the pavement, listening to Amy cry. She wasn't doing it fiercely, just whimpering and leaking tears.

JK bumped her shoulder with his, sympathy returning. It wasn't her fault. He'd felt the taste of her grief, knew how it lurked beneath everything, waiting to resurface when she least expected it.

Like living over a trap door. Exhausting.

He knew a little something about living like that. JK rallied himself and got back in the driver's seat. Still, Eleanor/Marietta lingered, a caustic tang to his thoughts, a wash of bile in his belly. He spat out the window, and thought if he intended to make a habit of this—which he wasn't!—he would need to invest in antacids and chewing gum.

Amy sniffled off and on throughout the drive, then switched just as rapidly to a muttering fury that had her hitting the door handle of his truck, apologizing, and doing it again. And his head barely seemed his at all, drifting between all the invading memories that he'd taken on in the past week.

JK dropped Amy off at Sabrina's with a sigh of relief, not just because it got her out of his cab, but because dropping her at the coffee shop might keep him out of trouble. If he let her out at her house, Ashford would notice—and dropping her at Zeke's dojo would be a fight waiting to happen.

JK got back to the Barton house and realized that he didn't want to be there either. For a single moment, he missed his basement in Maine, the blank white walls, the room that held nothing but what he'd put into it—his madness, his terror, his pain, his confusion.

He shuddered.

No, even living in a murder house, JK preferred this life.

He climbed out of the truck gingerly, and went inside, breathing deep, tasting the scent of change—sawdust, grout, wood polish, and industrial strength cleaners. Back to work. He might have screwed things up with Nick, with Amy, with the neighborhood. But he could make the house right.

12

JK had finished with the grout, had sealed off the kitchen with another round of plastic sheeting, and moved on to sanding the newly bared floors. He wanted to give the grout time to cure, but he didn't want the wet grout to pick up any sawdust. JK rigged up fans, opened all the windows, and blew dust and noise outside, a storm working its way outward.

He sat back every so often and imagined all the bad memories scoured out with the dust. It made him smile, and JK decided that he'd sand the baseboard and ceiling molding as well. If he screwed up? He could replace damaged molding. Hell, he felt like sanding the walls and ceiling. Whatever it took.

His phone vibrated at his hip, but JK ignored it, and kept working. He didn't want to deal with people.

The world had other ideas.

The sun began to set, turning the dirty dust clouds to tumults of gold spilling through the house, and JK's arms vibrated even when he wasn't holding the sander. Reluctantly, he admitted the job was done.

He turned the sander off, and the silence seemed as much a roar as the engine had been.

Someone knocked on the door, so promptly that JK got the feeling they'd been hovering, waiting for the sander to quit. He jumped, considered not answering it, but... a small hope surged. Maybe it was Nick.

That seemed about as likely as the odds of Marietta having been a real psychic.

He still couldn't help but hope.

This time it paid off.

Nick stood in the doorway, looking hesitant but not angry.

JK pulled down his respirator, pushed up the goggles, and said, "Is everything okay?" Then more cautiously, remembering their fight: "Did you need something?"

He kind of hated that he hoped the answer was yes, that Nick needed him. Wanted him.

"So I made a stupid amount of lasagna last night," Nick said. "You want some?"

JK got a flash of bad memory through entirely regular means; Nick, standing at the sink, accusing JK of getting Zeke out of Nick's life by fair means or foul. It soured the brief surge of happiness he'd had looking at Nick's pale eyes.

"I'm not hungry," JK said, but his stomach rolled over and growled at the idea of food.

Nick raised a brow. "You sure about that?"

"No," JK said. He slapped his hands against his thighs, spreading dust and aggravation. "I'm not sure. Last night you hated me—"

"I didn't hate you."

"You kicked me out."

"I did not!" Nick said.

"Might as well have."

Nick grimaced. The moment stretched. Then Nick sighed. He said, "I got pissed off, JK. I'm still pissed, but now it's split pretty evenly between you, me, and Zeke. You were right about some things. I did ask for your help. And I can see why you might think..." He winced. "Look. Zeke's not a murderer."

JK fidgeted, unwilling to give in on the topic. If he admitted he was wrong, then JK had called Conroy and wasted her time, and pissed off Nick for nothing. "You keep saying that. Do you really have no doubts at all? 'Cause I don't need any psychic touches to think that you do and just don't want to admit it—"

"That's bullshit," Nick said.

"Really? If I touched you right now, what memory would I find? Something suspicious?"

JK peeled off his glove, held out his hand in challenge. Nick recoiled, then his chin jutting out, he put his bare hand in JK's bare one. JK had a single moment to enjoy Nick's fingers linking up with his, the warmth of human contact in a place that never felt it, then...

Letting Zeke in, undoing the locks with shaking hands, only beginning to relax once Zeke was inside. Strong and solid and there, after a long day where Barton had been as savage as Nick had ever seen him, aiming his gun at Nick meaningfully, swaying on his feet. Angry and drunk, and God, would he have any restraint left?

"Easy, easy," Zeke murmuring. "You got to relax. He won't hurt you. I won't let him." Pouring Nick a drink from the bottle of whiskey he'd brought, turning up the TV loud and keeping his glass filled, until the entire night blurred and ran... and he woke in his room, tucked neatly beneath the covers, though he'd never felt Zeke move him. Staggering into the kitchen the next morning, hungover and ill, with no sign Zeke had ever been there, except for a note that read: "I'll take care of this. You won't have..."

"... to worry about Barton again," JK breathed.

Nick broke the touch, panting harshly as he recognized the note. "Jesus fuck, JK—"

Then the anger drained from his face, leaving him blanched and looking sick. "Look, I can't say I have no doubts. People can surprise you in terrible ways. But not like this. Zeke would have beaten Barton within an inch of his life if he'd gotten another chance. He probably *did* plan something to run him out of the neighborhood. That I believe."

Nick shook his head and continued. "Even killing Barton by accident. I could see that happening. Zeke's strong and fast and could have hit him wrong. But planning deliberate murder? Shooting the dogs? Shooting Barton? It's just not in his nature."

"He has a gun, so shooting has to be in his nature somewhere," JK pointed out.

Nick said, "His *parents* gave Zeke the gun. I don't think he's ever fired it, even at the range. And burying the bodies in the backyard? No fucking way. Zeke's not stupid; he's strong as hell and he owns a big-ass SUV. He'd have carted the bodies off where no one would have found him."

JK, listening to Nick painfully dissect his best friend's murderous tendencies, felt shame washing over him. Shame and a desire to believe. If he could believe in Zeke's innocence, then maybe he could keep Nick as a friend, as a lover, as part of his new life.

"Maybe I overreacted," JK allowed. "You were in trouble with the cops, and Zeke... yeah, he kind of scared me, then I had that look at his memories..."

Nick blew out a breath, coughing as he stirred fine sanding dust into the air, and said, "I guess the big thing is, how 'bout you ask me next time? If you see something that worries you about my friends, don't just run to the cops. Don't take it as the whole. I mean, look at Ashford. What do you think he thinks about you from the bits he's seen?"

JK scrubbed his face, setting his sweaty, dusty hair to standing on end; he could feel it pulling oddly against his scalp. He said, "Yeah, yeah. I get your point."

"Just come to me first. Trust me, if you don't trust my friends. Okay?"

"I do trust you," JK said. It didn't feel like a lie.

"Zeke stayed with me the night Barton got shot. The whole night, baby-sitting my hysterical ass. We stayed up watching *wuxia* movies all night long. So, it doesn't matter that he had a gun, that he hated Barton. I was with him."

A wave of numbness swept over JK's skin, a tiny shock running his nervous system. Nick had just lied. JK had heard Nick telling the cops he hadn't heard the gunshots, that his painkillers had knocked him completely out. Dead to the world.

If Zeke had been at Nick's house, but Nick had been drugged and sleeping, then Zeke could have killed Barton with ease. It put Zeke in the right place, at the right time. With the right motivation.

Nick said, "Anyway, what about dinner? I'd really like to get you out of here. You've been working in the house all day and you're looking a little... spacey. Time for a break?"

JK nodded, but felt like a disjointed doll. "Not all day. Amy and I went out." He cut that story off. Another thing he didn't really want to talk about, even though Nick's eyes sharpened with interest. "Yeah. Let me wash up, and I'm all yours."

He didn't call Nick on the lie; why bother? Nick believed in Zeke, and nothing JK could say would change that. He wasn't even sure he should try. Nick did have a point. None of JK's memories showed Zeke actually killing Barton and circumstantial evidence was just that. Circumstantial. Even more fragile when it came from a secondhand memory.

Nick said, "I called Zeke, and gave him the heads-up that the cops were probably going to want to talk to him."

"You tell him why?"

Nick shook his head. "Are you kidding me? I want you two to get along."

"I am sorry," JK said. "At least, for not talking to you first. I just freaked out."

Nick shrugged, deliberately casual. Fake casual. "Nothing's going to come of it. And hey, maybe it'll teach him to get a leash on that temper of his. Punching Barton I could understand. Punching you? Totally out of bounds."

❦

The topic lay between them even as they worked their way through a full third of the lasagna. It kept the conversation stilted, as one or the other of them lapsed into abstracted silences.

JK figured Nick just wanted to convince himself that Zeke wasn't in danger, that the whole thing would blow over as easily as he hoped. But the faked alibi made it clear that Nick wasn't nearly as calm as he pretended. And JK couldn't stop thinking that if Zeke had murdered Barton, Nick was never going to forgive JK for knowing it first.

JK knew he could change the tenor of the evening, just by telling Nick about his experience with Amy earlier, but it felt way too much like bartering. Like an apology. *I might have ratted Zeke out, but hey, look, I tried to help Amy!*

Though the silence verged on uncomfortable, JK, still working on sorting the new memories he'd picked up into the "not-mine" category, appreciated the respite. Sorting a memory took a weird sort of careful focus—not enough to make him relive it more than once, but enough to delineate all the edges, to enable him to slide the memory down the scale of emotional immediacy.

If JK managed it correctly, the memory would end up feeling as if he'd watched a particularly engrossing television show—something JK cared about while it was on the air, but something he could set aside when the episode ended.

The process would have been easier if he hadn't taken in more memories in the past week than he'd taken in over the past six months. He still hadn't properly sorted the nightmare landscape of Barton's last moments, Barton's threats to Nick, Nick's memories of Barton, memories of Nick's past lovers, Jesse's horrible dead-kid case, Hannah's concern for her patient, and all the Zeke nastiness.

Adding in Marietta's only made the mess worse. She woke echoes everywhere and made them harder to settle: found a resonance in the appliance dealer who'd tried to cheat Davis and JK, made Amy's grief sharper, made Zeke's rage brighter, which brought up the whole Barton parade again. It was like hammering in a board on a uneven surface: get one side nailed down and the other popped back up.

"JK?" Nick said.

JK realized he'd frozen mid-action, his fork raised high, lasagna growing cold, and he finished the motion started some minutes before. He said, "Sorry. May not be the best company.

Trying to sort things out." It felt odd and awkward to offer an explanation for something he usually tried to hide.

"We've been hard on you, huh?" Nick said. "Not such a peaceful neighborhood below the surface."

"Nothing's peaceful beneath the surface," JK said. "Nothing."

Nick's expression went soft and a little sad. He reached out and put his hand over JK's gloved one, rubbed his thumb over JK's wrist bone. "I think you've just been exposed to way too many stressful situations. People are complicated, yes, but they aren't all bad."

"You got beaten up by kids, and harassed by Barton until you couldn't leave your house. How the hell can you believe that?"

"Guess I'm an optimist," Nick said. "I teach, JK. I have to look at those young men and women and see good in them. Or there's just no point. But they're bright and interested and even the terrible students have things to offer."

JK's phone rang, saving him from having to come up with a coherent response. Nick rose from the table. "That's probably your brother. Better get it."

"Yeah," JK said. Nick slid behind him, and after a hesitant moment, kissed JK's shoulder.

JK found himself answering the phone with a smile. "Hey, Jesse."

"Oh, you sound good," Jesse said. "Thank God. I was worried."

"You're always worried," JK said. He rose and headed outside to Nick's deck, seeking a little privacy. He didn't know what Jesse wanted to talk about, but if it involved Zeke, he wanted to have the conversation out of Nick's earshot.

JK, aware of how sound could carry on a still evening—Nick *had* to have been drugged to miss gunshots—kept his voice low. "What's going on?" he asked.

Jesse said, "Heard Conroy cut your neighbor loose."

"Nick didn't kill Barton. Of course she let him go."

"You seemed pretty worried earlier."

"I like him. So sue me," JK said. "I'm fine now."

"In a murder house in a neighborhood with an unknown killer."

"Who killed Barton, a man no one liked. I'm likeable." JK shook his head at the contrariness of his mood. Nick, trying to encourage optimism in him, only woke skepticism. But in the face of his brother's nonstop pessimism...

"There is that," Jesse said.

"Jesse," JK said, "have you been looking into the Barton case?"

He replied, "I might have had lunch with Eva."

"Eva?"

"Gunnarson, to you. She said they've got other suspects. Mrs. Barton, who said she found him gone when she came home. And didn't wonder where he'd went. Your boy, Nick..."

"Not Nick," JK said. "Unless you think a guy with his dominant arm broken could have shot and killed two dogs and a man, then buried them."

"I'm just telling you what Eva gave me. But I'm with you. Nick's got a hell of a motive, but he's a crappy suspect. I looked into him. He's risk-averse, and respected. Zeke, on the other hand..."

"Zeke's got a temper," JK said.

"Yeah. And a gun license for a .22. Then there's Amy Sheridan."

"Amy?" JK said, his voice rising. She *had* flinched when Marietta had mentioned Barton's name. A brief scour through Marietta's restless memories didn't give him anything more. Why had Marietta mentioned him?

Nick, in the kitchen, raised his head and looked at JK, a question in his eyes. JK realized he was just standing there again, his phone squawking at him.

"Are you even listening?" Jesse asked.

"I'm here," JK said, and tried not to notice that his voice came out strained through Marietta's slight southern drawl. "You said something about Amy?"

"Yeah. Apparently, she and Barton had a screaming fight in the street and he slapped her."

JK felt a fierce protective surge rise through him, partly Zeke's, partly his own after the morning's events. "He was a real bastard, wasn't he?"

"The problem with bastards being murdered is the odds go up that you'll like their killer. I know you're gung-ho about justice for all," Jesse said. "Maybe I made you that way, but JK, sometimes the right ending isn't a happy one."

"I'm getting that," JK said.

The conversation lagged, Jesse's silence simmering with words he wasn't saying. JK knew what they were though; the same thing they had been for while. *Come home. Let me protect you.* For a moment, JK was tempted. It wasn't just the idea of walking away from the house, but the idea that no matter what happened with the police investigation, he wouldn't have to see the fall-out.

"No chance at all it was an outsider?" JK asked. "A bar buddy of his that got pissed and shot him? Someone who followed him home? If he made himself this hated to the people who knew where he lived, I got to think he'd be worse to strangers."

"There's always a chance," Jesse said.

"But you don't think it's likely."

"Not my case," Jesse said, then added, "Just be careful, okay? Don't get too involved."

JK looked through the kitchen window, at Nick tidying away with the absent-mindedness of habit, his hands quick and sure. Watching a man wash dishes shouldn't be sexy, but his mouth felt dry—sure sign that he'd been breathing a little faster—when he finally answered Jesse. "A little late for that."

Jesse put Hannah on the phone then, and she and JK made slightly stilted small talk, JK half afraid that she meant to turn the call into a counseling session/intervention. But Hannah kept the talk light—a new restaurant she'd tried, a movie she wanted to see, a funny video she'd send him a link to—and only at the end, did Hannah slip in her purpose. She said, "You know Jesse's just worried about you. He doesn't mean to ride roughshod over your life."

Nick had vanished from the kitchen at some point and JK sighed, missing the sight already. "Doesn't mean it isn't aggravating as fuck."

"It's guilt," she said. "Those years where he didn't know you were hurting. Where he believed what your parents were telling him. So, I'm not telling you to give in to his worries. You need to live your own life, make your own mistakes. Just be kind to him."

"Hannah," JK said, phone clenched tight in his gloves. "How am I ever going to get stronger unless I keep trying? Maybe I can get better control. Even with my hands. Learn to turn it on and off."

It sounded like a pipe dream. It had been almost a decade. If he was going to learn to control it, he would have done so by now. Wouldn't he? JK wouldn't be sitting here, shivering off and on, losing time to other people's memories that he'd taken in, incorporating pieces of them into him until he didn't know where the boundaries were.

Hannah said, "You know I believe in willpower and self-determination, JK, but sometimes the body just can't be ruled by the mind. No matter how much we want it. Or work on it. Some conditions just have to be accepted. Lived with." She said it like she'd been expecting the question for months. Anticipating him. She probably had.

JK swallowed hard. He loved Hannah. He just wished she wasn't so scrupulously honest.

"JK, you have to see how far you've come. Two years ago, you could barely walk down the street. Now you hold a job, have a life, friends. A boyfriend maybe?"

"You're fishing," he said. "You just want the sexy details." Trying to sound cheery in the face of the reality check she'd dealt him. Nick wandered back into sight, freshly showered, tidying up a few last things, the sinews in his shoulders catching shadows. A smudgy redness lingered on Nick's collarbone, a mark that JK had bitten into existence days before. He wanted to taste that mark again.

His attention wandered away from Hannah, and she laughed. "Something on your mind, JK?" she teased.

"Love you," he said. "Gotta go." Nick was not only freshly showered, but wearing the same soft pajama pants he'd had on when they met, and JK couldn't resist that temptation. He disconnected to Hannah's soft laughter, a whisper that might have been *be careful*, and moved back into Nick's orbit like a moth to a flame.

He'd shaved too, JK noted as Nick approached, had even taken the time to run a razor over his nighttime stubble. More than anything else, that made JK feel like things were good between them.

"Hey," Nick said, tugging JK close, fingers snagging in JK's dusty belt loops. "All good with your family?"

"Surprisingly, yes," JK said.

"Good," Nick said, then kissed him. JK breathed in the scent of clean skin and soap, rubbed his cheek against Nick's smooth jaw line, and bit gently at that red mark on Nick's collarbone, tasting the light sting of aftershave. "All good with us?"

"We making up?" JK asked.

Nick hummed happily beneath his teeth, and said, low in JK's ear, "I'm hoping. This past day's sucked."

"Getting better," JK murmured.

Nick pulled back, tugged on the hem of JK's t-shirt, and said, "I think it could improve even more. You want to fuck me?"

JK bit his lip hard on the splutter of *oh God, yes please* that wanted to erupt, giving his voice a chance to catch up to the sudden hunger in his blood, the leap of his heart.

Nick teased at the edge of JK's gloves, and smiled. "You going to make me beg for it?"

"That wouldn't be polite," JK said. He leaned in to that warm expanse of exposed skin, felt his hands were trembling against Nick's flesh. Ridiculous when he'd had so much of Nick's body in the past few days.

But this steady increase of intimacy was new.

"C'mon," Nick said. "You're overdressed for this party." He smiled, easy. Unafraid. JK followed his lead. Why not, when it seemed like he'd been following Nick ever since he'd met him.

JK pulled off his shirt, let it drop onto Nick's pristine floor.

"Good boy," Nick said.

JK's hands were already on the buttons of his jeans. They and his boxers decorated the hall outside Nick's bedroom door. Nick's PJ pants hit the floor just before the bed. JK's breath was quick in his chest with anticipation; his cock was a distracting weight between his thighs.

"Come here," Nick said, tugging JK down on the bed with him, pressing JK into the bedspread, and fitted himself between JK's legs.

JK groaned, dragged Nick closer, rutted up against him, and Nick laughed, breathless and pleased, pushed back. They lost themselves to that simple pleasure, until finally Nick made a concerted effort and squirmed away, digging out the condoms and lube from his bedside drawer.

"Here," Nick said, once they were sorted. "Like this." He slid out of JK's grasp, rolled to his side, gave JK his back, let JK press up behind him, spooning him.

It was deep and slow this way, a lazy man's fuck, and everything JK hadn't realized he'd wanted. He scraped his teeth along Nick's shoulder and nape, tasting sweat and salt, his arms drawing Nick tightly to him. Nick's low groans, intermittent and amazing, resonated through his chest and into JK's so that he felt the deep rumbles before he heard them voiced. Their right hands linked lazily, loosely near the headboard, and Nick rested his head on JK's biceps.

"There, right there," Nick murmured, arched his hips back, pressing them just that much closer.

JK bit at the knob of Nick's shoulder bone, let his gloved left hand slip easily from Nick's chest, where he could feel every throb and pulse of Nick's heart against his wrist, and closed his hand over Nick's where he was jerking himself off slowly, leisurely in time with JK's thrusts.

Nick groaned again, rolled his head back on JK's shoulder.

This might not be hard and fast, racing to the finish line, but somehow it was everything he wanted. Intimate in a way JK had never had.

In high school, he'd barely gotten past mutual masturbation and blow jobs. After the basement, it was clubbing for fast, hot fucks in restroom stalls and quiet corners. None of it compared to Nick clutched tightly in his arms, skin to skin, his breath beginning to hitch, his groans changing to broken-off words of encouragement and praise, and rolling his hips back in erratic surges.

JK gritted his teeth, swallowed his own body's urge to lose control, and kept to the same steady thrusting while Nick fell apart all around him. Only then did he duck his head, press his forehead hard against Nick's nape, and let himself go.

When they both had their breath back, the condom knotted off and tossed, cleanup out of the way, Nick lay facing JK and said, "So, that was you without the cheat sheet?" His cheeks and chest still had some high color, a fading blush; his eyes seemed insanely blue.

"Yeah," JK said. A weird sort of anxiety tried to seize him, but his body was too blissed to let it. "Just me. Gloves on. Psychic powers off. Or as off as they can be."

Nick smiled. "Nice to meet you, JK without a cheat sheet. I like your style."

13

He woke early to Nick's phone going off like a bomb, shattering the quiet, leaving his nerves shrieking. Nick swore, rolled across JK's body, and answered it. After his drowsy hello, he went silent, overpowered by whoever spoke on the other end.

Nick's muscles, pressed against JK's skin, went taut and unhappy. JK rested his gloved hand on Nick's back, offering reassurance. "All right, all right. I'll take care of this. I promise. It'll be all right." He hung up, and shrugged JK's hand off impatiently, sat on the edge of the bed, said, "Fuck, fuck, fuck!" and grabbed for the phone again.

"Lourdes?" Nick said. "I know it's early. The cops just arrested Zeke. They're going to charge him with Barton's murder."

JK's breath lodged in his throat, made him cough.

Nick's gaze cut to him, crystalline and hot. "Lourdes, I need you to get down there and keep him from shooting his mouth off. Remind him that he was with me all night, watching movies."

JK rolled out of bed and dressed, finding his clothes scattered where he'd left them the night before. His heart beat erratically, nervous and sick. If Zeke had been arrested because of him, Nick wouldn't forgive him. No matter how much he liked JK. Zeke was Nick's family, and Nick would lie to keep him safe if he had to.

Nick finally hung up again, and pinned JK in place with those burning eyes. He said, "He didn't do it, JK."

"Okay," JK said.

"Not 'Okay', he really didn't do this."

JK opened his mouth to agree, and no words came out.

Nick ran a hand through his hair; his hand shook, and JK wanted to look away. Couldn't. He'd created this mess. He'd sicced Conroy on Zeke, and maybe she'd have gotten there on her own, but this way... it was all on him. JK twisted his fingers around each other, gloves twisting, denting his flesh beneath.

Nick said, "You need to help me fix it."

"Fix it?"

"Prove he didn't do it," Nick said. "I know you don't trust him, but can you trust me? Help me. They've got to have other suspects."

"They do," JK said. "Not very many, but they do."

"Then it's easy! You just... touch them and find out. You said that people's memories were like category searches—"

"I also said it wasn't easy. That the memories are painful, and that it's dangerous. Remember that? Remember me spending most of last evening trying to sort them out?"

"It's Zeke, JK. *Zeke*. My best friend. My brother. If he's in trouble, it's because of me."

JK let out a pained breath. He knew what Jesse would say, knew that keeping himself safe meant saying no. Knew that even if he agreed, it might all be pointless. The cops were probably right and Zeke had been the one to kill Barton, and bury him; JK's read on Zeke could have been revelatory, not an outlier.

He closed his eyes, tested all the sore spots, the new memories he'd taken in. They were settled now, uneasy, but settled. He wanted to point out that he'd helped *Amy* and wasn't that enough? But one good deed didn't mean you never had to do others. "All right," he said. "I'll do it."

The tension in Nick's body drained out of him; he slumped forward and JK caught him. Nick rested his head against JK's chest, a weight on his heart, and said, "Thank you."

Nick rubbed at his eyes, leaned back. He said, "How do we start?" JK wasn't used to someone looking at him like he had the answers. Pity he didn't have an easy one.

JK replied, "I'm not really sure."

Nick shrugged. "The cops are done with the yard today, right? You saw his death before. Maybe if you were ready for it—"

JK shuddered. "You can't get ready for something like that. Besides, it doesn't work that way. I told you. Two types of memory. People and ambient. People are easier, clearer. Stronger. There's understanding behind events and that carries over, even if the images that come with it are a nightmare. It's like I'm getting a translation even as the memory comes. Zeke—" The name fell into the room like a weight, reminding them both what was at stake.

JK pushed on. "That first time. His memories came in like the view through a kaleidoscope. The girl crying. Zeke scared. Angry parents. The hospital. A blue blanket. A baby screaming. Zeke leaving. Zeke thinking of Amy."

"So, fragmentary," Nick said.

"Exactly. If you take a person's understanding out of the memories, when I'm picking up just the ambience—it comes without context. Just stuff. Feelings. Images. I got... *Barton* got knocked down. His attacker loomed above him. The dogs were black shadows in the dark and their fur moved in the breeze, even though they were dead." JK shivered, remembering that ghostly image, then went on.

"Someone carried a shovel. A gun. Someone dug a hole. There were gunshots. The dogs killed a cat. People shouted. None of it's in order. Mostly it flooded me with emotion. Rage. Pain. Terror. I couldn't breathe and everything hurt so much."

His throat rasped, dry. He stopped and Nick mutely passed him a bottle of water from the bedside.

JK drank it down, spilling a few drops from his trembling grip.

"So even if I were sadistic enough to ask you to go back in the yard again, try to pull up the scene of the crime?" Nick asked.

"Probably wouldn't work," JK said. "At best, I'd get the emotional terror again. The strong stuff. But I bet I'd also get a lot of crime scene techs walking around, us digging the dirt, maybe even Zeke punching me. Even traumatic events can get worn away by new ones. That's why I haven't quit this job. I can erase the things that happened here."

JK sat back down, the mattress sagging around him, and turned the bottle around and around in his hands. "So basically, I'm saying I don't know what to do next."

Nick leaned against him. "It comes down to people, then. You said there were other suspects?"

"A few," JK said. "Mrs. Barton, always suspect the spouse, right? And she said he left while she was out of town. Maybe she lied. Maybe she hired someone. It's disgusting how little it can cost to buy a killer. Jesse's told me stories."

"Okay. Mrs. Barton sounds good. I mean, she's a miserable bitch. Nearly as awful as Barton," Nick said. "She sure didn't do anything to keep a leash on his worst tendencies. Sometimes she laughed." Nick's mouth twisted. "Who else?"

"You and Zeke, naturally."

"Naturally," Nick echoed, making a face.

"Amy Sheridan," JK said. His lips felt sour just saying her name in this context. He'd helped her yesterday, roughly, ineptly, probably doing her damage in the process, but he'd tried. He wanted to keep thinking of Amy as worth helping, not a killer.

"Seriously?" Nick jerked to his feet, hands flying for his hair again, gripping tight. "What the fuck could she have to do with Barton?"

"Something unpleasant," JK said. "I don't know. Apparently she got into it with him. Marietta..." JK frowned. He'd picked up something from Marietta, but it wasn't clear, muddled beneath all the stuff he'd been actively hunting. "Marietta thought Amy cared about Barton's death. That's when she started talking about Amy being cursed. I didn't get why."

"Marietta? Who the fuck is Marietta?" Nick asked.

"The psychic," JK said. "Amy's psychic. Amy's ex-psychic."

Nick rocked back on his heels, closing brows darkening the pale blue of his eyes. "I missed something."

"Not really relevant," JK said. "Zeke told Amy I was a psychic. And I told Amy that Marietta wasn't."

"She believed you?"

"This whole... thing happened," JK said, flapping a gloved hand. "Messy. But according to Jesse, someone said that Barton slapped Amy after an argument in the street."

"How did I not hear about this? Jesus." Nick winced. "Did Zeke know?"

"Seems like," JK said.

"He didn't do it," Nick said, doggedly. JK wondered if he'd get sick of jumping to Zeke's defense.

"That's who we've got. Amy or Mrs. Barton. That's who Conroy and Gunnarson are looking at."

"Did you say the killer loomed over him? Amy's not tall. Then again, if your memory involved Barton looking up from the ground, how tall would the killer really have to be..." Nick flopped back onto the bed, let his legs sprawl off the edge, and covered his face. "Jesus. I can't believe I'm going there. Amy's my friend. She's Zeke's girlfriend. He loves her like crazy."

JK wanted to lie back down, to curl into the warmth of Nick's body and let the day start again. "Someone has to be guilty."

"Maybe someone Barton met in a bar. He came home with his own bruises often enough. Picked fights with other assholes."

JK said, "The police don't think that a stranger would have been unnoticed."

"Who says he had to have been unnoticed? I think you don't get how much people hated him. They might have looked the other way."

"I might buy that if he had just gone missing," JK said. "But now that it's obviously murder? And Ashford. You're telling me that the colonel wouldn't have said something?"

"There is that," Nick said. He stretched, sat up, wrapped his arms around his chest. "I could call Amy. Have her come over."

"Set her up for me to read," JK said. "She'll know what I can do. If she's guilty, I wouldn't think she'd let me..."

"I can distract her," Nick said, after a pause. He scrubbed a hand over his face, then said, "I've got to help Zeke. This is what I can do." He winced. "What *you* can do."

JK took a breath, another one, reassured himself. He couldn't imagine Amy as a killer; she'd been nothing but sweet and gentle since he'd met her. Nothing in her memories could be that bad. "All right. Call her."

⟡

JK showered and dressed carefully, feeling oddly like he was prepping for surgery of sorts. Making sure his hands were clean. Trying to tamp down all his own problems so he could better focus on Amy.

Nick had brewed coffee, strong and dark enough that JK added an extra splash of cream to it, and then they sat, waiting. JK fidgeted with the edges of his gloves. Thinking of the day ahead of him, he'd chosen the white silk ones because they would be easier to take on and off. But right now, as he folded his fingers around the coffee mug, the white gloves made his hands look like a magician's hands to him. Ready to pull rabbits out of a top hat. "Ugly murderous rabbits, though," he muttered.

He fell for Nick just that bit more when Nick looked at him, frowning, then said, "Rabbits out of hats. Finding the truth is a little like that, isn't it?"

"What's taking her so long?" JK asked.

"If we do find something out, what then?" Nick asked. "I mean, visions aren't evidence."

"To Conroy, they're a good place to start," JK said.

"She knows? Believes?"

"Seems to." JK squirmed in his seat. "She mentioned talking about other cases, and calling her any time."

Nick inched his mug around on the table in a circle, thinking. "You told her about your vision of Zeke and she just accepted that?" He grimaced. "Either she's got a thing for long-legged construction workers with a pretty smile, and who could blame her..."

"Or she's seeing a bunch of cold cases closed if I cooperate." JK shrugged, but refused to be flattered. He said, "Doesn't really matter. This is a one and done kind of thing. I don't have the nerve."

"Seem brave enough to me," Nick said. He graced JK with a smile, a kiss to the top of his head, and moved toward the front door. A moment later, JK heard his voice carrying back. "Aw, crap."

JK joined him at the front door, looking out. "Interception."

Amy stood on the colonel's manicured lawn, with Ashford leaning over her, frowning. Her body language screamed for rescue. From this distance, JK couldn't tell if Ashford was offering her comfort, interrogating her, or some emotional whiplash combination of both. In JK's limited experience, the colonel excelled at being both intimidating and reassuring.

Either way, time for them to spring into action. Nick opened the door. JK followed him out, slipped one of his gloves off and shoved it into his pocket. The air on his skin felt cool, full of potential. Amy jerked her head toward them as they approached, her expression equal parts dismayed and hopeful.

She wanted to be rescued, JK thought, but she didn't want them to overhear Ashford's conversation.

It was too late for that.

"... remember the day they took you away. You were only a baby, but Barton had fallen off the wagon. Again. Sofia was so sad to see you go; you were such a sweet baby, happy even with the cast on your arm. But you weren't safe in that house. I had to call."

JK hesitated, watching the flush rise on her face, the way Amy folded in on herself. She already felt vulnerable. And he planned on touching her, sneaking into her memories and finding out more than she would ever share in words.

"*You* called CPS?" Amy said.

"I did," Ashford said.

Amy nodded, once, twice, three times. Not okaying it, but filing that information away.

"Do the police know who you are?" Ashford asked. "I didn't tell them."

"They do," Amy said, her voice small and thin. She sent an apologetic look Nick's way; her gaze skittered over JK uneasily, yesterday still sharp in her mind. JK, the instrument of hurt.

"That's why the cops took Zeke. They knew. Honestly, the way they came after me, I expected to be the one they arrested. I guess they didn't think I had the right skill set." Her mouth trembled.

JK thought about a grave dug deep enough to hide three bodies and quickly enough to be done under cover of darkness, and agreed with the cops. Amy was in good shape, gym-fit, young and healthy, but digging even a shallow grave rapidly in this rocky soil at night took a more practical sort of strength.

"Why were they looking at you in the first place?" Nick asked.

Amy blew her bangs out of her face, misery and exasperation mingled. "Because I'm their kid. Born Amy *Barton*. Social Services took me away when I was eighteen months old. I don't even remember it. The Sheridans adopted me. Then when Mom and Dad died, I had no one left. But Mom and Dad had kept my adoption file. And I thought, maybe I'm not so alone, after all. So when the opportunity came up to live nearby, I took it." Her hands twisted in the air, trying to explain the inexplicable. Her wrists were thin, delicate.

JK reached out and took one narrow wrist in his hand, her skin smooth as silk beneath his. As easy as that. He lost the outer world all at once, only heard the tail end of the colonel asking, "Did they know you were their daughter?"

Heart burning in her chest, tears scalding her face, feeling rejection clear to her bones and Mrs. Barton's eyes, blankly looking at her. A wall of indifference.

"You didn't want me enough to choose me over him?"

"Couldn't afford you if I left him."

"You don't even care—"

In the living room at the Bartons' house, clutching the grocery bag tight against her chest, the frozen food nipping at her skin, her face flushing with humiliation and hurt. With anger.

"I could have killed him at the time, but now? So long ago. What do you even want? Money? 'Cause there isn't any."

Stumbling blindly out into the day, dropping the grocery bag at Barton's feet as he staggered up the stairs. He said, "What the fuck were you doing in my house, bitch? Think I don't know you're Collier's friend?"

Shoving away, fleeing. Grief. Missing her adoptive parents—her real parents—so much she thought she'd never be able to breathe again.

JK staggered, felt Nick's hand on his back. His ears popped and the world swam back into a mélange of sun, heat, and Ashford's scrutinizing gaze. Amy finished saying, "She did. Barton didn't."

A lie.

Another vision slamming into him.

"But you could leave him! He's dangerous. He's mean. You own the house, you could escape. Sell it, leave him—"

Mrs. Barton, can't think of her as Mom, staring blankly back. Not even listening. Not caring at all. Her eyes flickering over her shoulder.

Barton, his hand tight, so tight on her arm, bruising. Dragging her outside. "You think I don't know who you are? What you want? Spoiled little smartass, burned through one set of parents, now you want us back. Well, we don't want you."

Yanking away from him, screaming, can't even hear her own words through the pain...

He slaps her. Shock. Falling, running, scrabbling away. "I hope you die!"

JK's hand slipped from Amy's on a last flash: *Fear. Zeke. She told him. What did he do?*

Amy rubbed at her wrist absently, then her eyes flared wide. She turned to stare at JK. Her gaze flicked down to his bare hand.

Ashford said, "Barton wouldn't have welcomed you back."

It took JK a moment to remember that Ashford didn't know what he did, hadn't seen the truth behind Amy's quick, defensive lie.

"Hey," Nick objected for Amy. "Way to sugarcoat things, Colonel."

Amy's attention latched onto JK; her mouth trembled, then firmed. A flash of betrayal and hurt shone in her eyes: *You read me.*

"I *know* that," Amy answered Ashford, but spoke directly to JK. "Barton didn't want me back. But I didn't *kill* him. And I didn't ask Zeke to do it for me. Not for money, not for some weird-ass revenge. I just wanted to pretend they never existed. Especially once I realized how he treated Nick. I told the cops that, and I would have told anyone who *asked* me."

JK winced. Nick draped an arm over her shoulders, looked briefly at JK, a question in his eyes.

"I'm sorry, Amy," JK said.

She just shook her head, not forgiving him. Given how closely Ashford studied them, JK found himself glad to be on the receiving end of the silent treatment.

"You look shaky. Let Nick walk you home?" JK suggested. He could barely get the words out through a sore and ragged throat. But since he had strip-mined Amy's painful memories, the least he could do was get her out from under the colonel's scrutiny.

She clutched at Nick's t-shirt. "I need to talk to you about Zeke. About getting him out. What can I do? I've got cash if we need bail..." She glanced back at JK, remembering how she had acquired her new spending money, and her cheeks colored.

"Don't worry about him, right now. I called a good lawyer for him. C'mon, we'll talk about it later," Nick said, gently steering her away.

JK watched them go, watched Nick soothing Amy as they went so that by the time they were three houses away, her gait had shifted from unsteady to fluid. He envied Nick that, the ability to put people at their ease.

Amy's memories shivered and squirmed in his head, seeking acceptance. JK ignored them as best he could, stared at the short clipped grass of Ashford's lawn, tried to figure out if Bermuda or St. Augustine grass had been planted. Anything to keep the memories from gaining a foothold. But his arm ached dully with bruises he never had, and his cheek throbbed.

He thought about grass, thought about it hard.

Jesse planted St. Augustine, and he fought to keep it green in Dallas's dry heat. His parents, up in the Northeast, had fescue—

Amy's grief for her dead parents swarmed out of his brain and pounced, shocking his breath out of him, turning his knees to water. JK swayed, felt a calloused hand closing on his elbow. Someday, *his* parents would be dead, too, and the basement would never be resolved. Seven years of misery didn't erase eighteen years of happy life. But just thinking about them recalled the smell of bleached walls and his own fear sweat.

Ashford said, "Need a seat, Lassiter? You look like you're about to fall over."

"I'm good," JK said, and escaped the colonel's iron grip.

He wanted to put his glove back on, but couldn't think of a way to make it look normal. Ashford's gaze flicked down to that one bare hand, and frowned. Of course, wearing only one glove didn't look normal either.

JK flailed for a change of subject—too rude to just flee, and he felt another bolt of sympathy for Amy who'd been trapped talking to the colonel. "You think Zeke's arrest will stick? Did you see it happen?" JK asked.

"I do have better things to do than watch you all, you know," Ashford bit out with the heat of a man who really didn't have better things to do. "And what do I know about how the police think? I'm an old soldier, not a policeman. Stuart's troubles, he brought them on himself. I had to call."

"Had to call?" JK echoed. Did that mean what he thought it did? He wasn't the only one with doubts? "You called the police about Zeke?"

Ashford's mouth thinned until it looked like a paper cut, sore, ready to bleed. "I didn't want to. But they were going after Amy. Blaming that little girl. She wouldn't do that. Couldn't do it. Not my fault that Stuart's temper put him in a bad light."

"*And* he's an outsider," JK finished quietly.

"What's that?" Ashford said.

"Nothing," JK said.

Ashford lifted one rigid shoulder, dropped it again. A brittle shrug. "May come to nothing. Amy says she told the police that Zeke spent the night with her."

Ashford eyed him, a skeptical tilt to his jaw, a silent query as to what JK thought about that. But JK, still sagging under the weight of Amy's memories, found himself less affected than usual by the old man's questioning gaze. It was Nick all over again, wasn't it?

Nick would rather Amy get arrested than Zeke. Ashford would prefer Zeke to Amy. God knew, Amy's roommates probably preferred Nick as the killer rather than Zeke. And all of them muddling along, telling the cops what they wanted to be true.

Was JK any different? One vision: Zeke holding the gun, full of fury, and JK had been ready to hang the man if it meant Nick would be free.

"...ssiter? Lassiter!"

JK realized he was listing, knees giving, tipping him toward the grass. He jerked upright.

"You sure you're all right?" Ashford asked.

"Short on sleep," JK said. "Nick's upset."

Ashford scrubbed his face with a rough hand. "That boy's too damn sensitive for his own good. Life's gonna chew him up."

"Doesn't he have the right to be upset? Zeke's been arrested. For a crime he didn't do."

Ashford said, "Trust in the system, boy. Being questioned is not being arrested. If Stuart's innocent, he'll be freed."

"It's Texas," JK said. "I think I've got some reason to worry."

"Now you sound like Amy," Ashford said.

"Yeah," JK said. "I bet." Amy's adoptive mother had been an attorney. They'd been driving home and she'd been reading depositions while her husband drove. The papers had been scattered along the roadside for more than a mile after the accident. JK still felt sick whenever he saw a spill of paper flying in the highway current.

JK gritted his teeth. No, he didn't. *Amy* did.

"If you fall over on my lawn, I'm calling the ambulance," Ashford said.

"No!" JK said, backing away. "I'm gonna..."

He shook his head, forced the memories down, shoved aside that borrowed grief. His parents were alive and well—*flash of white, disorientation, scent of illness*—and JK wasn't in the basement. "I'm going to go check out my house. Get a soda. See what a mess the cops have made of my backyard. What kind of grass is this?"

He retreated on Ashford's lecture about centipede grass, and fled across the street, dodging a mail truck that wasn't actually there, but had been there the day Amy talked to Mrs. Barton. Twitchy memories filled his mind, just waiting to be explored.

Damn it, he thought, *pull it together*. It seemed like adding any new memories these days stirred up others. He needed to be better than this. JK could do this, and to hell with Hannah's limitations speech.

A scrap of crime scene tape fluttered from one of the remaining fence posts, drawing him on. He walked around the side and faced the core of the problem. The backyard.

The gaping hole had been filled in, the dirt sifted through and shoveled back. Dark crevices and gaps peppered the fill, and JK thought they looked a lot like dark veins, the blood beneath the skin. He skirted the edge of the yard, sat on the concrete stoop, then leaned up against the house. The Bartons' house. Amy's parents' house.

Amy.

His eyes felt wet, heavy, and he brought up his hand to touch, jerked back when instead of silk against skin, JK felt his lashes damp against his fingertips. In tears over a family drama he had no part in.

He fumbled his glove out of his pocket, and slid it back on. It felt like armor going on, and he wished he'd had the foresight to bring out the suede ones as well. Maybe two gloves deep, he'd feel safe.

Once JK got through Amy's grief, he still had to deal with her lingering fears: that maybe Zeke *had* done it, for her.

Her arm, where Barton had grabbed her, bruising black and green and tender for a week; and Zeke, livid, pacing the floor, muttering, "Should have broken his neck."

JK didn't think he'd tell Nick about that part. He felt a little too raw to start an argument.

"JK?" Nick called, tiptoeing into the yard. "Are you here?" On spotting JK in the shadows of the porch, he asked, "Are you okay?"

"How's Amy doing?"

"Inez was making her a Kahlua milkshake when I left. She'll be fine." His lips twisted. "For now anyway. Unless they make Zeke's arrest stick."

"Yeah," JK said. "Unless that happens."

"We won't let it happen," Nick reminded him.

"We're not any further ahead," JK said. "In fact, we're kind of worse off. Amy's scared he did it."

"Well, he didn't," Nick said. "And if she's so willing to believe he's guilty, then maybe she just doesn't know him as well as she thinks she does."

JK wanted to tell him about Ashford, about people being untrustworthy when facts ran counter to their desires, but his head was spinning.

Nick said, "Come on, my sofa's more comfortable than the dirt."

"Help me up?" He smiled, made a joke out of it, but he doubted he had fooled Nick.

Given how one cycle of painful memories had affected him, JK wasn't looking forward to dealing with their next target, Mrs. Barton. And after what he heard from Amy's memories—her cold admission that Mrs. Barton had thought about killing her husband—he had to wonder if she'd finally had enough.

"Can we wait until tomorrow for Mrs. Barton?" JK said, slumping into Nick's side much as Amy had.

Nick's lips tightened in misery at leaving Zeke's fate in the air for another twenty-four hours, but nodded. "I think that's a good idea."

14

JK sank into Nick's sofa gratefully, let the worn leather cushion his fall; he felt like Amy's memories were eating away at his bones, weakening him from the inside out. Nick's living room closed around him soothingly, the tall bookshelves like a shield against the world. The recessed lights illuminated the earth-tone colors of walls, easy chairs, and the house plants; the muted room felt like an oasis against the chaotic flash of his borrowed memories.

Nick draped a woolen throw over JK's feet, and JK rolled his eyes. "I'm tired, Nick. Not running a fever."

"Suck it up and deal," Nick said, and slipped an ivy-patterned pillow behind JK's head. He stroked fingers through JK's hair, and said, "Rest."

JK watched him disappear into the kitchen, phone in hand. Despite his best efforts, JK dozed to the sound of Nick arguing with his lawyer, trying to figure out when or if Zeke would be charged, when bail would be set, when they could get him out of there... Nick's voice went lower and tighter with each question, and JK fell asleep knowing that all the news was bad, heading for worse.

When he woke, it was with a galvanic start, kicking out, trying to avoid the slap Barton aimed his way.

Nick dropped to the sofa, a shadow in the dimly lit room, and said, "You awake?"

"Yeah," JK said.

"Want something to eat?"

"No," JK managed.

Nick rearranged JK so that his head rested on Nick's lap instead of the sofa cushion. His jaw jutted tightly, clenched on words he didn't say. Then he looked down at JK and his mouth eased.

He stroked JK's tangled hair back and said, "So, how bad is it on your end? 'Cause the legal side of things isn't looking so hot. Lourdes thinks this is not going away."

"I'm sorry," JK said. He turned his head, rubbed his cheek at Nick's wrist bone.

"For what?"

"God only knows. That Amy's not the killer, that I got Zeke arrested—"

"If you're worried that I'm still blaming you, don't." Nick's fingers moved in JK's hair, smoothing sleep knots away. "Are you up for dealing with Mrs. B. tomorrow? Amy wrecked you, and you thought she was going to be the easy one."

JK groaned, pushed himself to a sitting position. "Part of it's guilt, I think. She knew that I read her memories. I hurt her feelings."

Nick looked like he wanted to argue, but couldn't. JK wondered if he'd gotten an earful while he walked Amy home.

"Really, I'm okay. I've just got a bunch of foreign memory shuffling going on in my brain. Thinking about Amy's parents—either set—is bringing up memories of my own parents and that's a whole can of worms right there. When I push that away, then Zeke's memories start duking it out with Amy's. *I gave up my baby for adoption* and *they didn't want me* and both of them feel true and personal. It's making me dizzy, feeling both of them at once."

"Cognitive dissonance," Nick said.

JK said, "What?"

"Trying to sort out two conflicting impulses at the same time."

"That's about right. Gives me a headache."

Nick nodded. "I'm right there with you. I'm so worried about Zeke, I'm sick, but at the same time, I'm pissed at him. It's like he never thought about consequences at all. He's been shooting his mouth off for months that he'd punched Barton and wanted another chance. He knows better. He teaches the kids at his dojo better: you can't punch your problems out. And here he is. In jail. And I'm pissed at him, and scared it's my fault. I'm the one who brought Barton to his attention, made him more than just the jackass neighbor who dumped his dog shit and his cigarette butts on my lawn."

JK said, "To be fair, Barton did actually shoot at your house."

"Right." Nick rubbed his face, giving himself an excuse for reddening eyes. "I have an alibi for Zeke, and I want to make a statement, and Lourdes keeps saying, wait, wait... I don't know what she's waiting for."

"For it not to sound like a lie," JK said.

"What's that supposed to mean?"

JK bit his lip; he hadn't meant to get into that, but the downside of trying to rigidly control his brain—he lost control of his mouth. He shrugged, tried not to make it sound like a challenge, or like doubt. "You told Conroy the first time that you were asleep, under the influence of painkillers, and that's why you didn't hear the murder."

"When did I say that?" Nick asked.

"Right at the start, right after we dug him up."

"Must have been shock at the discovery," Nick said. "I couldn't sleep that night. We were watching movies. Me and Zeke. Had the volume cranked—"

"Amy told the police he spent the night with her."

Nick rocked back on his heels. He said, "What?"

JK hunched into himself. "I can tell you what my brother would. Stop helping. You and Amy are going to help him right into prison."

"But she's lying—"

"And you're not?"

"No. I just got confused when they first started asking. It was months ago. You try remembering a single night out of the blue when you're upset."

JK looked at Nick's tightly drawn mouth, the shadows behind his too-bright eyes, and rose to kiss him. The only kind of reassurance Nick would hear on the subject.

❧

JK woke early, the sun just rising, and despite Nick's warmth draped over him, he woke up chilled. Today he was going to confront Mrs. Barton. Today he might touch a murderer. And if he'd had trouble dealing with the mixed emotions—cognitive dissonance, Nick had called it—that Amy and Zeke had left, how would he cope with seeing Barton's murder from both sides? Victim and killer? Even if she'd hired someone, JK would absorb the rage, hate, and fear that had brought her to that point. Those memories would fight hard against each other, and do him damage in the process.

His mouth tasted of iron and dust and dirt, as if thinking about Barton's memories summoned the dead man's final one. Blood and burial.

If Nick hadn't asked him to do this, JK wondered if he would have volunteered. If Kate Conroy had asked him to look around… JK would have said no, but would he have stuck to that refusal?

The idea of getting inside Mrs. Barton's head scared him, but the idea of letting Barton's murderer get away scared him worse.

Before the basement, before his life had gone insane and taken his parents along for the ride, JK had been a believer in fixing the problems that fell into your lap instead of walking away. Believed that if you could help, you should.

The gift JK hadn't asked for gave him the ability to help. JK could try to protect himself, curl up and turn his back on the world, or he could make something of the hand he'd been dealt. He could help others.

He knew which one would let him sleep better at night.

JK eased himself out of the bed, out from under Nick's sheltering arm, and ghosted toward the guest bathroom to brush his teeth. He didn't want to wake Nick, not while he felt nervous and raw. Nick would want to talk about their plan for the day, and right now, JK couldn't bear the topic. Just because he was resolved to help didn't make the fear easier to stomach.

JK dressed, then went outside and sat in the rising sunlight, tried to figure out where his fear came from. So what if Mrs. Barton had killed her husband? That would be good news for Zeke. Good news for Nick. Good news for Conroy and Gunnarson. And good news for JK. The sooner the case was wrapped up, the sooner he'd get back on track with the renovations.

But he couldn't make himself feel anticipation.

Maybe, he thought, it wasn't fear that dogged him. It just felt like it. Confusion and dread, and how could people do that to someone they promised to love—

That was it.

Ever since he'd lived with Jesse, he'd heard the stats: most murders are committed by the spouse. JK had accepted those statistics as fact, never thought much about them. Never put a face to them. But now, with Nick... JK tried to imagine how you could get to that point. To look at someone you once cared for and kill them. To look at someone and think that it wasn't enough to walk away; to look at someone you loved and want them dead.

He thought about Jesse and Hannah, and the fights they had, with that current of love running so vibrantly underneath. He thought about how many marriages went bad for cops—divorce loomed for Jesse's partner right this moment—and shivered. Cops had guns.

Not all marriages ended in violence. Or in failure.

Not all love went twisty and wrong. JK tilted his head, stared up at the brightening sky, heard the rustle of birds rousing in the trees.

The air shifted, brought a tiny hint of old dirt and rot from his yard next door, and in the back of his mind, Barton stared blindly up at his attacker, at the gun. He was so full of rage and fear that JK couldn't tell if the residue of a dead love had lurked beneath the other emotions.

Mrs. Barton?

Supposedly, she'd been out of town, but she could have sneaked back; hell, if someone could evade the colonel's all-seeing gaze over the neighborhood, who would be more likely to do so? Someone who lived in the Bartons' house? Someone who was a common sight in the neighborhood at any hour? Or a stranger on the quiet street at night?

JK just couldn't believe in the hired killer scenario. Hired killers worked for money. Mrs. Barton didn't have enough. Amy didn't have any.

It was *too* easy to believe Zeke had killed Barton, that the cops weren't just assigning blame at random. He practically lived in the neighborhood, and he would have killed for Amy. For Nick. For *love*.

A hand landed on his bare shoulder, and JK jumped, jerked out of the chair, his heart rocketing.

"Crap. Sorry, JK, sorry!" Nick stepped back, looking as startled as JK felt.

JK tugged at the edges of his gloves, then shook himself. He said, "It's okay. I was just... someplace else, I guess. Trying to figure out the way people work."

"I've got a history degree, and I can tell you—no one really understands why people are the way they are. Shrinks talk a good game, but really? We're a mystery."

"I'm fucking psychic. Shouldn't that count for something?" JK sank back down into the chair, put his face in his hands, and felt Nick approach again. Felt his warm hands skim down the planes of his back, soothing at first, then just stroking for the sake of it.

"You're in a mood, aren't you?" Nick said.

JK's throat closed tight; what could he say? *I think I'm falling in love with you and is there anything in the world I can do to prevent you from falling out of love with me?* It happened. All the time, every day, even without violence. Even without reason.

"C'mon," Nick said. "You look miserable and that's no way to start the day. Blood sugar elevation coming up. You want Tex-Mex for breakfast or pancakes—"

JK turned and kissed him, soft and lingering, feeling a little frantic, fighting the need to cling. Nick seemed to read the desperation in his body; he dragged JK closer, threaded his fingers through JK's hair.

JK finally stepped away, lips tender, neck and chin pleasantly scratchy, and best of all—warmed all the way through. He said, "Omelets. I'll make them. You're in charge of the coffee."

"I can do that," Nick said.

As JK cooked, Nick leaned up against the counter and said, "Are you nervous about talking to Mrs. Barton? You think she's our man? Woman. Killer. You think she's too dangerous to talk to?"

"No," JK said. "How could she be? She's not going to know I'm reading her." JK *wanted* it to be Mrs. Barton—as much as he could want someone to be guilty of murder. That made him no better than Nick wanting it to be anyone but Zeke. He felt edgy, aware of affection's fragility.

Love was conditional.

At the moment, Nick wasn't blaming him for Zeke's situation. But if JK couldn't prove him innocent, if Zeke went to jail, convicted of murder... Nick could return to that first scorching anger he'd felt, remember that JK had called Conroy and first pointed the finger at Zeke. It wouldn't even matter if Zeke turned out to be guilty; that actually might make Nick hate JK more.

And despite Nick's confidence, the idea that Zeke wouldn't use a gun—because he had the strength and skill to beat Barton to death with his bare hands—didn't hold water. To fight Barton and two trained attack dogs, Zeke would have used a gun.

What had happened to Zeke's gun? The gun would remember who wielded it, if only he could find it.

"JK?" Nick said.

JK twitched, aware that the conversation had lagged, waiting on his response to a question he hadn't heard. Luckily, his body had moved on autopilot, flipping the omelets without letting them burn.

He replied, "Sorry. Just stuck in my head, I guess. What did you say?"

"How are we going to get Mrs. Barton's address?" Nick repeated. "I looked her up, but she's not listed."

"I've got it," JK said.

"How? You read it off of something?" Interest lit Nick's voice. "That's pretty cool."

JK found a rough laugh. "Hardly. Davis sent me a copy of the house sale paperwork. Her new address is on it."

He plated omelets while Nick retrieved JK's cell phone. "Your brother and sister-in-law are blowing up your texting plan," he said.

JK made a face at the piled texts on his screen, each of them a variant on "How's it going/keep in touch/just checking in!" He took the phone from Nick, and skipped over the texts. They'd have to wait. Texting was tricky, even with his tech-friendly gloves; his hands were just too big. And calling either of them back would mean lying to them. He didn't like lying.

His plans for the day?

Oh, nothing, just going to ask Mrs. Barton if she killed her husband... while holding her hand...

Yeah. Best to call them after the fact.

JK stared at his omelet, poked at it with a fork, and sighed. He wished he could believe in Zeke's innocence the way Nick did. Then maybe he wouldn't dread Mrs. Barton so much. All he knew of her were the grey images left behind in the house, a memory filtered through Amy's tears, and that single hostile phone call JK had endured to ask about her husband's belongings.

"Hey," Nick said, "Are you freaking out?"

JK dropped his fork. "What makes you say that?"

"The expression on your face?" Nick stirred his coffee, and watched the dark swirl of it. "We more or less just met and I asked you to help me, using your psychic abilities, and I just... Am I pushing? Are we moving too fast?"

"I don't know," JK said, because that was the truth.

"You haven't dated a whole lot. At least, I get that impression," Nick said.

"You're not wrong," JK admitted.

"Just... this is above and beyond the call of a new relationship. You can tell me to take a flying leap." Nick rested his chin on his hands, studied JK.

JK found himself twitching under that intent gaze, wanting to escape it. Nick was wrong about what worried him, but not that wrong; JK hadn't recognized how much their new relationship unsettled him until this moment.

"I didn't even know you a week ago." JK squared his shoulders. "But I've got no regrets so far."

"Good," Nick said, a small, genuine smile rising to his lips. "I'd hate to think I was in this alone."

15

Mrs. Barton's relocation put her in an apartment in a three-story complex that backed up onto a tennis court. Looking out of Nick's passenger window, JK couldn't imagine the woman—who had lived with stapled-down carpets and ancient linoleum—fitting in well in this neat, modern structure. He couldn't imagine the dull, bitter woman of Amy's memories carrying a bag full of rackets and balls, playing in white shorts and sneakers, spending her days on the courts. But then, maybe she'd just never had a chance. Maybe now, with her husband gone, she could start her life over.

Nick said, "She's in apt 38F."

JK said, "You're not coming? She doesn't even know me."

"I'm not one of her favorite people," Nick said. He drummed his fingers briefly on the wheel. "If I went with you, all we'd get is the door slammed in our faces."

JK nodded. He looked down at his gloved hands, then flexed his fingers.

"You don't have to—"

"Nick," JK said. "Been there, done that. I'm just trying to figure out if I should take the gloves off now, or at the door." Before Nick could weigh in, JK headed out of the car. Nick, who had been nothing but calm earlier, jittered with nerves now.

JK shut the car door, looking up at the apartment building with an assessing eye, and thought it looked nicely constructed. Solid without being blocky. Courtyards and open stairwells brought light and elaborate shapes to the otherwise rectangular complex, and the stucco façade gleamed creamy gold in the sunlight. All in all, about as different from the house she'd left behind as possible.

Distantly, he heard tennis balls being fired onto the courts; each tiny pop made him think of gunshots.

He knocked, then stripped his gloves off and tucked them into his pocket. Footsteps approached and JK wondered what he'd even say to her, if she'd even let him in. He hunched down, tried to look harmless.

When she first opened the door, her eyes were blank—puzzled, but unafraid.

He leaned away from her, trying not to intimidate her, and trying not to drown beneath the cloud of menthol and tobacco smoke she exuded. "Mrs. Barton," he said. "I'm JK Lassiter. I'm renovating your old house?"

"You're the one who found him." Her mouth pinched tight.

"Yeah," he said, tried to think of what to say next.

Mrs. Barton didn't have any such difficulties. She said, "What the hell possessed you to dig up the goddamn yard?"

"I was prepping to plant a tree," JK said.

"Nothing grows back there. Not after those goddamn dogs ruined the yard." She turned, walked back into the apartment, left the door open in an ungracious invitation. He sidled in after her, nudged the door shut with his shoulder.

"Those lady cops said the dogs were dead too. Can't say I'm sorry about that. They never minded for me. Only him."

Mrs. Barton sat down on her sofa—new, JK noticed, brightly floral and cheaply made—and said, "Well, don't loom. Sit, and tell me what brought you out here. Morbid curiosity, I bet. You look the type."

He thought about denying it, but he doubted she'd believe him. Besides, he wanted her thinking about Barton's death, and letting her assume curiosity had driven JK here would be one way to keep her mind on Barton.

"So. Spit it out," she said. "You always this tongue-tied?"

"You didn't report him missing."

"I didn't know he was," she said. "You're not a cop, what do you care?"

"Morbid curiosity, I guess," JK said. He didn't like Mrs. Barton, had a hard time keeping a lid on that dislike. Her sourness tainted everything around her.

She snorted, but didn't say anything, only reached for the pack of menthol cigarettes on the coffee table. She lit one, dropped the lighter back into the pack.

"Are you sorry he's dead?" JK asked, poking at her, trying to break through that sour shell. He wanted to get this done. The environment around Mrs. Barton had changed, gone from drab and worn to bright and new, but she hadn't. Still contemptuous. Still unhappy and bitter.

Her face flattened out—lips going tight, eyes squinting. "You came here to ask me that? You got a lot of nerve."

"You're the one who let me in," JK said.

She blew smoke into the space between them. "I've got manners."

Still no crack, no sign that Mrs. Barton was thinking about her husband. JK would only get one chance to touch her memories; he needed her to be thinking about the right set of them.

"I just don't get it," he said. "Why weren't you suspicious when he disappeared? When he left everything behind?"

Mrs. Barton looked at the apartment around her with sunken eyes that weren't seeing any of it. "Not that it's any of your goddamn business, but we... fought. I put up with his temper for too long. Bad enough when he lashed out at other people, but when he turned on me..."

Her hands started shaking; ash spattered the carpet, the sofa, her lap. JK reached out and laid his hand over hers. "I'm sorr—"

The memory swept over him like a flood, dark water, sucking cold, a cold he could die from. And woven through the icy pain, he burned with numb shock and anger and betrayal.

Shouting, turning to leave, and the dogs rising from the floor at his gesture, teeth bared, white teeth in the darkness. The clamp of jaws on her thigh, his hand dragging her back, dragging her down, the dogs howling around them—

JK jerked away, jerked to his feet, desperately trying not to let the memory take hold.

"Stop. You're hurting me. Please. Stop. Don't." Her husband's

face, bobbing blood-red over hers, his weight bearing her down, then pulling away, the satisfaction on his face fading to remorse. Staggering to her feet, straightening her dress, getting out of the house, getting away.

JK had thought her a potential murderer, but she was just another victim.

His stomach turned; his teeth locked tight against the memories. He wanted to get out of there, away from her pain.

Mrs. Barton went on, unheeding, her voice a dry rasp, sandpaper against his nerves. "He'd knocked me around some, but that's a husband for you. But this... I told him to get out. I went to my sister's, and he and those dogs were gone when I got back, and I didn't look a gift horse in the mouth. Guess I should have known it was too good to be true. Should have known the bastard would find some final way to be a pain in my ass." She took another drag of her cigarette, rose and walked toward the kitchen. "If that's all, you can let yourself out. I'm tired."

JK didn't remember getting the door open, fleeing down the stairs, back into the daylight.

Nick wrapped strong arms around his waist. "God, JK, are you all right?"

"No," JK said. He fell against the car, vomited half-digested omelet into the gutter, and wheezed for breath. "Just get me out of here. Now."

Nick got them home, driving faster than he should. JK closed his eyes, the better to feel the sway and jostle of the engine, trying to think only about that and not the violent memory lurching around inside him.

The engine cut off too soon, the screaming snarling memory rushing in to fill the silence. JK lurched out of Nick's car, and aimed himself at Nick's front door.

Nick hovered beside him, ready to offer aid, but obviously scared to touch him.

JK stumbled over his own feet, fell, pushed himself to his knees, bare hands pressed to the drive—*scrabbling dogs' claws and panting, leaping at the car door, snarling like thunder*—but those memories were faint glimmers, like candle flames at midday. He got himself to his feet, swaying.

"JK—"

JK leaned toward Nick, and Nick caught him. "I got you." Nick kept him moving, kept him on his feet, and got them both inside the house.

"She didn't do it," JK said. "Mrs. Barton. She didn't do it. He raped me. *Her.* Knocked me down. Her down. Tried to fight. Tried to run. Dogs brought her down. Bit my legs, my thighs. My wrists. Blood everywhere. She got out of town. Went to my sister's. I came back and he had gone. Not surprised. Went too far. Scared himself, the bastard. Kept asking if she needed a doctor. Saying he hadn't meant to." His throat felt scoured as if he'd been crying for hours. He wanted a shower desperately.

"Jesus, JK—"

JK's watch beeped. Noon. Time to take his pill, time to keep the memories at bay. He laughed without humor, without energy, and locked himself in the bathroom.

"JK?" Nick said, through the door.

"I'm good," JK said, stripping with haste, shoving the clothes aside. They were stained with Mrs. Barton's memories; the woman had gotten out of her marriage, out of the house, but she couldn't leave the memories behind, an addiction as dreadful as her nicotine, and now he had them stuck to him, prying into every cell of his body—

He turned the water to hot, pushed himself under it, hands bare; washing himself was a kaleidoscope nightmare of colliding memories. One moment, he scrubbed away Barton's blows, the next the ice broke beneath his feet, and JK breathed in gelid water, drowning; his heart locked up while Nick pressed kisses to the thin skin over his hip and belly, whispering words of endearment and the dog's jaw clamped down on his thigh, blood spraying.

When Nick popped the lock on the bathroom door, JK just blinked in exhaustion. "Put them on," Nick said, and handed him his nitrile gloves.

JK murmured, "Too late—"

"Put them on."

When JK only stayed leaning against the tiles, Nick did the job for him, slipping gloves on over his fingers and palms. "Pill," Nick said, fishing one out of the bottle.

JK swallowed it with shower water, tilting his head back, and letting the heat soak into his hair and face again.

"I'm freezing," he whispered.

"I think you're shocky," Nick said. "And very clean. Time to get out."

JK shook his head, but Nick dropped a towel around his shoulders, tied another around his waist.

"Why did he have to be such a bastard?" JK said, into the warmth of Nick's shoulder. "He always had a temper, but I never thought he'd sic the dogs on me—"

"Her," Nick said. "Her. Not you."

"Not me," JK repeated. He nodded. "I know. God, that poor—"

"Don't think about it," Nick said. "Right? That keeps you from making that memory yours? You don't want that memory. No one deserves that memory." Nick's blue eyes were insanely bright, glittering between their reddened edges.

Nick toweled JK's hair roughly, thoroughly, as if he could shake that memory loose with the water. JK went with it, and found himself dried, dressed, and settled on the couch before the surprise caught up with him. "You're pretty good at manhandling people," JK said. "In a nice way," he added hastily. He didn't want Nick to stop touching him.

"Once you ride herd on drunk frat brothers who want to walk on rooftops, you get good real fast," Nick said. "Hang on. I'm making you some coffee."

JK wrapped the couch blanket back around him and shivered. If Mrs. Barton had killed her husband, he'd have been hard-pressed to blame her for it. Even with Zeke taking the fall for her. But JK had gotten the whole horrible weekend in one compact package, and she hadn't killed him. Her sister hadn't been lying to the cops: Mrs. Barton had been with her, which meant she couldn't have killed him herself. The long, brittle conversations she'd had with her sister about the state of her bank account, and how she could afford the divorce argued she hadn't paid for his murder either.

His phone rang on the sofa arm. Jesse's name flashed on the screen. His big brother and his own sort of sixth sense: the one that told him JK had done something stupid, and someone needed to check that he was okay.

JK found himself crying. This time the tears were few and slow and all his. The phone rang twice more, before Nick got back with the coffee, heavily laced with sugar, and forced the mug into his hands.

His cell kept ringing, and he twitched.

Nick grimaced. "Jesse?" he asked.

"Master of timing, huh?" JK blinked back a few more tears, drank the coffee slowly. It helped. On the table, the phone cut off abruptly as Jesse gave up. JK let his breath out, a knot in his chest easing.

In the kitchen, Nick's phone rang.

"You have got to be kidding me," Nick said. "Does he have my number?"

"Hell," JK muttered, "he's probably got your tax returns."

"Fuck," Nick said. He went into the kitchen and grabbed up the phone. "Collier. Hi, Jesse. No, he's fine. He's in the shower."

JK winced. Nick was such a bad liar.

"Want me to have him call you? We're about to head out, so it'll be a little while. Yeah. Gonna catch a movie."

A *really* bad liar.

God, Detective Conroy was going to eat him alive: two alibis, neither of them true, each of them terribly delivered.

"... Zeke? Well, I can't do anything for him at the moment, so a movie... Yeah. No. Yeah, I hear you. I get it. I *get* it. I'll look after him."

Nick wandered back into the living room looking stressed, rubbing his brow. "Jesus. Not a trusting man, your brother."

"He's a cop," JK said. "What do you expect? And you're a crap liar."

"Hey, ouch," Nick said.

JK shook himself. "Sorry." He wasn't. The memories had settled as much as they were going to, as much as he would allow them to, and he found that the fear and nausea and betrayal had shifted toward something easier to express—anger.

Nick replied, "No, I get it."

"Do you?"

"Yeah. I asked far too much of you, and you're paying for it," Nick said. He dropped down onto the coffee table. "And for nothing. I got you mind-fucked and it's not going to do Zeke any good."

"Sorry I failed you—"

"That wasn't what I meant and you know it," Nick said. His hands clenched. JK eyed his fists, wondering morbidly if Nick would hit him when they fought, if JK goaded him, wondering if he could trust him.

Nick caught his gaze and deliberately relaxed his hands. "Well, it was a bad idea. *My* bad idea. But it's done now. The cops will have to find their man without help."

"Maybe they *have*," JK muttered, still angry.

"What?"

"Maybe they have," JK repeated.

"Fuck you," Nick snapped. "It's not Zeke. I don't know who it is, but it's not him. It can't be him." His voice cracked, tellingly, on *can't*. "Fuck you," he said again, but softer. Nick put his face in his hands.

JK felt his anger crack like Nick's voice had, baring the raw, scared center. He edged toward the coffee table. "Nick—"

Before he could apologize, a solid rat-a-tat sounded at the door. Nick jumped, looked spooked and said, "Tell me that's not your brother. He'll kick my ass from here to NYC if he sees you like this."

Like this? JK realized he was trembling from head to toe. Shocky still. He sipped at the cooled coffee, and said, "Not a cop knock."

"Then who the fuck—"

The front door opened, interrupting Nick, and JK realized how panicky Nick must have been on their return: he hadn't shot any of the bolts. Ashford poked his head in.

"You boys all right? Heard shouting. And your car door is open."

JK caught sight of Nick's wide eyes, and found himself on the emotional roller coaster again; he turned and hid his laughter in the couch. The colonel had to have been on Nick's *porch* to hear them arguing.

"We're fine," Nick said. "Just a little disagreement."

"Over Zeke Stuart?" Ashford said, coming in as if Nick's explanation had been invitation. "You don't think he killed Barton, do you?"

"No," Nick said. "I don't."

The colonel's dark eyes took in JK, bundled up on the couch, gloves bright blue against the plaid blanket. He came closer and dropped his voice as if he feared an eavesdropper.

He said, "Have you boys been investigating? Those two cops didn't seem like the kind to appreciate men stepping on their toes."

JK bit back more laughter. *Ashford* was the biggest snoop in the neighborhood.

"We're not, don't worry," Nick said.

Ashford studied him with a too-patient gaze, and said, "You're not too good a liar, are you, Collier?"

JK couldn't stop himself. He said, "See? I told you." Out of Ashford's line of sight, Nick made a rude gesture in response.

Ashford said, "I guess I'd be doing the same in your shoes. Some problems make you want to work on them yourself. Make sure they're dealt with in just the right way. Getting anywhere?"

"No," Nick admitted. "Amy didn't do it. Mrs. Barton didn't do it. And I know Zeke didn't do it."

"Stuart's got a hell of a temper on him," Ashford said, "but I admit, I didn't take him for the type to pick up a gun."

"He's not," Nick said.

Ashford scrutinized them as if they were his underlings in the army and he doubted they were up to snuff. "How do you know?" he asked.

"Know?" Nick asked.

"About Amy and Mrs. Barton. I agree with you, but I'm curious as to your reasoning." The colonel glanced over them, taking in JK's blanket again, and Nick's general twitchiness, and raised a brow. JK read that expression too easily. The colonel doubted either of them could reason their way out of a paper bag.

JK glared Nick to silence and said, "Amy's too small to manipulate dead weight like that, too soft to dig the hole in the dark. Mrs. Barton—the same, plus she was out of town. Neither of them have the kind of ready cash to hire a killer." He tried not to sound too invested, too certain.

"Sounds plausible," the colonel allowed. "Anything else? Anyone else?"

"It's not like the cops gave us a list of all their potential suspects," Nick said. "You got any ideas?"

"Wish I could help you out," Ashford said. "But I just don't have any ideas and that's the long and short of it. It's embarrassing. I try to keep an eye on things, and I missed this. I thought the man had left. Got into his friend's pickup truck—"

"And took his dogs," Nick and JK finished together.

"We all thought he left," Nick added. "Wish it were true."

"Do you know who started that story?" JK asked. "Someone must have said that. Someone *lied*. If we can track that back..."

Ashford fell silent. His face went remote as if searching through an extensive mental file marked *Barton*. After a time he said, "Lou Martinelli told me. That's how I heard."

"Mr. Martinelli?" Nick said. "Weird. He couldn't have seen Barton leaving. He's in bed by nine every night."

Ashford laughed. "You're a young man, Collier. When you're old, doesn't matter when you go to bed, you get up in the night to piss. Prostate." He laughed again, a dry rattle, and said, "Well, I got to get moving. Don't let your investigations get you so worked up you leave your car and house open. It's not safe. I shut your car doors by the way, but you make sure to lock them. You don't want the Sunitz boy getting in and accidentally putting it in gear."

"Yes, sir," Nick said. "Thank you."

Ashford stood there, looking at them, prolonging his stay for no reason that JK could tell. JK wondered if the old man felt lonely. He spent his widower's days always alone in a house for two. JK thought of Nick and how much he liked him already, and tried to imagine how much worse it would be to lose someone you'd loved for decades. To do everything you'd done in tandem, alone.

JK thought about suggesting that Nick bring Ashford a cup of coffee—the colonel's gaze kept dropping to JK's hands—when Ashford broke the silence again.

"You're staying here? With Collier? I thought the cops cleared Barton's house."

"Yeah," Nick said when JK hesitated, shooting him a questioning glance.

"That's a good thing to know," Ashford said. "I'll keep a close eye on Barton's house for you."

"It's not his house," JK said. "Barton doesn't own anything or anyone, anymore. And I can watch over the renovations just fine."

Nick cut in, "We're right next door. We can keep an eye on it."

"Didn't stop someone from killing Barton, did it? Or did you see something?"

Walked right into that one, JK thought. Nick's face tightened. JK wondered which of the hopelessly awful alibis Nick would try to sell this time, and intervened. "Really, I appreciate it, and I know my boss would," JK said. "But it's not necessary. I'll be over there during the days, and probably more than a few nights, working late."

"Of course," Ashford said. He stuck his hands in his pockets, turned all his attention to JK. "If you do find evidence that clears Stuart, you'll turn it over to the police, right?"

"If I find anything, yeah," JK said. He couldn't keep his mouth from dragging down. "I'm not real hopeful. I'm not a detective."

"Be careful," Ashford said. "You're young. Both of you. And young men are careless. Get themselves in trouble."

"Not me," Nick said. "Risk-averse after this year."

Nick escorted Ashford out, shut the door, shot the bolts, and slumped back against the frame. "Is it just me, or is it time for this damn day to be done already?"

Mrs. Barton's memory hiccupped in JK's mind, and he shoved it back with as much mental force as he could muster.

The memory faded obligingly. More obligingly than he would have expected. Maybe he was getting better at this. Improving.

Right now, that tiny improvement didn't feel like much. Despite the caffeine and sugar Nick had plied him with, he just wanted to crawl back into bed, and pretend he had never learned anything about Mrs. Barton, Amy, any of these people.

Jesse had been right: murder was an ugly business.

All he had to show for his efforts were painful new memories and the sense that he'd made Nick consider his oldest friend in the role of murderer.

But the house waited, and after what Mrs. Barton had gone through, JK wanted the house scrubbed clean.

"You're not going over there," Nick said, reading JK's glances toward the front door accurately.

"Work is work," JK said.

"You need company?"

JK didn't need to be a psychic to know that Nick wanted to stay behind. He didn't begrudge Nick that desire. "I might get · more done without. You're distracting." He forced a quick smile.

"I'll bring you lunch," Nick said.

JK hated to leave the cozy serenity of Nick's home, but if he could face Mrs. Barton's memories head on, he could face the lesser memories lingering in the house.

He could mark the kitchen essentials off his list, the flooring, the bedroom well underway, maybe it'd be a good day to tackle the bathrooms. Get that wiring dealt with, and since he'd been staying with Nick, it'd be no hardship for him to gut the rest. All his toiletries were at Nick's house anyway.

Trotting across the driveway, JK felt the colonel's eyes on him. He turned, waved, and the old man shook his head before retreating indoors. JK didn't know what the disapproval was for this time. For the house? For JK being in it? For the whole sorry state of the world...

He braced himself as he entered. The memories of the house blew past him, a buffet of unpleasant emotion, but failed to stick.

"Take that, Hannah," JK murmured. He was getting better. Stronger.

He hefted his toolkit and tackled the upstairs bath.

Fixing the sockets took him a couple minutes. After that, it was back to controlled destruction, tearing out the bathroom cabinets, tearing out the old tiled shower, and hard-water-caked fixtures.

"Getting rid of you," he said, as he hefted out another cigarette-burned section of countertop. "And good riddance."

Probably how everyone in the neighborhood had felt about Barton. Hell, anyone in the man's vicinity.

Curious Conroy's pool of suspects felt too small to JK. Not Zeke, definitely not Nick or Amy, not even Mrs. Barton, though JK wouldn't have blamed her for pulling the trigger. There had to be more than those four.

Who else, though?

JK wanted to help, but felt directionless. The police thought someone in the neighborhood had killed him. JK got that; he really did. JK figured if he'd been living here, he'd have wanted Barton dead also.

Running his mind through the neighbors didn't make him feel any better. Ashford said Mr. Martinelli had been the one to pass the story around, to make sure no one missed Barton. JK couldn't imagine either of the Martinellis good with guns. Shovels, yes. And Almira Sunitz went nowhere without her son; JK just couldn't see the woman committing murder with Devi in tow. Olivia? When would she have the time between her work, class, and working out? Inez? JK laughed. The Treanors? The neighbors who were on vacation?

Fleeing the scene of the crime?

JK briefly envisioned a conspiracy; someone declaring enough, straws drawn, duties meted out. You, lie about his disappearance to his wife, to everyone. You, bury the body deep. You... lure him out into the dark and shoot him, and watch out for the dogs...

Ridiculous. Like something out of a thriller movie. He got back to work, carting out the stained sink.

JK caught his hand between the edge of the door and the porcelain, and got slammed with two pains: the purely physical, and a memory of being shoved into the door.

Wincing, he shook the feelings off.

A lifetime of petty cruelties in this house. JK wondered if it would be like that in the next one Davis wanted to renovate. If there were an endless array of houses stretching before him, full of lurking misery. People held onto what made them happy, after all. Made sense that the homes like Nick's—restful, soothing—stayed in the families.

But renovating a whole series of miserable houses like this one... JK put that trouble off for later. He worked with the skills he had and that meant construction. Or maybe... the thought glimmered across his mind like a firefly streak, there and gone.

Maybe he could do more. If one cop wanted to work with him, there might be others.

In the interim, the bathroom tiles needed removal.

16

A little past midnight, JK jerked awake to Nick swearing under his breath. "... the fuck is it now?"

JK heard the knocking through a fog of exhaustion. Rhythmic. Loud. Even. Impatient. "*That*," he muttered, "is a cop knock."

Nick put his face in his pillow and groaned. "Not going to go away?"

"Not in their nature," JK said. He flailed for escape from the sheets. He rolled out of the bed, took the t-shirt Nick passed him to go with the PJ bottoms he'd borrowed earlier.

Nick, just that minute more awake, beat JK to the door, peered through the peephole and said, "Oh, you've got to be kidding me."

Nick opened the door, stepped aside and let Jesse in.

"What?" Jesse said, to Nick's glare. "If JK would return my calls, I wouldn't have to stop by. I just got off work."

"What do you want?" JK said, stepping out of the hallway shadows. His words slurred; he could hear the drag in his own voice. Exhaustion, an extra pill, and bad memories combined to slow him down.

Jesse's gaze lasered toward him.

"Christ, you couldn't leave it alone, could you?" He brushed past Nick, who bowed to inevitability and shut the door behind him. "The Barton woman called to complain you were harassing her. You're just lucky Gunnarson and I are friends."

"Does she actually have friends—" JK started.

Jesse grabbed JK's shoulder, pulled him closer to the light, tilted his head up.

"What are you doing?" Nick asked.

"Looking my little brother over for damage," Jesse said. "Do you mind?"

"Jesus! Fuck off," JK said, jerking away.

Nick muttered something under his breath and headed for the kitchen. Light flashed on, added brightness to the scene and let JK see the worry lines etched deeply into Jesse's face.

"I'm okay," JK said, relenting. "Yeah. I did something stupid. But I'm going to be fine."

"What'd you do?"

"I read Mrs. Barton," JK said. "On purpose."

"You're right. That was damned stupid," Jesse said. "That woman sounds like a mess."

"Come on now," Nick said, returning to the living room, three bottles in hand. He passed Jesse a beer, JK a water, and kept a beer for himself. "Chill out. Leave JK alone."

Jesse said, "You're going to tell me how to—"

"Hey," JK said. He dropped the water bottle, put his hands on Jesse's knotted forearms. Jesse didn't lose his temper for real all that often, but JK recognized the signs. "Jesse. Lay off, okay? Please?"

Jesse's mouth tightened; Nick carefully said nothing, only sipped at his beer, and eyed him sidelong.

"Jesse," JK repeated. "It's not Nick's fault. I wanted to help Zeke."

Jesse said, "Was it worth it? Did you find out who killed Barton?"

JK was getting really sick of that question. Of admitting he'd failed. "I would have called you if I had."

"Even if it meant getting caught bare-handed, so to speak?"

"Jesse, what the fuck—"

"We need to talk about Zeke," Jesse said to Nick. He set the beer, unopened, down on the arm of the couch.

Nick said, "I'm getting sick of saying it. He didn't do it."

"Well, Gunnarson's beginning to believe he didn't do it *alone*." Jesse studied JK. "No smartass response to that?"

JK shivered.

"They're looking at me," Nick said. "Aren't they?"

"Your motive is strong and your story weak. And Zeke is your friend," Jesse said.

Nick turned his beer around and around in his hands, picking at the label. "My *story*?" he said.

Jesse leaned on the back of the sofa, and said, "Yeah. They don't like that you didn't report hearing gunfire or the dogs barking or the grave-digging. They don't like that you told them Zeke was with you when Amy told them Zeke was with her. It stinks of cover-up. They don't like Zeke being *somewhere* on the scene and not reporting gunfire either—"

Nick set down his beer with a thump on the bookshelf nearest him. "*No one* reported gunfire—"

"You live right next door. They found your fingerprints in Barton's house, on a dog collar in his stuff that they got back from the DAV, and since you're so close, they think it'd have been easy for some nosy neighbor to have missed you in his yard. In his house. Hell, for all I know they think you vaulted the fence to lure Barton out into the yard while Zeke did the dirty work."

"And here I thought cops were supposed to lack imagination," Nick said.

Jesse lunged off the sofa, got into Nick's face, flung a hand out to ward JK off when Nick quailed. "Quit fucking around, Collier. It's not fucking funny. Did you help Stuart kill Barton?" he asked.

"No," Nick said. "God. No." His hands grasped air for a second before pushing gingerly at Jesse's shoulders. "Really. Not a killer. You can back off now."

Jesse did, easily, and JK had the confusing sensation that maybe Jesse's anger had been for show.

He said, "That's what JK said. Said you're not the violent type."

Nick rolled his shoulders, wincing as he shook off the impact with the wall. "And what, you thought you'd test me? See if I threw a punch? At my lover's brother?"

"Maybe it wasn't the best idea," Jesse said, looking tired.

"You think?" JK said. His heartbeat rabbited in his chest, driving the fog of exhaustion away. "Hannah's going to kick your ass when I tell her."

"You want to start that game? What do you think she'd say about you playing detective until your brain broke? Don't you tell me you didn't have another episode. You think she'd get on me for yelling at the person who enabled that?" Jesse's growl rumbled in the room.

"Okay," JK said. "Okay. Truce. But just for the record, I didn't have another episode."

"Really?" Jesse looked to Nick for confirmation. Nick obliged by nodding.

"Really," JK said. "It wasn't fun but I didn't lose myself completely."

Silence settled on the room. Nick looked between the two of them, then reclaimed his beer and drank steadily. Jesse's black scowl slowly eased enough for JK to yawn, and say, "So let me break this down for Nick's sake. Despite your bad cop routine, you rushed over here after your shift to warn him that Zeke's probably going to have company in the hot seat."

Nick raised his brows, and JK nodded at him. Yes, his brother was that guy.

"Do you have a lawyer?" Jesse asked, brushing everything under the rug. "Or explanations? 'Cause I have to say Gunnarson is getting pretty hacked off at not solving this bastard. She likes her cases cleared and fast."

"Barton liked to take potshots at my house with an old .22 and if I went out to complain, he sicced his dogs on me. I stopped going out. I touched the damn dog collar once when the dog lunged at me. Lourdes Constanza's my lawyer."

Jesse nodded. "Don't say anything without her. And don't tell them I gave you the heads-up. I like my job. And for all that is holy, do not ask, coax, or—"

"Hey," JK objected, and Jesse bulled onward without hesitation.

"—let JK touch anyone or anything else related to murder. Because Gunnarson also does not like the fact that you two couldn't get your statements straight about why you two, along with their prime suspect, were digging up the yard in the first place."

"C'mon, Jesse, how many times have you told me that people rarely agree in their accounts? It doesn't mean anything."

"When it's a small difference, it doesn't mean anything. But you said you were helping install a water feature and you—" Jesse paused to point at JK, then continued, "—said you were digging a hole for a tree."

"What did Zeke say we were doing?" JK asked.

"Well, JK, it's funny you should ask. After several hours of questioning, Zeke said that he was there because you had had some kind of psychic vision about there being a body buried in the yard," Jesse said. "Of course no one believes that."

JK shuddered, horrified and furious that Zeke had been so loose-lipped. A heartbeat later, JK realized that Jesse's aim had been distraction from the topic at hand. To scare JK into retreat. For his own good.

"Jesse, I'm not just going to stand by and do nothing if I can help," JK said. "You've drummed it into my head often enough. Good people should always try to help."

"Other good people," Jesse said. "You've got enough to deal with."

Nick blew out his breath, ran a hand through his rumpled hair. He said, "Jesse, I appreciate the warning. No matter how you delivered it. But it's late. And your wife's probably expecting you home, right?"

"Yeah," Jesse admitted.

"Then go there," JK said, when Nick hesitated on the brink of kicking Jesse out of his house. "Seriously, bro. Don't make her worry. I'm fine. We're fine. Gunnarson and Conroy are solid, right? They won't railroad anyone?"

"They're ambitious. Hot shots," Jesse said. "But honest as far as I know. Even better, they're not gossips. Zeke's comment about the neighborhood psychic won't get around."

"You hope," JK said. "They told you; they put it on Zeke's statement, right?"

"Yeah." Jesse sounded exhausted again, all his worry sapping his anger, his energy. He picked up his beer bottle, still unopened, and passed it back to Nick; he said, "Hold that for another time, huh? JK, stay safe."

Once he had left, and Nick had relocked the doors, they stood at loose ends in the living room, shocked awake and exhausted at the same time. Nick raked his hair out of his face again with nervous fingers and said, "Don't take this the wrong way, but your brother's an asshole."

JK said, "He means well."

"Yeah. Except now I'm expecting the cops to come break down my door and arrest me at any moment. Not exactly conducive to sleep."

"Couch?" JK suggested, drifting toward it, slumping over the familiar cushions. Nick joined him, shifted until they were shoulder to shoulder, and tilted his head back, closing his eyes.

"Nick," JK said, watched those dark lashes flutter open again.

"Hmm?" he said.

"What can I do? If it's not Amy or Mrs. Barton or... or Zeke. How can I prove it's someone else? I can't touch everyone Barton ever fought with."

Nick took his hand, rubbing at the seam of JK's glove, and said, "Maybe there's nothing you can do."

"It just..." JK shifted uncomfortably. "It seemed like it had purpose, you know? Everything made sense. The whole fucking thing. Falling through the ice, the basement, this nightmare ability that I can't get rid of. I met you and found Barton's body, and you needed answers. It finally made sense."

Nick tugged JK down, let his weight sag against his shoulder. He kissed his temple, sighed out into his hair. "Purpose or sheer random chance, I'm glad you're here."

Despite his words, Nick fell asleep relatively quickly, but JK awake and alarmed, couldn't find rest, no matter how leaden his body felt. He didn't like Zeke, but he didn't want him to be a killer.

But maybe it wouldn't come to that. Gunnarson and Conroy didn't have any actual evidence against Zeke. Loads of motive. Opportunity. Ability. But actual physical evidence?

Problem was, JK thought, looking at Nick's t-shirt-covered chest, at the university logo on it, evidence might not matter in the long run. Sure, Zeke's lawyer might get him freed, might point out the weakness of a case based on circumstances, might run circles around a prosecutor if it went to trial: Barton made enemies like he breathed. But would a clever lawyer be enough?

Zeke taught kids as well as college girls—would his dojo fold if he got a bad reputation? Would Nick's career last? A professor implicated in a cover-up?

JK didn't think Nick had even considered that. Nick believed in guilty and innocent. Black and white. But the world was never that clear-cut. Nick worried about Zeke, about himself, his head full of the splashy fears—corrupt cops, tainted evidence, a jury swayed by emotion instead of facts—but he hadn't gotten to the real meat yet. The danger to their reputations. If Nick's shifting alibi got out, went viral, would the college keep him on? A gay professor who lied to defend an accused murderer...

"Ouch," Nick muttered, and JK realized he had pulled Nick tighter against him, bending his arm a way it didn't want to go.

Nick blinked blurry eyes at him and said, "Still awake?"

"Yeah," JK said.

"Want me to make you coffee?"

JK shrugged. "No. I think I'm going to work."

"In the house? It's 3 a.m."

"So I won't use power tools," JK said. He shifted out from beneath Nick's weight, stretched. His back protested. So did Nick, reaching out to catch JK's arm.

"Really," JK said. "I need to do something. I can't just sit here and stress. It's making me nuts. Go back to bed. I'm going to dust-mop the floor, prep it for staining."

"All right," Nick said. He let JK go, and yawned. "Take the house keys. You know where they are."

❀

The morning crept up on him, changing the lamplight in the living room from incandescent to something softer, and more golden. It brought out unexpected highlights in the stripped, sanded wood, and JK caught his breath, really seeing the possibilities for the first time. The renovated house wouldn't only be clean and neat; it could be gorgeous.

Car doors closing outside serially, one, two heavy thumps, made JK's heart leap in his chest. Nothing good came of such early arrivals here. JK had internalized the rhythms of this neighborhood, and the only doors opening at 6 a.m. should be neighbors staggering through their front doors to pick up their newspapers, or Olivia going for her early morning run—not cars pulling up.

He opened the front door and startled Detective Conroy into taking a precipitous step back. She teetered on the edge of the porch, and JK caught her automatically.

Conroy regained her balance and yanked her arm out of his hand, her lips thin. "Please don't touch me," she said.

"Next time I'll let you fall, then?" he asked.

"I didn't come here to argue," she said.

"Then why..."

"To let you know this was not my idea." Conroy eased past him, heading into the house; JK turned to keep watching her. She touched things as she went, tapping the edge of the wall with her fingernails, running her hands over the new paint,

picking up a piece of broken tile with a crow's curious acquis-
itiveness. Having a detective in the house felt a bit like having
a wild animal trapped in the same room as you; you needed to
keep an eye on it.

"I know you and I, we have a rapport. A mutual thing happening. Trust. But Eva... she's impatient and she's sick of thinking about Barton. She wants the case closed."

He said, "She has Zeke—"

"And a lawyer who's chewing our asses." Conroy tilted her
head, then looked up at him. "This is what you need to know,
and remember, I argued against it. Eva's arresting Nick Collier
on charges of conspiracy to commit murder, of accessory after
the fact, of obstruction, anything she thinks will stick."

JK went cold. He headed for the open door, and Conroy
stepped before him, blocking him, her hand sliding over her
weapon. "Don't be stupid, JK. You can't stop the arrest."

He could see her now, Gunnarson waiting on Nick's front
lawn, her pale hair a blaze in the morning sunlight. It made him
think of torches and mobs. Behind her, two uniformed cops
stood, ready to act.

"The thing is," Conroy said, "I don't think Eva believes he's
really involved. But she's waiting to see what you do."

"What *I* do?" JK lost his voice on the last word, went breathy.

"It's about the gun, JK. We need the gun. Now, I know that
Nick's fingerprints aren't going to be on it. He's a shit liar, but he'd
be even worse if he were involved in the murder. And well... you've
been up-close and personal with him. You'd know, wouldn't you?"

She waited, waited long enough that he knew she wasn't
going to say a thing more until he acknowledged the question.
"Yes," JK gritted out. "I'd know."

"So we want the gun. You find it. Then you call us." At his
intake of breath, Conroy said, "If that's too hard, you could
come to the station. Visit Zeke. Find out what he did with it?"
She said it like it was a reasonable request.

"How am I supposed to do that?"

"You found the body."

"Conroy, finding that body didn't take skill. It took ten minutes with a shovel. Anyone would have found it."

"Right… While planting trees," she said, with a wry smile.

He couldn't return the smile even if he'd wanted to. Nick had stepped out of the house, still in his sleepwear, and Gunnarson closed in on him. Nick looked up, saw JK standing on his porch, and even at this distance, JK saw or imagined the alarm in those beautiful eyes.

"I can't solve this for you," he said. "I've tried. Please."

"JK," she said. Conroy reached out and took his gloved hands carefully between her small, strong ones. She squeezed gently. "Try harder."

17

JK followed Conroy out of the Barton house, hot on her heels, watching the tension rise in her back at his closeness. He felt meanly glad of it. She wasn't playing by the rules. She blamed Gunnarson for everything, but he thought they were playing that old classic—bad cop/good cop. Both of them working in lockstep.

One of the uniforms had escorted Nick into the house. Ice Queen Gunnarson's implacable shell had cracked enough that she betrayed her impatience. She tapped her foot on the sidewalk, scowling as she noticed the front doors around the block cracking open.

Mrs. Martinelli came out, dawdling as JK had never seen her dawdle before, and picked up her paper, squinting at them the whole time.

"How long does it take for a grown man to dress himself?" Gunnarson muttered to Conroy as she and JK approached. Gunnarson eyed JK warily and said, "You, stay on the curb."

"This is ridiculous," JK said, keeping his voice steady, all too aware of the guns on the scene.

Ashford stood on his porch, deep in the shadows, his expression unreadable, but judging by his tightly crossed arms, he didn't like what he saw. JK nearly called out to him, but really, what could Ashford do?

Nick stepped out of the house, wearing a suit but stubble dotted his chin and throat. Obviously, the uniformed officer dogging his heels hadn't given him the time to shave. Nick's face looked set in miserable but determined lines.

Testing the waters, Nick moved toward his car, and Gunnarson said, "Nope. You ride with us. You know we'll get you there."

Nick let out a slow breath, a heartbeat of enforced calm, and said, "Of course." He shot JK a desperate look. "JK, Lourdes's number is on my desk. Would you call her? Her office opens at 9:00."

"Yeah," JK said. "I will."

He watched Nick duck his head, slip into the back of the sedan, and moved forward automatically.

Gunnarson turned on her heel, and slipped into the passenger seat as neatly as a knife sheathing itself. She smiled at him, and Conroy raised her hand in an unmistakable gesture. Thumb and pinky extended, fingers tucked, hand up by her ear. *Call me.* A cheery and jaunty gesture that expected him to do the impossible.

Find the gun.

Solve the case for them.

Soon.

❈

After the unmarked car and the squad car had driven away, JK stood watching the road like they might turn around, come back, say *ha, just a joke, we got you,* but he knew it wouldn't happen.

He needed time and space to think this through, but just like the day he moved in, he had an audience, and no time to spare.

Amy came barreling down the road at him, lurching with panic, and staggered to an awkward halt. JK reached out to steady her, but she jerked away, away from his touch. "Don't. I saw the police. Why did they take Nick?" she asked.

"Well, come inside, for God's sake," JK said, looking at the neighbors he could see. Both Mrs. Martinelli and Ashford looked like they might join them at any moment.

Amy nodded, but she wouldn't come any further than the front entryway of Nick's house. "Tell me."

"They think he and Zeke were working together," JK said, then ran out of steam. He felt as panicked as she did. Murder charges were one thing; he had faith in Nick's lawyer, in the legal system that Nick would be all right if charged outright with murder. Nick hadn't done it.

But conspiracy charges were a sneaky sort of thing; hard to disprove a lack of something. Especially, JK thought with a sick little jolt, when this wouldn't be a conspiracy fueled by money, but friendship and love. Old friends, new loves, one murder, two of them trying to cover up for their friend... It seemed all too easy to believe.

"What are we going to do?" she asked. Amy seemed small suddenly, hunched into herself. She reminded him terribly of Mrs. Barton, her birth mother, beaten down and bitter.

"First, I'm going to call Nick's lawyer."

"Isn't there anything else we can do?" Amy asked. "I feel like I should be storming a castle or something, alerting the media—"

"Oh God, don't do that," JK said. "Their reputations."

"I'm not stupid," she said. "I know that. It was just an example." She scrubbed tears out of her eyes, sniffed wetly. "I just don't have anyone to call for help, you know? I always go to Zeke, and Nick, but—"

"They're not here," JK finished. Certainty settled in his stomach like lead shot. He didn't think he could do what Conroy expected of him, but he had to give it a try.

Amy said, "Your brother's a cop. Can't you call him?"

"I will. If the lawyer doesn't solve the problem." At her betrayed gaze, he said, "What do you think he can do? Ask his colleagues to free them just because his baby brother says Nick's a nice, honest guy who wouldn't cover up for Zeke, and oh, by the way, Zeke's not a killer either."

"Do you really think that? About Zeke?"

JK stared at her, flat-footed. He'd expected anger, a fight. Instead she just repeated herself. "Zeke. Do you think he's innocent?" She jerked her chin upward.

"I... want to," he said.

"Yeah. Me too." Amy's chin dropped. She hugged herself tightly, then scrubbed a flight of tears from her face. "I want to say he couldn't have done it. But... the gun Zeke gave me is gone. And he really hated Barton. I mean, really. Like the kind of hatred that made you sick to the stomach. That's the kind of hate that makes you crazy. I told the cops he was with me, but..."

"He was with Nick," JK said.

"Was he? For sure?" she asked.

JK shrugged. "Nick might have been asleep. Not a reliable witness."

Amy's mouth pulled tight. Then she sniffed wetly again, and said, "I'm so scared." The words came out flat like she'd run out of energy. "Can your brother keep an eye on Zeke and Nick? Make sure they're okay?"

"Yeah, oh definitely," JK said, relieved to be asked something so doable. Jesse would bitch and moan, but he would keep JK up to date on the case. Only... JK couldn't call his brother yet.

He wanted to. Wanted to dump the whole mess in Jesse's lap, no matter how much it would make him feel like a boy running to his brother, tattling on bullies. But if JK called Jesse, if he told him what Gunnarson and Conroy expected him to do, what would happen? Jesse couldn't intervene in the case without solid evidence that Conroy was doing something actively illegal. Calling Jesse would only result in him trying to keep JK from clue-hunting, gloves off. And JK couldn't afford to be stopped.

If he admitted it to himself, he didn't *want* to be stopped. He wanted to wrangle his gift into being useful if it killed him. JK just needed to figure how to approach the problem.

The body was gone, his suspects were cleared, the gun hidden or disposed of... somewhere.

There had to be something he could do.

He showed Amy back out, watched her head slowly back toward her house, dragging her feet.

Made sense, JK thought grimly. Her urgency had transmitted itself to him, making his hands shake, his breath go short in his chest. He turned, inexorably, toward the Bartons' house.

The damned house had been working against him ever

since he first set foot in it. Now, the house needed to help him save Nick. Save Zeke. Expose the murderer.

JK stepped off Nick's porch steps with the sense that he was stepping off a cliff.

❀

First things first. The yard. Though he'd told Nick that the discovery of Barton's body, and the ensuing crime scene investigation would have cleared all traces of past events from the yard, a lot of it had been wishful thinking.

Find the gun?

How about starting with seeing if he could "see" the killer. If Zeke had murdered Barton, if JK could get that straight for once and for all, maybe things weren't so bad. If Zeke had killed Barton, and Nick and Amy were dragged into his mess, he'd confess to spare them. Wouldn't he?

People did all sorts of regrettable things in the name of self-preservation.

The yard had started out a wreck, and had only worsened after the excavations made by JK and the crime scene techs. The soil had been disturbed so often, he wasn't sure that he hadn't been right after all, telling Nick there was nothing left to find.

Gingerly, he wandered into the yard, near the grave site, and knelt. He took off his gloves; he didn't want to go fingers first into the dirt, but taking off the gloves served double duty—exposing his hands seemed to expose the nerves that were so sensitive to atmosphere.

Sound hit JK first, a montage of noise sweeping in on him like a summer storm.

The dogs: barking, snarling, fighting, growling, yelping.

The sound of a shovel slicing rhythmically into the dirt.

A mix of voices: *"Hope to God Conroy is right—that the home owner's not part of this. He's fucking big."*

"Fucking spooky."

"Scared she'll hate you."

"Should call the cops."

"Leave well enough alone."

"You killed my dogs!"

JK jolted out of his near trance, then tried to dive back in, tried to catch that outraged exclamation that had been Barton's last words.

It was like trying to catch the wind.

He retrieved the grating memory of shovels, digging bodies into the ground, digging bodies out of the ground, *digging digging digging.*

Cigarette butts made red contrails across his vision.

A slammed door like a shock wave. Shouting. Barking.

Gunshots. Distant percussion. He spun, trying to find the killer...

Nothing but a sickness in his gut, *Barton's rage turning to shock, to pain, to—*

JK gasped for air, bent around the phantom bullet, trying not to clutch at his shirt, half afraid he'd find blood. If he touched, he thought he might. His gloves were off, and an episode lurked. Another go 'round with someone else's death.

He forced himself to straighten. He was JK, uninjured—not Barton, shot and bleeding out.

Maybe JK could find where the killer had stood. It would have to be a space within the fence. The killer would have to have come in through the gate, gone out through the house— common sense. Barton would never have let him come in. Assume he buried Barton pretty much where he fell...

JK stood on a likely spot, a rare space where the soil wasn't milled under or covered over. A few tufty tough strands of grass slowly sprang back to life between his feet. He closed his eyes.

Digging. Barking.

Nothing more.

He knelt, as slowly as an old man, and let his hand come to rest on the grass. For a moment, the unfamiliar, amazing tickle of grass against his palm and between his fingers took his breath away, the delicate sharp smoothness of it. Then he felt swept back to his feet, braced, the gun in his hands, the dogs lunging across the yard at him.

Patience.

Gunfire.

Confidence.

Barton rushing out into the yard, half-blind in the dark, slow to understand, then lunging. "Just like his dogs. Dangerous. Put him down. Put them all down."

Gunfire.

JK shuddered. Fell back on his ass, his hand ripping from the ground. He had connected with the killer, but... the touch had been too brief. It gave him nothing to grab hold of, nothing to identify him by. Only that confidence. No real emotion had been associated with the murder.

Maybe they should revisit the hit man idea.

Or maybe the dirt's memory had degraded, corrupted by all that had come after.

"That's that then," he murmured.

Another failure. He couldn't find the gun from that memory—it had never hit the ground. Couldn't even ID the killer. A man. A patient man. A calm man.

JK got to his feet, shook dirt from his hand, tucked himself back into gloves. He kicked at the ground in frustration. He knew nothing more than he could have figured on his own. It took a cool head to shoot two dogs charging through the darkness.

A cool, collected killer.

So... why would Mr. Calm and Collected bury the bodies so shallowly? That confused JK. If he hadn't found Barton with his abilities, he would have found him in purely ordinary ways when it came time to landscape the yard.

Had the sun been coming up? The grave taking longer to dig than they'd assumed? Because someone would have seen? At the barest edge of dawn, Olivia started her run, moving directly through the cul-de-sac. Would she have seen the killer through the open gate if she'd known to look?

Had the burial been a temporary measure? A quick cover-up that he meant to come back to and never got the chance to? It could have been a neighbor who knew that Mrs. Barton had left town, who realized that Ashford spent his nights watchful and restless; could it have been Lou Martinelli? He had a shovel, knew how to dig effectively. The neighbor that had started the story about Barton leaving. Retired, Ashford had said about him. Retired from what?

Martinelli had played coy when JK asked. And he admitted to using a shovel in anger against the dogs before.

Martinelli with a shovel would be unnoticeable to the neighbors. Even to Ashford.

But why would he kill Barton?

No reason at all that JK could see.

JK considered that maybe Martinelli was just so offended about Barton's lawn that he had to kill him... then groaned. He was going insane, and he was no closer to finding the gun than before.

Zeke had given his gun to Amy long before the murder, so she said, taking it from Nick's frightened hands—but then Amy said she'd lost it. Really lost it? Or covering for the boyfriend who took it back.

Where would Zeke have gotten rid of the gun?

Zeke showed reasonable smarts; he would have ditched the gun in one of the city's dumpsters. The moment in the backyard where JK had touched the killer's consciousness—that cool blankness—had done what all of Nick's protests hadn't. JK couldn't imagine hot-tempered Zeke reaching that point of murderous Zen.

The gun just seemed impossible to find. But it wasn't the only distinctive tool that had been out here. The shovel.

It hadn't been Barton's. The killer had dragged the shovel through the house—JK recalled the scraping sound—and a shovel wasn't like a gun. Everyone owned one. The killer hadn't used it to do anything but bury Barton. There'd be no blood on it, no reason to get rid of it, no evidence for the cops to find. For JK...

The shovel would remember.

That'd be enough for Conroy, surely.

He turned and headed into the house.

The Bartons hadn't been sociable, not likely to invite people in. And after he shot and buried Barton, the killer had come through the house with the shovel, dragging it alongside him. If JK could sense the trace of someone in the house who had no reason to be there, could link them with the shovel, then that would be a start. Then he could knock on a door, ask to borrow their shovel... perfectly normal. Then he'd know.

Then he could bargain with the police, get Curious Conroy on his side, and thaw the Ice Queen's frosty suspicions.

Because so far, the only thing he had to offer wouldn't make either of them happy at all—his new conviction that they had the wrong guy.

Inside, JK looked at his sanded, scraped, smoothed floor and grimaced. The shovel had dragged across the carpet in here, pulling up the pile after it. He remembered that. Remembered remembering it. The carpet was gone, but maybe he could...

JK put a bare hand on the floor board, wincing. He expected the worst. He got only a reflection of his own anxiety, his worries, his stress, then and now, laid over the nearly lost scuttle of scrabbling dog paws, barking... The killer dragging the shovel, that one-time event, had been purged.

"Oh, good job, JK," he muttered.

He crept toward the wall, crawl-creeping on two knees and a gloved hand, sweeping his bare hand before him like a metal detector.

An explosion of glass, a thrown bottle, shouting... a woman screaming.

JK cringed, expecting the blow, expecting the dogs, to be bitten and savaged and shoved to the floor, raped while the dogs snapped at her flailing limbs...

He gagged, shuddered, and flailed back to consciousness. He jerked back with a shout—someone stood in the open doorway, watching him. His heartbeat pounded in his ears; he scrambled for his footing, failed.

"What in God's name are you doing, Lassiter?" Ashford said. "Are you ill?"

"No," JK said, and the roughness in his voice made him realize he was one step from tears again. He collapsed back to a slump, hiding his face in his upraised knees.

"You know, of all the places for you to stop wearing your gloves, this is the last one I'd expect."

JK gaped, yanked his head up to stare at Ashford—what did he know?—and the old man said, "Splinters, Lassiter. Splinters. Or is that how you check if your sanding job is good?"

"I..." JK fumbled for words, for his glove. He pulled it on in awkward silence, horribly aware of Ashford watching him.

"Oh hell," Ashford said. "You'd better come with me and tell me what's got you so screwy. Though I can guess. Saw the police haul Collier back in for questioning."

"Not just questioning. They *arrested* him," JK blurted out. He couldn't imagine how Ashford had misinterpreted the scene, but the shock on the old man's face made it clear he had.

Ashford turned grey-tinged. "For what? They arrested Stuart for Barton's murder. What the hell do they want with Collier?"

"Conspiracy charges," JK said.

"Damn it all," Ashford said. He sounded as savage as JK felt. "Come on, I'll make you some coffee and you can fill me in."

JK rose, wobbly on his feet, but he teetered after the old man with a growing sense of relief. Ashford knew the ins and outs of the neighborhood. He'd help.

18

"Come in," Ashford said again as JK hovered just outside. "I've got a pot on if you think you can handle an old soldier's brew." He held his door open and gestured impatiently.

Nothing for it but to follow him. Ashford's house lived up to most of JK's expectations, being not only neat and clean, but obviously organized. It lacked the bachelor feel JK had thought he might find from a widower living on his own for nearly a year.

Ashford watched JK looking around, looking at the warm rosy color on the wall, the cream-colored lampshades, and the delicately floral furniture. "Sofia died last winter," Ashford said. "It's pure sentiment, I suppose, but I've kept the house the way she left it."

"I'm sorry," JK said.

"I had forty years with her, should have had more. She was a patient woman. Never got tired of my stories."

He headed into the kitchen, brought JK back a china cup with a rose on the side. Ashford drank out of a metal camping cup, and JK winced at the idea of heat transfer to his mouth.

"Sit, sit," Ashford said.

JK, careful not to spill, obeyed. He sipped at the coffee, kept his face straight with an effort. It was hot enough to qualify as boiling and gritty with grounds. It made him grateful for his gloves, even if they dwarfed the china cup and made it hard to hold.

"All right, enough palaver. Tell me what the hell is going on. You said they arrested Collier? Really arrested him or just took him in for questioning?"

"I don't know—" JK let out an unsteady breath. He didn't know how far Gunnarson and Conroy's act went. Would they really charge Nick in an attempt to make JK heel? Or was the act for JK's benefit. Maybe Gunnarson wasn't playing. Maybe she really thought Nick and Zeke were her murderers.

"Either way, that's not good," Ashford said. He sucked his lips in, which turned his face into a death's head, teeth tight against his thin skin.

"I don't know what to do. I mean, call the lawyer, great. But there has to be *something*. Some way I can prove his innocence." Some way that didn't depend on his abilities, or finding a weapon that could be anywhere.

Ashford studied him, shoved the sugar dispenser his way, pushing it across the narrow coffee table. "Add that to your coffee. Steady yourself, boy. Getting emotional on the eve of battle is always a bad idea."

"This isn't a battlefield. I'm not a soldier," JK said. "This is my life. Nick's life. And I want to fix it. I'm going to fix it." He tightened his hands around the mug, watched the surface of the coffee tremble.

Ashford sighed, his shoulders rounding forward. He scowled into the tin coffee cup. "You ever think they might be right? Not Collier—" He held up a hand, forestalling JK's instant protest. "But Stuart? People can do terrible things in the name of protection."

JK shook his head. "Zeke's not the one."

"You sound awfully certain. Collier's loyalty wearing off on you? Come on, Lassiter. Your brother's a cop. He arrest the wrong man often?"

"Hardly ever," JK said, refused to let Ashford put doubt back into his mind. He knew what he'd felt in the yard. "You changed your mind awfully fast. I thought you said Zeke wasn't the type. He's still the same man he was yesterday."

Ashford let out a crack of unamused laughter. "Maybe I'd rather see Stuart in jail than Collier. Stuart can handle himself. Collier—"

"Neither of them should be in jail," JK snapped, and set down his cup, but his gloves caught the edge and tipped it over. He hadn't drunk more than a sip or two, so the mess spread fast.

"Shit," he swore. "I'm sorry." He grabbed at the picture on the table, got it out of the way. "God, I'm really sorry."

"It's just coffee," Ashford said. He rose as JK slid to his knees, blocking the flow with his gloves. "Relax. I'll get a rag."

He left JK and JK tried to calm down. He didn't know where this fear came from. Spilling his coffee was just an annoying accident, a tiny flaw in an already bad day, and yet, his heart pounded.

The recognition of his feelings woke another spurt of anxiety and something that felt terribly like surprise.

Scared?

Of an old man?

Not just an old man.

A soldier.

The head of the neighborhood, the one everyone trusted.

The one who stayed up late at nights.

Who better to spread the word that Barton had left, who more *believable* than Ashford?

Ashford, the soldier. A man trained to shoot. An *old* soldier, who might be too frail to remove the bodies or bury them deep.

JK jerked to his feet, knocked the picture off the couch where he'd put it for safe-keeping, fumbled it again, the frame catching between wet gloved fingers. The photograph within— Ashford and his wife—made his fear seem foolish. Ashford and his wife looked so happy, and this house felt... kind, right down to the welcoming sofa. The love in Ashford's face as he looked at his dying wife made JK sigh. No love gone bad here.

Ashford was a kind man. Compassionate. Bossy. Caretaking. A killer?

He wished he could dismiss that thought. He couldn't.

Ashford tossed a rag in JK's direction, making him jump. JK knelt to mop up the last remnants, aware of Ashford watching him.

He said, "There, you see. Nothing that can't be fixed. Your gloves are wet. I imagine you'll be keeping them on, though."

"Thanks for the coffee, sorry I spilled it," JK said. "I need to get going, anyway. Got to call Nick's lawyer." He wanted out of this nice room in this nice house. Out from under Ashford's too-steely gaze.

A gaze like a gun sight.

He'd been blind. Worse. He'd been stupid. Too damned trusting. He'd walked right into the lion's den.

"Who's Collier's lawyer? Not the same woman who couldn't get a good sentence on those hooligans who beat him up?"

"I guess," JK swallowed. "Nick likes her. I need to call her. Now."

"I've met a few lawyers." Ashford said. "I could look one up."

"You don't need to. Thanks," JK tacked on. Politeness trapped him. He wanted desperately to leave, to get some space to think.

Hard to believe Ashford could be the killer, when JK saw those thickened knuckles, the age-whittled build. Then JK glanced up again and met his eyes.

Not so hard to believe.

JK swallowed. Steadied himself. Shoved the panic down. No way Ashford could know what JK was thinking. It gave him an opportunity he couldn't pass up.

"Actually," JK said. "I *would* like those names. Options are always good."

"Right." Ashford studied him a long moment, then said, "It'll take me a minute. Have a seat."

JK settled, hands in his lap, and waited for Ashford to disappear into the back of the house. Then he sprang to his feet and started searching. End table. Ashford spent all his time watching; wouldn't an old soldier keep his weapon close?

The drawer didn't squeak... kept in perfect condition, it eased open into his wet gloved hands; JK grimaced. He left wet prints where he touched, an obvious sign of his snooping. But he didn't find a gun. The only things inside the drawer were more pictures of Sofia, kept close, but kept out of sight—too painful?—and a bank calendar opened ahead to November, the eighteenth circled in red.

He heard Ashford in the back, the metal clank of filing cabinets being opened. How long would it take him to find a number? JK held his breath, heard the rumble of another cabinet being opened, and hot-footed it through the kitchen to the garage door.

Ashford's car blocked most of the garage from view, but JK's eyes were drawn inexorably to the shovel, hung neatly with the rest of the yard tools. Even from here, it vibrated with the echoes of frantic digging. He sidled around the hood of the car, caught a glimpse of his reflection in its glossy black surface; he looked determined but blurred, a figure in a dream. Or nightmare.

He reached for the shovel handle, and heard the faintest of sighs. It took JK far too long to realize that it wasn't an echo of long-ago effort, but coming from behind him. "Don't touch that," Ashford said. "Come back inside."

There, JK thought, *there was the gun.*

He'd been looking for it; he hadn't wanted to find it this way—not pointed directly at him. He'd seen bigger weapons, more overtly menacing ones, but it still made his blood turn to winter slush, his brain go blank and small.

"Come inside," Ashford said.

The garage door opener couldn't be reached from JK's side of the garage; he couldn't flee outward. JK surreptitiously tugged the sedan's door handle. Locked.

"I'm losing patience. Come on. We need to talk."

JK roused his legs to motion, slipped around the car, and Ashford pulled back as he approached, staying out of JK's reach. Back in the living room, Ashford gestured JK to the sofa. JK sat, his knees making the descent faster than he'd meant. He clutched at the sofa arm, and said, "What are you doing?"

Ashford shook his head, once. He said, "I don't know, Lassiter, and that's the long and short of it. I've seen some peculiar things on a battlefield, see men show strange sides of themselves."

JK gaped, trying to follow. He felt slow and stupid beneath the gun's muzzle, and this change of topic just made it worse. "What?" he asked.

"A young officer on my base started to get a reputation. Men going to see him in secret. So my superior told me to fix it." A tight half-smile for the memory, for the long-ago time. "He didn't want to know what the situation was; drugs, smuggling, cutthroat gambling, sex... he just wanted the problem to stop. So I went and I asked around."

Ashford waited and waited, and JK roused himself to say, "What did you find out?" If the old man wanted to talk, he'd talk and buy himself some time. Maybe keep himself from taking a bullet.

He knew no one would be in position to help him. No one would be looking through Ashford's windows. No one would have thought twice about JK going into Ashford's house; everyone trusted the colonel. The best he could hope for involved Jesse making another surprise visit.

Ashford said, "Crazy thing. Turned out it wasn't any of the above. This officer made predictions about when the men were going to die. He'd take your hand between his and give you a date."

A tiny charge ran down JK's spine. A shock of sudden attentiveness, as if he'd heard his name used in another room. He started paying attention, instead of letting the words wash over him.

"Parlor games. I expected him to be charging for the predictions. But he wasn't profiting from it. Bad for morale though. Too many dates too soon. He promised to stop. I let it go. But men kept going. As long as they did it without drawing attention, what could I do? Isolate the soldier? I had to let it go.

"The thing that kept me up at nights... he was always right," Ashford said. "So much so that men used his warnings to write goodbyes to their loved ones."

JK's heart had stopped beating. It lodged in his throat, insurmountable.

"Don't know how, but he could tell you when you were going to die with a touch."

Ashford picked up his coffee with his free hand and slurped it down. The gun stayed steady; his eyes over the rim of the cup never left JK. Ashford nodded pointedly at JK's wet, gloved hands.

He said, "You got that kinda touch yourself, don't you? But you don't see upcoming death, you see... what exactly? You've been poking around. Finding Barton. Asking questions. Wanting to prove Nick innocent. Telling people you know Amy couldn't have done it. Or Mrs. Barton. What's your touch tell you?"

JK's heart thudded. Would it make it worse or better to admit to being a psychic? Every decision, every word, every movement seemed fraught. Would this be the moment the colonel decided to shoot him?

"Well?" the colonel said, eyes like steel. "Don't be shy, Lassiter. It doesn't suit you."

"I see the past," JK said. "People, places."

"So you *knew*. The minute you set foot inside. You knew all this time."

"I knew someone had died," JK said. "That's all. Then later, in the yard, I knew where and how. I never knew who did it. Not until now. I actually thought about blaming Lou Martinelli."

"Until now," Ashford repeated. He sounded suddenly old and tired. "You didn't know? You didn't *see* me. You wouldn't have followed me into my house otherwise." He sighed, rubbed at his temple with his free hand. The gun never wavered. "Never get old, Lassiter. It makes you error-prone. And murder. It changes you. Different than killing men in war. Murder makes you paranoid. Makes you selfish."

"Why did you—" *Murder* was such a terrible word; it stuck in his throat.

"I didn't set out to," Ashford said. "I don't even own a gun. When I retired, Sofia asked... We were going to adopt kids. Couldn't have guns with kids in the house, Sofia said. But then Amy comes around, dropping this gun out of her purse, shrugging, and says Zeke gave it to her. So shortsighted. Thinking with his heart. Gave her the gun. Didn't ask if she wanted it.

Didn't ask if she knew how to use it. She carried it around like a toy. I appropriated it to keep her from hurting herself. But then Barton—"

JK looked at the door. It wasn't that far away. Fifteen feet. But Ashford had taken down two charging dogs in the dark. JK didn't move. Couldn't move. His blood felt like it had been replaced with ice.

Ashford said, "I went there to kill the *dogs*. They were dangerous. It needed to be done. I saw his wife limping away, leaving blood on the driveway. She said the dogs had attacked her. If they had turned on her... I knew they'd shred Collier, turn on anyone. The Martinellis. The Sunitz boy. Or Amy."

The colonel's voice softened on Amy's name, and JK took in a much needed breath.

Then Ashford's expression tightened again. "Barton made this neighborhood a battlefield. I had to do it. Barton wouldn't listen to me. Called me an old fossil. Out of step with the modern world. As if there were ever an appropriate era to abuse your wife, to make war on your own people. I waited until he let them out, then killed them. Barton came out boiling mad. He pulled his gun, and then I killed him. I just... reacted."

"I'm not attacking you. Not mad. Not fighting. You don't have to shoot me," JK said, keeping as calm as he could. "I'm your people. Your neighbor."

Ashford studied him, the gun muzzle steady in its aim. Silently, JK cursed his large frame for making him such a damned good target.

"I'm torn, Lassiter. You seem like a decent kid. But God help me, I'm furious at you. I had a *plan*." His voice barely showed any signs of that admitted fury, only dipped a little into a deeper register, went a little flatter. That scared JK more than anything else had. It made him remember that cool professional blankness that had preceded Barton's murder.

JK's hands clenched on the sofa edge. It was hard to think of a way out of this when that gun and Ashford's steady stance held all of his attention. "Someone would have found him. Sooner, rather than later. You didn't bury him deep enough. He stank."

"I didn't plan on burying him," Ashford said. "I hadn't planned on shooting him. But he gave me no choice. At first, I figured I'd turn myself in. Wouldn't have that long to pay for my crime."

JK shivered, remembering that circled date on a calendar tucked out of sight. "You asked that psychic way back when. You've got a death date, don't you?"

Ashford didn't deny it.

JK whispered, "You *buried* him. You didn't turn yourself in."

"It's my *life*," Ashford said. The gun wavered briefly, not enough to make JK think he had any chance of running for it. Ashford might be old, but he was far from harmless.

He added, "Why should I waste my last months dealing with police and lawyers and doctors arguing over my sanity? No one needed to know. Unless someone got blamed for it, then I would confess."

"But you didn't," JK said. "You *haven't*. Zeke and Nick are in jail."

"I *know*," Ashford snapped. "It's your fault. Digging him up. God damn it. The housing market is so bad, and that house is so ugly... I figured no one would buy the house for years."

"But Davis snapped it up and so here I am." Urgency chewed at JK's nerves, adding another vibrating layer to the fear that shook him through.

"I'll leave a note. Clearing them after my death."

JK's eyes were dry; he couldn't seem to blink, couldn't stop staring at the gun, at the shame plain on Ashford's face. "You haven't written it yet, have you?" he asked him. Ashford was lying to JK, and lying to himself. He probably believed each of his lies. At least, he wanted to.

"I will write it. Don't say that like I won't."

"Do it now, then," JK suggested. "Or just let me leave. You don't even have to put pen to paper—" He didn't sound like himself, a collection of cracked words in a strained throat. "Just let me go. This... this is nothing. Doesn't need to come up with the cops. If you confess, they'll probably take that into—"

Ashford said, "I have an unblemished military career. My father was army before me, and my grandfather. Generations of honor. I killed a man. People won't understand."

"And killing me would make that better?" JK asked.

"I don't know, Lassiter, and that's the damn truth. I just don't know."

On the couch, JK shuddered, hearing the despair in Ashford's voice.

"What will you tell them? If you kill me? You can't make me disappear—no one would believe it. Even coming from you."

"I don't think I'd have to explain much. You've got some kind of condition, the neighborhood knows that. Saw you get violent with your family. With Nick. I could tell them you were crazy, dangerous."

"So dangerous you shot me with the same gun that killed Barton?" JK tried to think faster than he ever had. "That might raise questions you don't want to answer, don't you think?"

Ashford's mouth twitched. Irritated.

But arguing with Ashford wouldn't last long. Not if the old man was so locked into his self-preservation. Buying himself time wasn't going to be enough.

JK didn't have Zeke's martial arts skills, had no idea how to disarm a man, even an old one; he didn't have Jesse's training in keeping calm in the face of violence. He lacked Hannah's skills with people and their broken minds. JK didn't even have the benefit of Nick's years of acquaintance with Ashford. All he had were his bare hands and a psychic gift that liked to turn on him. Maybe that would be enough.

JK wriggled his wet, clinging glove down, terrified Ashford would shoot him while he tried to read the house, that he'd die while living someone else's memories, but desperate enough to try. To look for something that could reach Ashford. Reach below the surface.

The glove fought him, and Ashford tilted his head, watching, just watching.

If he died here... Nick. Well, getting himself shot with the same gun that killed Barton would be one way to prove Nick innocent.

Not the way JK would choose.

JK shucked the glove and put his hand on the coffee table. He *dove* into the memories of the house, years of routine, Sofia and Ashford sitting on this couch, at this table, inscribing it with emotion and memory. JK let go of everything that held him to himself; it wasn't going to be enough to just read a random memory. He needed a potent one. One that would help him. Words whispered to him, luring him this way and that—*cancer* and *love* and *I'll always take care of you* and *honor*.

JK latched onto that single word. Honor.

When he surfaced again, dizzy with the memories he'd absorbed, Ashford stood right in front of him, the gun muzzle resting dead center at his forehead. JK was too stunned to flinch.

"Did you see her?" Ashford asked, stepping back as he spoke. "She's everywhere in this house. I see her, even without gifts. Did you see her, my Sofia?"

"Sofia," JK breathed. "So beautiful. Even at the end." Cancer, her life lost by inches, the painful downward slope of it. Her thick white hair sparse, her body thinning to bone and sinew, but her dark eyes were so kind...

"She was beautiful. Always," Ashford said.

"She wouldn't want you to do this," JK said.

Ashford huffed. "You would say that—"

"No, no. The court-martial, remember? Sofia and I, sitting here, the meatloaf cold on the dining room table because I couldn't settle myself..." JK shook space between himself and the memory. "*You* couldn't settle yourself enough to eat. You were too angry at that soldier—Fletcher—who committed crimes and tried to flee. You said...it wasn't honorable. It wasn't what the soldiers were trained to be. Bad enough to rob someone, you said. Downright dishonorable to run when caught. To flee your just desserts."

Ashford stared at him, face blank. JK got the feeling if he touched him right now, he'd be getting an up-close and personal look at all the men the colonel had ever killed.

He curled his fingers into his palm, gathering the memories in.

Sofia whispering, "*You hold people to a high standard, Edwin. But you hold yourself to a higher one. It's one of the things I've always loved about you.*" He breathed her words across his lips. Ashford grew as still as stone.

JK felt ill, caught in conflicting emotions. Sofia's trust, love, and admiration versus his own gut-clenching fear.

"*Edwin,*" he said, a plea, her plea at the very end. "There's no honor in seeing other people blamed for your crime," JK said. "Zeke. Nick. They've been dragged through the wringer for something you did."

"There is no evidence. They'll be cleared even if I never confess."

"Are you sure?" JK said. "You set them up for a perfect conspiracy charge. Amy might even get sucked into it. She's sure busy telling the cops lie after lie."

"No!" Ashford's hand tightened on the gun, and JK shuddered.

Distantly, he thought he'd be etching his own terror into this spot, ruining the peace and love that Sofia and Edwin had together. His presence would leave a stain over the years of happiness.

JK said, "Even if they are cleared, suspicion lingers. Men's reputations, their honor—it's so fragile. You know it, or you wouldn't be fighting so hard to keep your own. It's all they have. Even outside the army. You think Nick's job can stand the suspicion? That parents would let their kids be taught martial arts by a suspected murderer?"

As he spoke, his fear became a distant thing. These words felt familiar. He had dug into the house's past to learn about Ashford, but the memories taught him more and more about

Sofia, about the way she used her words, the way she talked so fluidly, the confidence and certainty she had when dealing with her rigid, slow-to-change husband. Gaining the veneer of her emotions gave him relief—strange, but welcome—from the churning dread in his belly.

"And what about me? You know I won't stay silent if they're going to be blamed. You can't leave me behind and protect your reputation. You know you'll have to kill me. And I... I've died enough. I don't deserve it. You didn't mean to kill Barton—"

Ashford laughed without humor. He said, "I know how to aim a gun, Lassiter. When I shot, I meant to kill him."

JK swallowed as he lost ground. "I mean... it wasn't pre-meditated. You were just trying to protect the neighborhood. You always have. You don't want to become the neighborhood threat. Please. Let me go. Turn yourself in."

Ashford moved and JK's borrowed confidence fled him. He flinched, expecting the bullet, his bare hand flying before his face like it could deflect a headshot. His heartbeat thundered. The moment stretched.

A creak. Ashford slowly, stiffly, settled himself down in the armchair opposite the sofa, the gun cradled in his lap. "The phone is over there. Call the police."

JK's breath locked up. He wasn't sure he could stand, much less walk. But Ashford nodded him forward with a jerk of the gun, and JK moved toward the wall phone. The phone, he noticed sickly, kept him in range of Ashford's line of sight. A perfectly easy shot to take. JK eyed the door... but Ashford twitched and JK stopped looking in that direction. It'd be idiotic to get shot when he might be freed because he'd triggered Ashford's trained response.

He dialed Conroy's number, fumbling it twice, trying to remember it. Trying to hold the phone to his ear while dialing, horribly aware of Ashford's gun at his back, the crawling sensation between his shoulder blades. All his stirred memories swirled upward: Barton's too-late fear of the man standing above him. The shovel scraping through the house as an old man with a stiff back wearily went home to his empty house, exhausted by burying two dogs and a man in the dark hours.

He wanted to call Jesse, wanted his brother so bad he sweated with it. But if Ashford changed his mind again, if he decided to skip *this* confession as he had all the other opportunities, if he decided to kill JK—JK didn't want Jesse to hear his baby brother murdered.

Conroy picked up, casual and disinterested, faced with Ashford's number on her cell. JK couldn't speak for a moment and Conroy said, "Hello?" with mounting impatience.

"Conroy—" JK choked. His voice broke, cracking like a teenager's. "*Kate.*" He couldn't help but turn toward the colonel, trying to see if the old man was going to change his mind. Ashford only nodded.

"Lassiter? You got something for me?" Avid. She sounded avid. He hated her a little bit right then.

"Ashford killed Barton," JK said. Breathed it out one distinct word at a time. Two names and a verb. Nothing worth dying over. Clear enough that if JK did die, there'd be no confusion. No more chances for Ashford to change his mind.

Behind him, Ashford groaned. JK's back seized, muscles spasming in anticipation of a bullet that didn't come.

"JK?" The avidity shifted toward something shriller. Something that sounded like worry.

"I found the gun," he told her. "I'm looking at it right now. Up close. I'm at Ashford's," he said.

"Stay on the line, JK. I'm coming."

❂

JK didn't think he'd ever heard anything as sweet as the sirens heard in stereo over fiber optics and simultaneously from outside.

He hung up, looked over at Ashford, and said, "You should put the gun away." JK wanted to sound strong, cautionary. It just sounded small. It had been a long twenty minutes, with the only sounds Conroy's shouts and cursing at the other end, swearing—*no one call Jesse!*—tinny and distant, and his own erratic breathing. Panic warred with moments of numb shock.

Ashford seemed to have turned himself to steel, nothing but duty and discipline in his face, and JK hadn't been able to do more than clutch the phone and breathe.

"You think they'd shoot an old man in cold blood?" Ashford asked.

JK said, "I'm a well-liked cop's baby brother. At risk. How cold do you think their blood is right now?"

The bullhorn made them both jump, and Ashford cursed as the gun jerked in his grip.

"Let JK out, Colonel Ashford!" Gunnarson's voice. If Gunnarson was manning the bullhorn, Conroy would be moving close to the house, preparing to force her way in if necessary.

Ashford set the gun down on the floor before his chair. "You'd better go."

JK darted for the door, opened it into Kate Conroy's face, a mask of pallor and burning black eyes. She grabbed JK's sleeve and slung him off the porch with surprising strength. JK staggered, and a uniformed officer caught him, dragged him away from Ashford's house, off his lawn, and propped him up against one of five squad cars.

Conroy disappeared inside the house, Gunnarson in her wake, the bullhorn still rolling across the roadway.

JK turned his head from the flashing lights, shuddered. "Are you all right?" the officer said. That damned rookie again. The young man seemed to have aged in the few days since JK first met him. "Are you hurt?"

"I'm fine, I'm fine," JK said. "Don't touch me." He'd left his glove inside, and the rookie kept grabbing at his hand. JK realized he was cradling his bare hand protectively—the officer probably thought he'd injured it. He tucked his hand behind his back, fingers closed in over the palm.

Last week, the glove being off in public would have been enough to send him into a panic. Now... he couldn't be bothered to care.

In the end, it took JK six months to remodel and renovate the house, longer than he had intended. He'd been slowed not only by Barton's murder, and the house ambience that required him to spend half his days elsewhere, but by the neighborhood's insistence on being part of Ashford's trial. JK had been dragged to every hearing, every sentencing, helped chase away reporters. He'd even joined the rank of visitors to the jail, managing to go once before Ashford's death date came around, though Jesse protested: *He held a gun on you!*

JK countered with *He didn't use it*, feigning confidence he didn't feel. But it felt necessary to see Ashford, to shake the terror of that last interaction from his bones.

On his visit, JK had surprised himself by talking freely to the old man who had terrified him, sharing memories of Sofia with him.

After that visit, JK had found the nerve to make the long, overdue call to his parents. After Ashford, JK had a better understanding of how people could want to do the right thing and have it go so wrong. The conversation had been short and stilted—his parents cried; he didn't—but it was a start. They were glad he had a job he enjoyed, and asked him to send pictures of the house, the neighborhood, and especially pictures of Nick. JK didn't tell them anything about Ashford.

When Ashford died, on November 18th, of a sudden heart attack, he left one last surprise for the neighborhood. He left his house to Amy Sheridan, maybe in thanks for her repeated visits at the jail, or maybe just stepping up one last time to help out, maybe even for Sofia's joy in the happy infant Amy had been.

JK had found himself overseeing repairs in Ashford's house, too, when Amy, despite all expectations, chose not to sell it. She told JK—while he knelt, ripping up carpet—that Ashford and Sofia had been happy in the house for years, and Amy thought she and Zeke would be happy there too. JK, who carried memories of the Ashfords' marriage, couldn't argue. Amy still insisted on repainting every room, and she wouldn't let him paint any of them bordello red.

And then there was Kate Conroy, who didn't give up easily, if at all.

Three times she wandered by, just "in the neighborhood"— taking JK for coffee and asking if JK wanted to take a ride to a crime scene. He'd put her off each time, and the fourth time, when he'd weakened enough to consider going, he had a flashback to Barton's violent death throes and spilled his coffee all over her lap. It didn't stop her from calling. JK figured it was only a matter of time before he joined her at a crime scene.

The summer and fall passed by in a haze of work and weekly barbecues in various neighborhood backyards. By the fifth one, Zeke had stopped bristling at JK—and by the tenth, he'd unwound enough that when Olivia's date had questioned JK's gloves, the man got a faceful of Zeke telling him to mind his own goddamned business.

Close to Christmas, JK had the first open house and the realtor was cautiously optimistic. She left on a cloud of possibilities, and JK ambled around the house, looking at all the differences he'd made with clean paint, hardwood floors, updated appliances, and new windows. It looked good; better than good. It looked and felt welcoming.

Davis had offered him first dibs on putting down a down payment if he wanted, told JK he'd discount the property for him. JK thought about it briefly, but demurred. The house might not have bad memories any longer, but he still did.

"Knock, knock," Nick said from the open doorway. He'd been teaching, and JK thought he looked edible—his dark hair tousled, his blue shirt open at the neck, giving JK a tempting glimpse of collarbone, and doing good things to show off his pale eyes. His charcoal slacks hugged his hips and thighs. JK missed Nick's casual wear less and less every time Nick put on those slacks.

He said, "Did I miss the whole open house? Sorry, student advising ran over."

JK said, "You're lucky, really. Most people just wanted to nitpick the furnishings—no granite countertops! A few people wanted to ask about the murder. Loudly of course. While there were other viewers in the room."

"That sucks," Nick said.

"Well, I did have at least three people tell me it didn't look like a murder house. Still, it's going to be a harder sell than Davis had hoped. No wonder he wanted me to buy it."

"Hey, more time for you to stick around. I don't know anyone who'd object to that," Nick said. "But you're moving on."

"Yeah," JK murmured, reaching out to drag Nick to him for a kiss.

Nick evaded him and said, "How about moving in, instead of moving on?" His tone shifted, went from easy to nervous in a few words.

"Nah, I'm done with this house."

"Not move in here. With me. Move in with me," Nick said, rushing the words.

JK blinked; his heart thumped.

"Seriously, JK. I know Davis is looking for another place for you to renovate. That's great. But stay here. Live with me. At least between projects. I think it'd be great. The Sunitzes love you since you helped build the playground for Devi, and God knows the Martinellis would be crushed under subpar woodworking if you didn't build their trellises for them, and you exercise the Treanors' ridiculous dog so they don't have to—"

JK put a gloved hand over Nick's mouth. "Are you going to give me time to say yes?"

"Yeah?" Nick said. The tension in his body eased. He swayed into JK's body. JK draped his arms around Nick's neck, pressed his forehead to Nick's hair.

He said, "Yeah. Everything I want is here."

About the Author

Lane Robins was born in Miami, Florida, the daughter of two scientists, and grew up as the first human member of their menagerie. She attended the Odyssey workshop and has a BA in Creative Writing from Beloit College. She returned to Odyssey as writer-in-residence in 2012. She is the author of *Maledicte* and *Kings & Assassins*. Under the name Lyn Benedict, she writes an urban fantasy series beginning with *Sins & Shadows*.

Her short fiction has been published recently in *Strange Horizons, Penumbra*, and in *Nightmare Magazine*. She currently resides in Lawrence KS, but lives in worlds full of cannibal fairies, modern knights, psychic construction workers, and little girls who can turn their pigtails into snakes.

BLIND
EYE
BOOKS

blindeyebooks.com